THE SIGNALMAN
AND OTHER HORRORS

The Best Victorian Ghost Stories of
CHARLES DICKENS

Edited, Annotated, and Illustrated By
M. GRANT KELLERMEYER, M.A.

CR

EXPAND YOUR SUPERNATURAL FICTION COLLECTION
By Acquiring These
— ANNOTATED AND ILLUSTRATED EDITIONS —

WWW.OLDSTYLETALES.COM

WEIRD FICTION & HORROR BY:
Algernon Blackwood
Robert W. Chambers
F. Marion Crawford
William Hope Hodgson
Arthur Machen
Guy de Maupassant
Fitz-James O'Brien
Edgar Allan Poe
H. G. Wells

CLASSIC GHOST STORIES BY:
Charles Dickens
Sir Arthur Conan Doyle
W. W. Jacobs
Henry James
J. Sheridan Le Fanu
E. Nesbit
Robert Louis Stevenson
Bram Stoker
Washington Irving

CLASSIC GOTHIC NOVELS:
Dracula
Frankenstein
The Phantom of the Opera
Dr. Jekyll and Mr. Hyde
The Turn of the Screw
The Invisible Man
The Picture of Dorian Gray

FIRESIDE HORROR SERIES:
Ghost Stories for Christmas Eve
Victorian Ghost Stories
Supernatural Cats
Demons and the Devil
Mummies and Curses
Pirates and Ghost Ships
Werewolves

OLDSTYLE TALES

This edition published 2016 by
OLDSTYLE TALES PRESS
2424 N. Anthony Blvd
Fort Wayne, Indiana
46805–3604

*For more information, or to request permission
to reprint selections or illustrations from
this book, write to the Editor at*
oldstyletales@gmail.com

NOTES, INTRODUCTIONS, AND ILLUSTRATIONS
COPYRIGHT © 2016 BY MICHAEL GRANT KELLERMEYER

Readers who are interested in further titles from
Oldstyle Tales Press are invited to visit our website at

— WWW.OLDSTYLETALES.COM —

— TABLE *of* CONTENTS —

Concerning What
You Are About to Read

ENGLISH literature is punctuated by a series of inescapably titanic figures – one or two per century – who overwhelmingly defined the mood, tone, and standards of their eras. Chaucer, Shakespeare, Milton, Swift, and Wordsworth dominated their respective eras, and the chief don of the mid-19th century was Charles Dickens (1812 – 1870). His works are unrelentingly required for any survey of British literature during the period called the Victorian Era. His novels began with the Irvingian sketchbook of humoresques, *The Pickwick Papers*, followed by his socially conscious *Oliver Twist*, the anti-Malthusian social allegory, *A Christmas Carol*, the virtually autobiographical *David Copperfield*, an acidic attack on the ineptitude of British courts crying for legal reform in *Bleak House*, the stark and gloomy social criticisms of *Hard Times*, the historical meditation on parallelism and redemption, *A Tale of Two Cities*, and his world-weary bildungsroman, *Great Expectations*. Born to penny-poor middle classed parents, Dickens knew keenly what it was to feel on the fence between two existences: one secure and fashionable, and one chaotic and scandalous. It was this feverish play between poles that he fed into his supernatural fiction, investing it with a gravity that pulled between sanity and madness, good and evil, normal and uncanny, without ever securing a firm footing. He suffered from a scandalous love life which saw his wife abandoned, his mistresses scandalized, and his children divided; he endured lifelong bouts of manic-depression – sometimes in productive spurts, sometimes in paralyzing waves; he grew weary and jaded with industrial society, capitalism, and commercialism – forces he struggled against valiantly if vainly; and while keenly religious he loathed the hypocrisy of the church, the charlatanism of spiritualists, and the selfishness of affluent Christians. All of these passions and fears and resentments were gradually – then forcefully – channeled into his speculative fiction, resulting in a number of invasive ghost stories that entice with pleasant language and characters, but cling to the imagination like a baited barb.

Dickens enjoyed, for the better part of a century, a reputation as one of the greatest writers of ghost stories in the language. Aside from the obvious *Christmas Carol*, he was well known for his light hearted satires ("The Lawyer and the Ghost"), his dark humored allegories ("The Baron of Grogzwig"), and his conventional spiritualist episodes ("The Trial for Murder"). His tales were regularly anthologized alongside Edward Bulwer-Lytton, Wilkie Collins, Sir Walter Scott, Henry James, Robert Louis Stevenson, and Rudyard Kipling. It is a reputation which he has unquestionably lost. As time has proceeded, these relatively conventional supernaturalists have fallen out of fashion in favor of masters of slow-burning terror and plot control such as M. R. James, Oliver Onions, E. F. Benson, J. Sheridan Le Fanu, Edith Wharton, and H. Russell Wakefield. Even among the Victorians, the great female writers (Amelia B. Edwards, Mrs J. H. Riddell, Rhoda Broughton, Mrs Oliphant, Elizabeth Gaskell, Miss Braddon, Maria Louisa Molesworth, Mary E. Wilkins Freeman, E. Nesbit, and Sarah Orne Jewett) have overwhelmingly dominated the respect and attention of contemporary critics. But Dickens contributions to the field of speculative fiction continue to prove considerable, from his influence on Edgar Allan Poe, M. R. James, and J. Sheridan Le Fanu, to his genuine masterpieces of horror – some four expert ghost stories (*To Be Read at Dusk, The Hanged Man's Bride, The Trial for Murder, The Signal-Man*), three still-effective supernatural allegories (*Baron Grogzwig, A Christmas Carol, The Goblins Who Stole a Sexton*), and two grisly tales of psychological horror (*A Madman's Manuscript, The Mother's Eyes*). Dickens' tales – many of which were modelled after the whimsical, character-driven supernatural tales of Washington Irving and the historically-set Gothic episodes of Sir Walter Scott – were almost always either social satires, social allegories, or contained undercurrent social themes, causing them to tread the borderlands between pure supernatural fiction (like that of M. R. James) and pure social realism (like that of Thomas Hardy). Elizabeth Gaskell, Mrs Oliphant, and Edith Wharton would follow his example, generating some of the century's best socially conscious ghost stories. His early tales especially were concerned with basic human dignity, the plight of the poor, and humanist celebrations of life and loss, but as he aged his stories began to darken and broaden from social critiques to existential anxieties. His best ghost stories mourned the loss of divine justice, the impotence of the law, and the corruption of authority, concluding either with pyrrhic victories (the evil are punished, but only after true justice is impossible) or – as in "The Signal-Man" and "To Be Read at Dusk" – disturbing, mysterious riddles which refused to yield answers to their tragic plots. Almost Lovecraftian in their sinister worldview, these later stories draw far away from the jolting whimsy of his early tales, creating a chiaroscuro universe of deep shadow closing in around weak points of light.

As previously mentioned, Dickens' influence on speculative fiction was sizeable. The most obvious benefactor was the American critic, poet, and Gothic writer Edgar Allan Poe, whose tales of madness and murder were undeniably impacted by Dickens' similarly themed "A Madman's Manuscript," and "The Mother's Eyes" which presaged "The Black Cat," "The Tell-Tale Heart," "Berenice," "Ligeia," "Morella," "The Imp of the Perverse," and to degrees "The Fall of the House of Usher," "William Wilson," "Hop-Frog," and "The Cask of Amontillado." Dickens returned the favor by modelling his story "The Hanged Man's Bride" loosely off of "Metzengerstein" and "The Black Cat," while "The Baron of Grogzwig" bears notable similarities to "Metzengerstein," "Bon-Bon," "The Devil in the Belfry," and "Never Bet the Devil Your Head." Other writers built on top of Dickens supernatural works (especially "Trial" and "Signal-Man"), but the most notable are his contemporary J. Sheridan Le Fanu – the unrivaled master of the Victorian ghost story – and the former's 20th century protégé, M. R. James. Le Fanu appears to have been inspired by "The Trial for Murder," creating "Mr Justice Harbottle" while James constructed on top of both stories to forge his eerie courtroom drama "Martin's Close." "The Hanged Man's Bride," a decidedly Lefanuvian tale of guardian abuse, greed, ghostly revenge, and just desserts heralds bevies of Le Fanu stories (especially "The Haunted Baronet," "Squire Toby's Will," "Harbottle," "Madam Crowl's Ghost," and "Schalken the Painter") and became reworked in many of James' best known grotesqueries (particularly "The Ash Tree," "Martin's Close," "The Story of a Disappearance and an Appearance," "Lost Hearts," and "The Stalls of Barchester"). His influence is also clearly felt in E. F. Benson, Wilkie Collins, Amelia B. Edwards, H. Russell Wakefield, E. Nesbit, Mrs Oliphant, and droves more.

For his part, Dickens' supernatural fiction was chiefly inspired by the earlier work of the American humorist, historian, and sketch writer Washington Irving and the Scottish writer of historical romances, Sir Walter Scott. Irving's touch can be easily glimpsed in "The Bagman's Uncle" – loosely formed in the model of the half-credible narratives of *Tales of a Traveler*, some of which are blatantly humorous distortions of the truth (the sex-themed "Adventure of My Grandfather") while others offered mysterious suggestions of either madness or genuine horror ("The Adventure of My Uncle," "The Adventure of the German Student"). "The Goblins Who Stole a Sexton" unabashedly suggests Irving's two most popular tales – "The Legend of Sleepy Hollow" and "Rip Van Winkle" – consisting as it does of an antisocial ne'er-do-well who roams into a cemetery, is spirited away by the supernatural, becoming a legend in his own right when his affects are found abandoned hard by, and returns years later, a changed man. "The Baron of Grogzwig" bears stark similarities to several of Irving's German tales ("The Spectre Bridegroom" especially), and the character of Fezziwig from *A Christmas Carol* is all but a caricature of Irving's Christmas-loving Squire Bracebridge (*Bracebridge Hall*, with its nostalgic affection for Yuletide, inspired Dickens to write the *Carol*, and the two authors – with some help from Prince Albert – virtually singlehandedly revived Christmas in England after two centuries of dormancy).

Dickens continued to write prolifically until the railroad accident which inspired "The Signal-Man." After this life-shaking event, his moods worsened, and his creativity dried up rapidly. His son credited the horror of the crash with abbreviating his father's life. On 9 June 1865, a boat train driving passengers from the Kentish coast to London was derailed near the town of Staplehurst when it crossed over a section of rail which had been removed during a sloppy repair process. A signalman had attempted to wave the train to a halt, but he was located half the legal distance from the repairs, and the engine could not stop in time. Dickens' car was among the seven which derailed, and after he had rescued his mistress and her mother, he frantically began tending to the injured. Several died in his company, ten in total, while forty were injured. The event robbed him of his voice for two weeks, and left him scarred until his death five years later to the day.

His most important work remains literary fiction, social realism, and historical fiction, with horror and supernaturalism occupying a terribly small portion of his vast oeuvre. But those stories which continue to circulate in anthologies such as this do so because of their unmistakable artistry – whether due to their humor, their allegorical significance, their psychological depth, their existential vision, or –

though rarely – their abject horror. His tales can be charming, disturbing, haunting, and charismatic. They can be fine pieces to read to small children by cheery candlelight on October 31 (or December 24), or grim episodes to be mulled over by world-weary adults as they contemplate the role of fate, social responsibility, free will, and cosmic charity in their own lives. Like Irving whom he adored, and James who adored him, Dickens' supernatural work continues to charm and thrill regardless of its lack of octopoid aliens, fiery skeletons, or blood-drenched vivisections. He is not Stephen King. He is not H. P. Lovecraft. He is not Ramsey Campbell or Clive Barker or Dean Koontz. He is Dickens, Boz, and his speculative fiction is propelled, not by gore, or horror, or sadism, but by its subtle roots in the human unconscious – his stories which cause us to chuckle disarmedly while we read, but to furrow our brow in confused discomfort when we put the book aside and leave the room.

M. Grant Kellermeyer
Fort Wayne, Christmas Eve 2014

THE SIGNAL-MAN and OTHERS
The Best Victorian Ghost Stories of

Charles Dickens

WRITING on Christmastime, a season that he (partnering with Washington Irving and Prince Albert) largely revitalized in the English-speaking world, Charles Dickens apportioned roughly a third of his Yuletide essay, "The Christmas Tree," to a survey of English ghost lore, tropes, summaries, and exemplars. While the literary ghost story is the only remnant of Victorian supernatural fiction that this volume concerns itself with, we happily open the scene with a glimpse into the parlor of a typical middle-classed family on a night in November or December. The fire is red and low, and the company has decided to spend the night rather than risk the nocturnal drive through the blizzard. While wassail and Indian tea are passed around, a favorite uncle settles into his favorite wingback chair. He lights his pipe with a cinder from the hearth, and while the children pool at his feet and the adults settle into the shadows, you will hear some of these tales issue from his mustachioed lips...

Christmas Ghost Stories
EXCERPTED *from the* ESSAY "THE CHRISTMAS TREE"
{1850}

THERE IS PROBABLY A SMELL OF ROASTED CHESTNUTS and other good comfortable things all the time, for we are telling Winter Stories — Ghost Stories, or more shame for us — round the Christmas fire; and we have never stirred, except to draw a little nearer to it. But, no matter for that. We came to the house, and it is an old house, full of great chimneys where wood is burnt on ancient dogs upon the hearth, and grim portraits (some of them with grim legends, too) lower distrustfully from the oaken panels of the walls. We are a middle-aged nobleman, and we make a generous supper with our host and hostess and their guests — it being Christmas-time, and the old house full of company — and then we go to bed. Our room is a very old room. It is hung with tapestry. We don't like the portrait of a cavalier in green, over the fireplace. There are great black beams in the ceiling, and there is a great black bedstead, supported at the foot by two great black figures, who seem to have come off a couple of tombs in the old baronial church in the park, for our particular accommodation. But, we are not a superstitious nobleman, and we don't mind. Well! we dismiss our servant, lock the door, and sit before the fire in our dressing-gown, musing about a great many things. At length we go to bed. Well! we can't sleep. We toss and tumble, and can't sleep. The embers on the hearth burn fitfully and make the room look ghostly. We can't help peeping out over the counterpane, at the two black figures and the cavalier — that wicked- looking cavalier — in green. In the flickering light they seem to advance and retire: which, though we are not by any means a superstitious nobleman, is not agreeable. Well! we get nervous — more and more nervous. We say "This is very foolish, but we can't stand this; we'll pretend to be ill, and knock up somebody." Well! we are just going to do it, when the locked door opens, and there comes in a young woman, deadly pale, and with long fair hair, who glides to the fire, and sits down in the chair we have left there, wringing her hands. Then, we notice that her clothes are wet. Our tongue cleaves to the roof of our mouth, and we can't speak; but, we observe her accurately. Her clothes are wet; her long hair is dabbled with moist mud; she is dressed in the fashion of two hundred years ago; and she has at her girdle a bunch of rusty keys. Well! there she sits, and we can't even faint, we are in such a state about it. Presently she gets up, and tries all the locks in the room with the rusty keys, which won't fit one of them; then, she fixes her eyes on the portrait of the cavalier in green, and says, in a low, terrible voice, "The stags know it!" After that, she wrings her hands again, passes the bedside, and goes out at the door. We hurry on our dressing-gown, seize our pistols (we always travel with pistols), and are following, when we find the door locked. We turn the key, look out into the dark gallery; no one there. We wander away, and try to find our servant. Can't be done. We pace the gallery till daybreak; then return to our deserted room, fall asleep, and are awakened by our servant (nothing ever haunts him) and the shining sun. Well! we make a wretched breakfast, and all the company say we look queer. After breakfast, we go over the house with our host, and then we take him to the portrait of the cavalier in green, and then it all comes out. He was false to a young housekeeper once attached to that family, and famous for her beauty, who drowned herself in a pond, and whose body was discovered, after a long time, because the stags refused to drink of the water. Since which, it has been whispered that she traverses the house at midnight (but goes especially to that room where the cavalier in green was wont to sleep), trying the old locks with the rusty keys. Well! we tell our host of what we have seen, and a shade comes over his features, and he begs it may be hushed up; and so it is. But, it's all true; and we said so, before we died (we are dead now) to many responsible people.

There is no end to the old houses, with resounding galleries, and dismal state-bedchambers, and haunted wings shut up for many years, through which we may ramble, with an agreeable creeping up our back, and encounter any number of ghosts, but (it is worthy of remark perhaps) reducible to a very few general types and classes; for, ghosts have little originality, and "walk" in a beaten track. Thus, it comes to pass, that a certain room in a certain old hall, where a certain bad lord, baronet, knight, or gentleman, shot himself, has certain planks in the floor from which the blood WILL NOT be taken out. You may scrape and scrape, as the present owner has done, or plane and plane, as his father did, or scrub and scrub, as his grandfather did, or burn and burn with strong acids, as his great-grandfather did, but, there the blood will still be — no redder and no paler — no more and no less — always just the same. Thus, in such another house there is a haunted door, that never will keep open; or another door that never will keep shut, or a haunted sound of a spinning-wheel, or a hammer, or a footstep, or a cry, or a sigh, or a horse's tramp, or the rattling of a chain. Or else, there is a turret-clock, which, at the midnight hour, strikes thirteen when the head of the family is going to die; or a shadowy, immovable black carriage which at such a time is always seen by somebody, waiting near the great gates in the stable-yard. Or thus, it came to pass how Lady Mary went to pay a visit at a large wild house in the Scottish Highlands, and, being fatigued with her long journey, retired to bed early, and innocently said, next morning, at the breakfast-table, "How odd, to have so late a party last night, in this remote place, and not to tell me of it, before I went to bed!" Then, every one asked Lady Mary what she meant? Then, Lady Mary replied, "Why, all night long, the carriages were driving round and round the terrace, underneath my window!" Then, the owner of the house turned pale, and so did his Lady, and Charles Macdoodle of Macdoodle signed to Lady Mary to say no more, and every one was silent. After breakfast, Charles Macdoodle told Lady Mary that it was a tradition in the family that those rumbling carriages on the terrace betokened death. And so it proved, for, two months afterwards, the Lady of the mansion died. And Lady Mary, who was a Maid of Honour at Court, often told this story to the old Queen Charlotte; by this token that the old King always said, "Eh, eh? What, what? Ghosts, ghosts? No such thing, no such thing!" And never left off saying so, until he went to bed.

Or, a friend of somebody's whom most of us know, when he was a young man at college, had a particular friend, with whom he made the compact that, if it were possible for the Spirit to return to this earth after its separation from the body, he of the twain who first died, should reappear to the other. In course of time, this compact was forgotten by our friend; the two young men having progressed in life, and taken diverging paths that were wide asunder. But, one night, many years afterwards, our friend being in the North of England, and staying for the night in an inn, on the Yorkshire Moors, happened to look out of bed; and there, in the moonlight, leaning on a bureau near the window, steadfastly regarding him, saw his old college friend! The appearance being solemnly addressed, replied, in a kind of whisper, but very audibly, "Do not come near me. I am dead. I am here to redeem my promise. I come from another world, but may not disclose its secrets!" Then, the whole form becoming paler, melted, as it were, into the moonlight, and faded away.

Or, there was the daughter of the first occupier of the picturesque Elizabethan house, so famous in our neighbourhood. You have heard about her? No! Why, SHE went out one summer evening at twilight, when she was a beautiful girl, just seventeen years of age, to gather flowers in the garden; and presently came running, terrified, into the hall to her father, saying, "Oh, dear father, I have met myself!" He took her in his arms, and told her it was fancy, but she said, "Oh no! I met myself in the broad walk, and I was pale and gathering withered flowers, and I turned my head, and held them up!" And, that night, she died; and a picture of her story was begun, though never finished, and they say it is somewhere in the house to this day, with its face to the wall.

Or, the uncle of my brother's wife was riding home on horseback, one mellow evening at sunset, when, in a green lane close to his own house, he saw a man standing before him, in the very centre of a narrow way. "Why does that man in the cloak stand there!" he thought. "Does he want me to ride over him?" But the figure never moved. He felt a strange sensation at seeing it so still, but slackened his trot and rode forward. When he was so close to it, as almost to touch it with his stirrup, his horse shied, and the figure glided up the bank, in a curious, unearthly manner — backward, and without seeming to use its feet — and was gone. The

uncle of my brother's wife, exclaiming, "Good Heaven! It's my cousin Harry, from Bombay!" put spurs to his horse, which was suddenly in a profuse sweat, and, wondering at such strange behaviour, dashed round to the front of his house. There, he saw the same figure, just passing in at the long French window of the drawing-room, opening on the ground. He threw his bridle to a servant, and hastened in after it. His sister was sitting there, alone. "Alice, where's my cousin Harry?" "Your cousin Harry, John?" "Yes. From Bombay. I met him in the lane just now, and saw him enter here, this instant." Not a creature had been seen by any one; and in that hour and minute, as it afterwards appeared, this cousin died in India.

Or, it was a certain sensible old maiden lady, who died at ninety- nine, and retained her faculties to the last, who really did see the Orphan Boy; a story which has often been incorrectly told, but, of which the real truth is this — because it is, in fact, a story belonging to our family — and she was a connexion of our family. When she was about forty years of age, and still an uncommonly fine woman (her lover died young, which was the reason why she never married, though she had many offers), she went to stay at a place in Kent, which her brother, an Indian-Merchant, had newly bought. There was a story that this place had once been held in trust by the guardian of a young boy; who was himself the next heir, and who killed the young boy by harsh and cruel treatment. She knew nothing of that. It has been said that there was a Cage in her bedroom in which the guardian used to put the boy. There was no such thing. There was only a closet. She went to bed, made no alarm whatever in the night, and in the morning said composedly to her maid when she came in, "Who is the pretty forlorn-looking child who has been peeping out of that closet all night?" The maid replied by giving a loud scream, and instantly decamping. She was surprised; but she was a woman of remarkable strength of mind, and she dressed herself and went downstairs, and closeted herself with her brother. "Now, Walter," she said, "I have been disturbed all night by a pretty, forlorn-looking boy, who has been constantly peeping out of that closet in my room, which I can't open. This is some trick." "I am afraid not, Charlotte," said he, "for it is the legend of the house. It is the Orphan Boy. What did he do?" "He opened the door softly," said she, "and peeped out. Sometimes, he came a step or two into the room. Then, I called to him, to encourage him, and he shrunk, and shuddered, and crept in again, and shut the door." "The closet has no communication, Charlotte," said her brother, "with any other part of the house, and it's nailed up." This was undeniably true, and it took two carpenters a whole forenoon to get it open, for examination. Then, she was satisfied that she had seen the Orphan Boy. But, the wild and terrible part of the story is, that he was also seen by three of her brother's sons, in succession, who all died young. On the occasion of each child being taken ill, he came home in a heat, twelve hours before, and said, Oh, Mamma, he had been playing under a particular oak-tree, in a certain meadow, with a strange boy — a pretty, forlorn-looking boy, who was very timid, and made signs! From fatal experience, the parents came to know that this was the Orphan Boy, and that the course of that child whom he chose for his little playmate was surely run.

{17}

Legion is the name of the German castles, where we sit up alone to wait for the Spectre — where we are shown into a room, made comparatively cheerful for our reception — where we glance round at the shadows, thrown on the blank walls by the crackling fire — where we feel very lonely when the village innkeeper and his pretty daughter have retired, after laying down a fresh store of wood upon the hearth, and setting forth on the small table such supper-cheer as a cold roast capon, bread, grapes, and a flask of old Rhine wine — where the reverberating doors close on their retreat, one after another, like so many peals of sullen thunder — and where, about the small hours of the night, we come into the knowledge of divers supernatural mysteries. Legion is the name of the haunted German students, in whose society we draw yet nearer to the fire, while the schoolboy in the corner opens his eyes wide and round, and flies off the footstool he has chosen for his seat, when the door accidentally blows open. Vast is the crop of such fruit, shining on our Christmas Tree; in blossom, almost at the very top; ripening all down the boughs!

DICKENS, who almost single-handedly revived the tradition of old fashioned Christmases (as opposed to the virtually secular bank holiday it had become after the Puritan Revolution) was himself inspired by the Christmas stories of another ghost story writer, the godfather of American literature, Washington Irving. His depiction of old fashioned English Christmases in The Sketch Book of Geoffrey Crayon, Gent. (the same collection that contained "The Legend of Sleepy Hollow" and "Rip Van Winkle") and Bracebridge Hall charmed the young Dickens – an Irving devotee – and was incorporated into the imagery and rhetoric of A Christmas Carol. Irving also adored the ghost story – though he often lampooned it. In the beginning of Tales of a Traveler (much of which is the 19th century version of the Scary Movie franchize), a lover of English ghost lore rhapsodizes about the tropes of the literature. In his beaming catalog we can detect the inspiration for Dickens loving homage above:

" By my soul but I should not be surprised if some of those good-looking gentlefolks that hang along the walls [in picture frames] should walk about the rooms of this stormy night; or if I should find the ghost of one of these long-waisted ladies turning into my bed in mistake for her grave in the church-yard... Oh, I should like it of all things... Some dark oaken room, with ugly, wo-begone portraits that are dismally at one, and about which the housekeeper has a power of delightful stories of love and murder. And then a dim lamp, a table with a rusty sword across it, and a spectre all in white to draw aside one's curtains at midnight..."

DICKENS wrote several types of ghost stories, and most were more rhetorical exercises or moral parables rather than horror stories, but that makes them no less important or even chilling than the most haunting narratives of M.R. James, H.R. Wakefield, or Robert Aickman. The first ghost story he is known to have penned is, at face value, a simple joke, but the humor behind this dwarfish episode is deep and black with bitter cynicism. Presaging Mark Twain, Guy de Maupassant, Ambrose Bierce, and other misanthropists who blended the supernatural and the humorous to snipe at humanity, Dickens' first ghost story may appear to be a soft chuckle in a can, but the echoes boom.

The Lawyer and the Ghost
EXCERPTED *from* THE PICKWICK PAPERS, CHAPTER *Twenty-One*
{1837}

I knew a man - forty years ago - who took an old, damp and rotten set of chambers, in one of the most ancient Inns, that had been shut up and empty for years and years before. There were lots of stories about the place, and it was certainly far from being a cheerful one; but he was poor, and the rooms were cheap, and that would have been quite a sufficient reason, if they had been ten times worse than they really were.

The man was obliged to take some mouldering fixtures, and, among the rest, was a great lumbering wooden press for papers, with large glass doors, and a green curtain inside; a pretty useless thing, for he had no papers to out in it; and as to his clothes, he carried them about with him, and that wasn't very hard work either.

Well, he moved in all his furniture - it wasn't quite a truckful - and had sprinkled it about the rooms, so as to make the four chairs look as much like a dozen as possible, and was sitting down before the fire at night, drinking the first glass of two gallons of whisky he had ordered on credit, wondering whether it would ever be paid for, if so, in how many years' time, when his eyes encountered the glass doors of the wooden press.

'Ah,' says he, speaking aloud to the press, having nothing else to speak to; 'if it wouldn't cost more to break up your old carcase, than it would ever be worth afterwards, I'd have a fire out of you in less than no time.'

He had hardly spoken the words, when a sound resembling a faint groan appeared to issue form the interior of the case; it startled him at first, but thinking that it must be some young fellow in the next chamber who had been dining out, he put his feet on the fender and raised the poker to stir the fire.

At that moment, the sound was repeated: and one of the glass doors slowly opening, disclosed a pale figure in soiled and worn apparel, standing erect in the press. The figure was tall and thin, and the countenance expressive of care and anxiety, but there was something in the hue of the skin, and gaunt and unearthly appearance of the whole form, which no being of this world was ever seen to wear.

'Who are you?' said the new tenant, turning very pale, poising the poker in his hand, however, and taking a very decent aim at the countenance of the figure.

'Who are you?'

'Don't throw the poker at me' replied the form: 'If you hurled it with ever so sure an aim, it would pass through me, without resistance, and expend it's force on the wood behind. I am a spirit!'

'And, pray, what do you want here?' faltered the tenant.

'In this room,' replied the apparition, 'my worldly ruin was worked and I and my children beggared. In this room, when I had died of grief, and long-deferred hope, two wily harpies divided the wealth for which I had contested during a wretched existence, and of which, at last, not one farthing was left for my unhappy descendants. I terrified them from the spot, and since have prowled by night - the only period at which I can revisit the earth - about the scenes of my long misery. This apartment is mine: leave it to me.'

'If you insist on making your appearance here', said the tenant, who had had time to collect his presence of mind, 'I shall give up possession with the greatest pleasure, but I should like to ask you one question if you will allow me.'

'Say on,' said the apparition sternly.

'Well', said the tenant, 'it does appear to me somewhat inconsistent, that when you have an opportunity of visiting the fairest spots of earth - for I suppose space is nothing to you - you should always return to the place where you have been most miserable.'

'Egad, that's very true; I never thought of that before', said the ghost.

'You see, sir,' pursued the tenant, 'this is a very uncomfortable room. From the appearance of that press, I should be disposed to say not wholly free from bugs; and I really think you might find more comfortable quarters, to say nothing of the climate of London, which is extremely disagreeable.'

'You are very right, sir,' said the ghost politely, 'it had never struck me till now; I'll try a change of air directly.

In fact, he began to vanish as he spoke: his legs, indeed had quite disappeared!

'And if sir,' said the tenant calling after him 'if you would have the goodness to suggest to other ladies and gentlemen who are now engaged in haunting old empty houses, that they might be much more comfortable elsewhere, you will confer a very great benefit on society.'

'I will', replied the ghost, 'we must be dull fellows, very dull fellows, indeed; I can't imagine how we can have been so stupid.'

With these words, the spirit disappeared, and what is rather remarkable, he never came back again.

A onetime favorite of ghost story anthologies, "The Lawyer and the Ghost" has since developed a reputation for being a disappointing joke rather than a spooky foray into the supernatural. But in it was laid the foundation for Dickens' truly chilling tales such as "The Signal-Man," "To Be Read at Dusk," "The Hanged Man's Bride," and "The Trial for Murder," which similarly use their ghostly situations to expose a disturbing element of human society. The dark background to this little jest is the concept that there are people living in modern, industrial cities who would be happier – or at least have a better quality of life – if they were dead. A dead man can escape his misery, and while many some people are capable of improving their circumstances, there continue to be some whose only recourse is death: after having advised the spirit in changing his circumstances, we may wonder if the tenant took his own advice and committed suicide. Dickens' ghost stories almost unanimously are used to critique Victorian society through satire, metaphor, analogy, and symbolism. His first foray into speculative fiction is hardly scary, but it is haunting, calling into question the humanity of a society that offers more to its ghosts than its poor.

A perfectly charming ghost story, "The Bagman's Uncle" treads the line between humoresque, fantasy, and dreamscape, wrought perfectly in the model of a Washington Irving's ambiguous ghost tales (especially the dreamy fantasies "Rip Van Winkle," "Dolph Heyliger," "The Adventure of the Black Fisherman," "The Adventure of My Grandfather," "The Adventure of the German Student," "The Adventure of My Uncle," "The Legend of Sleepy Hollow," and "The Spectre Bridegroom") which wove deep layers of uncertainty around their spectral events. Whether these phantasms were generated by drunkenness, insanity, tricksters, miscommunication, or genuine spooks are largely contingent on the reader's interpretation and cynicism. At this point in his literary career – continuing up to the allegorical "Goblins Who Stole a Sexton" – Dickens used supernaturalism purely as a vessel for humor and social satire, much like Mark Twain, Stephen Crane, and Jack London would later in the century. Whether the bagman's uncle is a drunk (highly suggested), a napper (also hinted at), or the victim of a whirlwind supernatural visitation is open to interpretation, but the overwhelming sense that Dickens hopes to convey is one of wistful fantasy and quixotic reverie.

The Ghosts of the Mail
Or, The Story of the Bagman's Uncle
EXCERPTED *from* THE PICKWICK PAPERS, CHAPTER *Forty-Nine*
{1837}

'MY uncle, gentlemen,' said the bagman, 'was one of the merriest, pleasantest, cleverest fellows, that ever lived. I wish you had known him, gentlemen. On second thoughts, gentlemen, I don't wish you had known him, for if you had, you would have been all, by this time, in the ordinary course of nature, if not dead, at all events so near it, as to have taken to stopping at home and giving up company, which would have deprived me of the inestimable pleasure of addressing you at this moment. Gentlemen, I wish your fathers and mothers had known my uncle. They would have been amazingly fond of him, especially your respectable mothers; I know they would. If any two of his numerous virtues predominated over the many that adorned his character, I should say they were his mixed punch and his after-supper song. Excuse my dwelling on these melancholy recollections of departed worth; you won't see a man like my uncle every day in the week.

'I have always considered it a great point in my uncle's character, gentlemen, that he was the intimate friend and companion of Tom Smart, of the great house of Bilson and Slum, Cateaton Street, City. My uncle collected for Tiggin and Welps, but for a long time he went pretty near the same journey as Tom; and the very first night they met, my uncle took a fancy for Tom, and Tom took a fancy for my uncle. They made a bet of a new hat before they had known each other half an hour, who should brew the best quart of punch and drink it the quickest. My uncle was judged to have won the making, but Tom Smart beat him in the drinking by about half a salt-spoonful. They took another quart apiece to drink each other's health in, and were staunch friends ever afterwards. There's a destiny in these things, gentlemen; we can't help it.

'In personal appearance, my uncle was a trifle shorter than the middle size; he was a thought stouter too, than the ordinary run of people, and perhaps his face might be a shade redder. He had the jolliest face you ever saw, gentleman: something like Punch, with a handsome nose and chin; his eyes were always twinkling and sparkling with good-humour; and a smile—not one of your unmeaning wooden grins, but a real, merry, hearty, good-tempered smile—was perpetually on his countenance. He was pitched out of his gig once, and knocked, head first, against a milestone. There he lay, stunned, and so cut about the face with some gravel which had been heaped up alongside it, that, to use my uncle's own strong expression, if his mother could have revisited the earth, she wouldn't have known him. Indeed, when I come to think of the matter, gentlemen, I feel pretty sure she wouldn't, for she died when my uncle was two years and seven months old, and I think it's very likely that, even without the gravel, his top-boots would have puzzled the good lady not a little; to say nothing of his jolly red face. However, there he lay, and I have heard my uncle say, many a time, that the man said who picked him up that he was smiling as merrily as if he had tumbled out for a treat, and that after they had bled him, the first faint glimmerings of returning animation, were his jumping up in bed, bursting out into a loud laugh, kissing the young woman who held the basin, and demanding a mutton chop and a pickled walnut. He was very fond of pickled walnuts, gentlemen. He said he always found that, taken without vinegar, they relished the beer.

'My uncle's great journey was in the fall of the leaf, at which time he collected debts, and took orders, in the north; going from London to Edinburgh, from Edinburgh to Glasgow, from Glasgow back to Edinburgh, and thence to London by the smack. You are to understand that his second visit to Edinburgh was for his own pleasure. He used to go back for a week, just to look up his old friends; and what with breakfasting with this one, lunching with that, dining with the third, and supping with another, a pretty tight week he used to make of it. I don't know whether any of you, gentlemen, ever partook of a real substantial hospitable Scotch breakfast, and then went out to a slight lunch of a bushel of oysters, a dozen or so of bottled ale, and a noggin or two of whiskey to close up with. If you ever did, you will agree with me that it requires a pretty strong head to go out to dinner and supper afterwards.

'But bless your hearts and eyebrows, all this sort of thing was nothing to my uncle! He was so well seasoned, that it was mere child's play. I have heard him say that he could see the Dundee people out, any day, and walk home afterwards without staggering; and yet the Dundee people have as strong heads and as strong punch, gentlemen, as you are likely to meet with, between the poles. I have heard of a Glasgow man and a Dundee man drinking against each other for fifteen hours at a sitting. They were both suffocated, as nearly as could be ascertained, at the same moment, but with this trifling exception, gentlemen, they were not a bit the worse for it.

'One night, within four-and-twenty hours of the time when he had settled to take shipping for London, my uncle supped at the house of a very old friend of his, a Bailie Mac something and four syllables after it, who lived in the old town of Edinburgh. There were the bailie's wife, and the bailie's three daughters, and the bailie's grown-up son, and three or four stout, bushy eye-browed, canny, old Scotch fellows, that the bailie had got together to do honour to my uncle, and help to make merry. It was a glorious supper. There was kippered salmon, and Finnan haddocks, and a lamb's head, and a haggis—a celebrated Scotch dish, gentlemen, which my uncle used to say always looked to him, when it came to table, very much like a Cupid's stomach—and a great many other things besides, that I forget the names of, but very good things, notwithstanding. The lassies were pretty and agreeable; the bailie's wife was one of the best creatures that ever lived; and my uncle was in thoroughly good cue. The consequence of which was, that the young ladies tittered and giggled, and the old lady laughed out loud, and the bailie and the other old fellows roared till they were red in the face, the whole mortal time. I don't quite recollect how many tumblers of whiskey-toddy each man drank after supper; but this I know, that about one o'clock in the morning, the bailie's grown-up son became insensible while attempting the first verse of "Willie brewed a peck o' maut"; and he having been, for half an hour before, the only other man visible above the mahogany, it occurred to my uncle that it was almost time to think about going, especially as drinking had set in at seven o'clock, in order that he might get home at a decent hour. But, thinking it might not be quite polite to go just then, my uncle voted himself into the chair, mixed another glass, rose to propose his own health, addressed himself in a neat and complimentary speech, and drank the toast with great enthusiasm. Still nobody woke; so my uncle took a little drop more—neat this time, to prevent the toddy from disagreeing with him—and, laying violent hands on his hat, sallied forth into the street.

'It was a wild, gusty night when my uncle closed the bailie's door, and settling his hat firmly on his head to prevent the wind from taking it, thrust his hands into his pockets, and looking upward, took a short survey of the state of the weather. The clouds were drifting over the moon at their giddiest speed; at one time wholly obscuring her; at another, suffering her to burst forth in full splendour and shed her light on all the objects around; anon, driving over her again, with increased velocity, and shrouding everything in darkness. "Really, this won't do," said my uncle, addressing himself to the weather, as if he felt himself personally offended. "This is not at all the kind of thing for my voyage. It will not do at any price," said my uncle, very impressively. Having repeated this, several times, he recovered his balance with some difficulty—for he was rather giddy with looking up into the sky so long—and walked merrily on.

'The bailie's house was in the Canongate, and my uncle was going to the other end of Leith Walk, rather better than a mile's journey. On either side of him, there shot up against the dark sky, tall, gaunt, straggling houses, with time-stained fronts, and windows that seemed to have shared the lot of eyes in mortals, and to have grown dim and sunken with age. Six, seven, eight storey high, were the houses; storey piled upon storey, as children build with cards—throwing their dark shadows over the roughly paved road, and making the dark night darker. A few oil lamps were scattered at long distances, but they only served to mark the dirty entrance to some narrow close, or to show where a common stair communicated, by steep and intricate windings, with the various flats above. Glancing at all these things with the air of a man who had seen them too often before, to think them worthy of much notice now, my uncle walked up the middle of the street, with a thumb in each waistcoat pocket, indulging from time to time in various snatches of song, chanted forth with such good-will and spirit, that the quiet honest folk started from their first sleep and lay trembling in bed till the sound died away in the distance; when, satisfying themselves that it was only some drunken ne'er-do-weel finding his way home, they covered themselves up warm and fell asleep again.

'I am particular in describing how my uncle walked up the middle of the street, with his thumbs in his waistcoat pockets, gentlemen, because, as he often used to say (and with great reason too) there is nothing at all extraordinary in this story, unless you distinctly understand at the beginning, that he was not by any means of a marvellous or romantic turn.

'Gentlemen, my uncle walked on with his thumbs in his waistcoat pockets, taking the middle of the street to himself, and singing, now a verse of a love song, and then a verse of a drinking one, and when he was tired of both, whistling melodiously, until he reached the North Bridge, which, at this point, connects the old and new towns of Edinburgh. Here he stopped for a minute, to look at the strange, irregular clusters of lights piled one above the other, and twinkling afar off so high, that they looked like stars, gleaming from the castle walls on the one side and the Calton Hill on the other, as if they illuminated veritable castles in the air; while the old picturesque town slept heavily on, in gloom and darkness below: its palace and chapel of Holyrood, guarded day and night, as a friend of my uncle's used to say, by old Arthur's Seat, towering, surly and dark, like some gruff genius, over the ancient city he has watched so long. I say, gentlemen, my uncle stopped here, for a minute, to look about him; and then, paying a compliment to the weather, which had a little cleared up, though the moon was sinking, walked on again, as royally as before; keeping the middle of the road with great dignity, and looking as if he would very much like to meet with somebody who would dispute possession of it with him. There was nobody at all disposed to contest the point, as it happened; and so, on he went, with his thumbs in his waistcoat pockets, like a lamb.

'When my uncle reached the end of Leith Walk, he had to cross a pretty large piece of waste ground which separated him from a short street which he had to turn down to go direct to his lodging. Now, in this piece of waste ground, there was, at that time, an enclosure belonging to some wheelwright who contracted with the Post Office for the purchase of old, worn-out mail coaches; and my uncle, being very fond of coaches, old, young, or middle-aged, all at once took it into his head to step out of his road for no other purpose than to peep between the palings at these mails—about a dozen of which he remembered to have seen, crowded together in a very forlorn and dismantled state, inside. My uncle was a very enthusiastic, emphatic sort of person, gentlemen; so, finding that he could not obtain a good peep between the palings he got over them, and sitting himself quietly down on an old axle-tree, began to contemplate the mail coaches with a deal of gravity.

'There might be a dozen of them, or there might be more—my uncle was never quite certain on this point, and being a man of very scrupulous veracity about numbers, didn't like to say—but there they stood, all huddled together in the most desolate condition imaginable. The doors had been torn from their hinges and removed; the linings had been stripped off, only a shred hanging here and there by a rusty nail; the lamps were gone, the poles had long since vanished, the ironwork was rusty, the paint was worn away; the wind whistled through the chinks in the bare woodwork; and the rain, which had collected on the roofs, fell, drop by drop, into the insides with a hollow and melancholy sound. They were the decaying skeletons of departed mails, and in that lonely place, at that time of night, they looked chill and dismal.

'My uncle rested his head upon his hands, and thought of the busy, bustling people who had rattled about, years before, in the old coaches, and were now as silent and changed; he thought of the numbers of people to whom one of these crazy, mouldering vehicles had borne, night after night, for many years, and through all weathers, the anxiously expected intelligence, the eagerly looked-for remittance, the promised assurance of health and safety, the sudden announcement of sickness and death. The merchant, the lover, the wife, the widow, the mother, the school-boy, the very child who tottered to the door at the postman's knock—how had they all looked forward to the arrival of the old coach. And where were they all now? 'Gentlemen, my uncle used to SAY that he thought all this at the time, but I rather suspect he learned it out of some book afterwards, for he distinctly stated that he fell into a kind of doze, as he sat on the old axle-tree looking at the decayed mail coaches, and that he was suddenly awakened by some deep church bell striking two. Now, my uncle was never a fast thinker, and if he had thought all these things, I am quite certain it would have taken him till full half-past two o'clock at the very least. I am, therefore, decidedly of opinion, gentlemen, that my uncle fell into a kind of doze, without having thought about anything at all.

'Be this as it may, a church bell struck two. My uncle woke, rubbed his eyes, and jumped up in astonishment.

'In one instant, after the clock struck two, the whole of this deserted and quiet spot had become a scene of most extraordinary life and animation. The mail coach doors were on their hinges, the lining was replaced, the ironwork was as good as new, the paint was restored, the lamps were alight; cushions and greatcoats were on every coach-box, porters were thrusting parcels into every boot, guards were stowing away letter-bags, hostlers were dashing pails of water against the renovated wheels; numbers of men were pushing about, fixing poles into every coach; passengers arrived, portmanteaus were handed up, horses were put to; in short, it was perfectly clear that every mail there, was to be off directly. Gentlemen, my uncle opened his eyes so wide at all this, that, to the very last moment of his life, he used to wonder how it fell out that he had ever been able to shut 'em again.

"'Now then!" said a voice, as my uncle felt a hand on his shoulder, "you're booked for one inside. You'd better get in."

"'I booked!" said my uncle, turning round.

"'Yes, certainly."

'My uncle, gentlemen, could say nothing, he was so very much astonished. The queerest thing of all was that although there was such a crowd of persons, and although fresh faces were pouring in, every moment, there was no telling where they came from. They seemed to start up, in some strange manner, from the ground, or the air, and disappear in the same way. When a porter had put his luggage in the coach, and received his fare, he turned round and was gone; and before my uncle had well begun to wonder what had become of him, half a dozen fresh ones started up, and staggered along under the weight of parcels, which seemed big enough to crush them. The passengers were all dressed so oddly too! Large, broad-skirted laced coats, with great cuffs and no collars; and wigs, gentlemen—great formal wigs with a tie behind. My uncle could make nothing of it.

"'Now, are you going to get in?" said the person who had addressed my uncle before. He was dressed as a mail guard, with a wig on his head and most enormous cuffs to his coat, and had a lantern in one hand, and a huge blunderbuss in the other, which he was going to stow away in his little arm-chest. "ARE you going to get in, Jack Martin?" said the guard, holding the lantern to my uncle's face.

"'Hollo!" said my uncle, falling back a step or two. "That's familiar!"

"'It's so on the way-bill," said the guard.

"'Isn't there a 'Mister' before it?" said my uncle. For he felt, gentlemen, that for a guard he didn't know, to call him Jack Martin, was a liberty which the Post Office wouldn't have sanctioned if they had known it.

"'No, there is not," rejoined the guard coolly.

"'Is the fare paid?" inquired my uncle.

"'Of course it is," rejoined the guard.

"'It is, is it?" said my uncle. "Then here goes! Which coach?"

"''This," said the guard, pointing to an old-fashioned Edinburgh and London mail, which had the steps down and the door open. "Stop! Here are the other passengers. Let them get in first."

'As the guard spoke, there all at once appeared, right in front of my uncle, a young gentleman in a powdered wig, and a sky-blue coat trimmed with silver, made very full and broad in the skirts, which were lined with buckram. Tiggin and Welps were in the printed calico and waistcoat piece line, gentlemen, so my uncle knew all the materials at once. He wore knee breeches, and a kind of leggings rolled up over his silk stockings, and shoes with buckles; he had ruffles at his wrists, a three-cornered hat on his head, and a long taper sword by his side. The flaps of his waist-coat came half-way down his thighs, and the ends of his cravat reached to his waist. He stalked gravely to the coach door, pulled off his hat, and held it above his head at arm's length, cocking his little finger in the air at the same time, as some affected people do, when they take a cup of tea. Then he drew his feet together, and made a low, grave bow, and then put out his left hand. My

uncle was just going to step forward, and shake it heartily, when he perceived that these attentions were directed, not towards him, but to a young lady who just then appeared at the foot of the steps, attired in an old-fashioned green velvet dress with a long waist and stomacher. She had no bonnet on her head, gentlemen, which was muffled in a black silk hood, but she looked round for an instant as she prepared to get into the coach, and such a beautiful face as she disclosed, my uncle had never seen—not even in a picture. She got into the coach, holding up her dress with one hand; and as my uncle always said with a round oath, when he told the story, he wouldn't have believed it possible that legs and feet could have been brought to such a state of perfection unless he had seen them with his own eyes.

'But, in this one glimpse of the beautiful face, my uncle saw that the young lady cast an imploring look upon him, and that she appeared terrified and distressed. He noticed, too, that the young fellow in the powdered wig, notwithstanding his show of gallantry, which was all very fine and grand, clasped her tight by the wrist when she got in, and followed himself immediately afterwards. An uncommonly ill-looking fellow, in a close brown wig, and a plum-coloured suit, wearing a very large sword, and boots up to his hips, belonged to the party; and when he sat himself down next to the young lady, who shrank into a corner at his approach, my uncle was confirmed in his original impression that something dark and mysterious was going forward, or, as he always said himself, that "there was a screw loose somewhere." It's quite surprising how quickly he made up his mind to help the lady at any peril, if she needed any help.

'"Death and lightning!" exclaimed the young gentleman, laying his hand upon his sword as my uncle entered the coach.

'"Blood and thunder!" roared the other gentleman. With this, he whipped his sword out, and made a lunge at my uncle without further ceremony. My uncle had no weapon about him, but with great dexterity he snatched the ill-looking gentleman's three-cornered hat from his head, and, receiving the point of his sword right through the crown, squeezed the sides together, and held it tight.

'"Pink him behind!" cried the ill-looking gentleman to his companion, as he struggled to regain his sword.

'"He had better not," cried my uncle, displaying the heel of one of his shoes, in a threatening manner. "I'll kick his brains out, if he has any—, or fracture his skull if he hasn't." Exerting all his strength, at this moment, my uncle wrenched the ill-looking man's sword from his grasp, and flung it clean out of the coach window, upon which the younger gentleman vociferated, "Death and lightning!" again, and laid his hand upon the hilt of his sword, in a very fierce manner, but didn't draw it. Perhaps, gentlemen, as my uncle used to say with a smile, perhaps he was afraid of alarming the lady.

'"Now, gentlemen," said my uncle, taking his seat deliberately, "I don't want to have any death, with or without lightning, in a lady's presence, and we have had quite blood and thundering enough for one journey; so, if you please, we'll sit in our places like quiet insides. Here, guard, pick up that gentleman's carving-knife."

'As quickly as my uncle said the words, the guard appeared at the coach window, with the gentleman's sword in his hand. He held up his lantern, and looked earnestly in my uncle's face, as he handed it in, when, by its light, my uncle saw, to his great surprise, that an immense crowd of mail-coach guards swarmed round the window, every one of whom had his eyes earnestly fixed upon him too. He had never seen such a sea of white faces, red bodies, and earnest eyes, in all his born days.

'"This is the strangest sort of thing I ever had anything to do with," thought my uncle; "allow me to return you your hat, sir."

'The ill-looking gentleman received his three-cornered hat in silence, looked at the hole in the middle with an inquiring air, and finally stuck it on the top of his wig with a solemnity the effect of which was a trifle impaired by his sneezing violently at the moment, and jerking it off again.

'"All right!" cried the guard with the lantern, mounting into his little seat behind. Away they went. My uncle peeped out of the coach window as they emerged from the yard, and observed that the other mails, with coachmen, guards, horses, and passengers, complete, were driving round and round in circles, at a slow trot of about five miles an hour. My uncle burned with indignation, gentlemen. As a commercial man, he felt that the mail-bags were not to be trifled with, and he resolved to memorialise the Post Office on the subject, the very instant he reached London.

'At present, however, his thoughts were occupied with the young lady who sat in the farthest corner of the coach, with her face muffled closely in her hood; the gentleman with the sky-blue coat sitting opposite to her; the other man in the plum-coloured suit, by her side; and both watching her intently. If she so much as rustled the folds of her hood, he could hear the ill-looking man clap his hand upon his sword, and could tell by the other's breathing (it was so dark he couldn't see his face) that he was looking as big as if he were going to devour her at a mouthful. This roused my uncle more and more, and he resolved, come what might, to see the end of it. He had a great admiration for bright eyes, and sweet faces, and pretty legs and feet; in short, he was fond of the whole sex. It runs in our family, gentleman—so am I.

'Many were the devices which my uncle practised, to attract the lady's attention, or at all events, to engage the mysterious gentlemen in conversation. They were all in vain; the gentlemen wouldn't talk, and the lady didn't dare. He thrust his head out of the coach window at intervals, and bawled out to know why they didn't go faster. But he called till he was hoarse; nobody paid the least attention to him. He leaned back in the coach, and thought of the beautiful face, and the feet and legs. This answered better; it whiled away the time, and kept him from wondering where he was going, and how it was that he found himself in such an odd situation. Not that this would have worried him much, anyway—he was a mighty free and easy, roving, devil-may-care sort of person, was my uncle, gentlemen.

'All of a sudden the coach stopped. "Hollo!" said my uncle, "what's in the wind now?"

'"Alight here," said the guard, letting down the steps.

'"Here!" cried my uncle.

'"Here," rejoined the guard.

{31}

"'I'll do nothing of the sort," said my uncle.

"'Very well, then stop where you are," said the guard.

"'I will," said my uncle.

"'Do," said the guard.

'The passengers had regarded this colloquy with great attention, and, finding that my uncle was determined not to alight, the younger man squeezed past him, to hand the lady out. At this moment, the ill-looking man was inspecting the hole in the crown of his three-cornered hat. As the young lady brushed past, she dropped one of her gloves into my uncle's hand, and softly whispered, with her lips so close to his face that he felt her warm breath on his nose, the single word "Help!" Gentlemen, my uncle leaped out of the coach at once, with such violence that it rocked on the springs again.

"'Oh! you've thought better of it, have you?" said the guard, when he saw my uncle standing on the ground.

'My uncle looked at the guard for a few seconds, in some doubt whether it wouldn't be better to wrench his blunderbuss from him, fire it in the face of the man with the big sword, knock the rest of the company over the head with the stock, snatch up the young lady, and go off in the smoke. On second thoughts, however, he abandoned this plan, as being a shade too melodramatic in the execution, and followed the two mysterious men, who, keeping the lady between them, were now entering an old house in front of which the coach had stopped. They turned into the passage, and my uncle followed.

'Of all the ruinous and desolate places my uncle had ever beheld, this was the most so. It looked as if it had once been a large house of entertainment; but the roof had fallen in, in many places, and the stairs were steep, rugged, and broken. There was a huge fireplace in the room into which they walked, and the chimney was blackened with smoke; but no warm blaze lighted it up now. The white feathery dust of burned wood was still strewed over the hearth, but the stove was cold, and all was dark and gloomy.

"'Well," said my uncle, as he looked about him, "a mail travelling at the rate of six miles and a half an hour, and stopping for an indefinite time at such a hole as this, is rather an irregular sort of proceeding, I fancy. This shall be made known. I'll write to the papers."

'My uncle said this in a pretty loud voice, and in an open, unreserved sort of manner, with the view of engaging the two strangers in conversation if he could. But, neither of them took any more notice of him than whispering to each other, and scowling at him as they did so. The lady was at the farther end of the room, and once she ventured to wave her hand, as if beseeching my uncle's assistance.

'At length the two strangers advanced a little, and the conversation began in earnest.

"'You don't know this is a private room, I suppose, fellow?" said the gentleman in sky-blue.

"'No, I do not, fellow," rejoined my uncle. "Only, if this is a private room specially ordered for the occasion, I should think the public room must be a VERY comfortable one;" with this, my uncle sat himself down in a high-backed chair, and took such an accurate measure of the gentleman, with his eyes, that Tiggin and Welps could have supplied him with printed calico for a suit, and not an inch too much or too little, from that estimate alone.

'"Quit this room," said both men together, grasping their swords.

'"Eh?" said my uncle, not at all appearing to comprehend their meaning.

'"Quit the room, or you are a dead man," said the ill-looking fellow with the large sword, drawing it at the same time and flourishing it in the air.

'"Down with him!" cried the gentleman in sky-blue, drawing his sword also, and falling back two or three yards. "Down with him!" The lady gave a loud scream.

'Now, my uncle was always remarkable for great boldness, and great presence of mind. All the time that he had appeared so indifferent to what was going on, he had been looking slily about for some missile or weapon of defence, and at the very instant when the swords were drawn, he espied, standing in the chimney-corner, an old basket-hilted rapier in a rusty scabbard. At one bound, my uncle caught it in his hand, drew it, flourished it gallantly above his head, called aloud to the lady to keep out of the way, hurled the chair at the man in sky-blue, and the scabbard at the man in plum-colour, and taking advantage of the confusion, fell upon them both, pell-mell.

'Gentlemen, there is an old story—none the worse for being true—regarding a fine young Irish gentleman, who being asked if he could play the fiddle, replied he had no doubt he could, but he couldn't exactly say, for certain, because he had never tried. This is not inapplicable to my uncle and his fencing. He had never had a sword in his hand before, except once when he played Richard the Third at a private theatre, upon which occasion it was arranged with Richmond that he was to be run through, from behind, without showing fight at all. But here he was, cutting and slashing with two experienced swordsman, thrusting, and guarding, and poking, and slicing, and acquitting himself in the most manful and dexterous manner possible, although up to that time he had never been aware that he had the least notion of the science. It only shows how true the old saying is, that a man never knows what he can do till he tries, gentlemen.

'The noise of the combat was terrific; each of the three combatants swearing like troopers, and their swords clashing with as much noise as if all the knives and steels in Newport market were rattling together, at the same time. When it was at its very height, the lady (to encourage my uncle most probably) withdrew her hood entirely from her face, and disclosed a countenance of such dazzling beauty, that he would have fought against fifty men, to win one smile from it and die. He had done wonders before, but now he began to powder away like a raving mad giant.

'At this very moment, the gentleman in sky-blue turning round, and seeing the young lady with her face uncovered, vented an exclamation of rage and jealousy, and, turning his weapon against her beautiful bosom, pointed a thrust at her heart, which caused my uncle to utter a cry of apprehension that made the building ring. The lady stepped lightly aside, and snatching the young man's sword from his hand, before he had recovered his balance, drove him to the wall, and running it through him, and the panelling, up to the very hilt, pinned him there, hard and fast. It was a splendid example. My uncle, with a loud shout of triumph, and a strength that was irresistible, made his adversary retreat in the same direction, and plunging the old rapier into the very centre of a large red flower in the pattern of his waistcoat, nailed him beside his friend; there they both stood, gentlemen, jerking their arms and legs about in agony, like the toy-shop figures that are moved by a piece of pack-thread. My uncle always said, afterwards, that this was one of the surest means he knew of, for disposing of an enemy; but it was liable to one objection on the ground of expense, inasmuch as it involved the loss of a sword for every man disabled.

"'The mail, the mail!' cried the lady, running up to my uncle and throwing her beautiful arms round his neck; "we may yet escape."

"'May!' cried my uncle; "why, my dear, there's nobody else to kill, is there?" My uncle was rather disappointed, gentlemen, for he thought a little quiet bit of love-making would be agreeable after the slaughtering, if it were only to change the subject.

"'We have not an instant to lose here," said the young lady. "He (pointing to the young gentleman in sky-blue) is the only son of the powerful Marquess of Filletoville." "'Well then, my dear, I'm afraid he'll never come to the title," said my uncle, looking coolly at the young gentleman as he stood fixed up against the wall, in the cockchafer fashion that I have described. "You have cut off the entail, my love."

"'I have been torn from my home and my friends by these villains," said the young lady, her features glowing with indignation. "That wretch would have married me by violence in another hour."

"'Confound his impudence!" said my uncle, bestowing a very contemptuous look on the dying heir of Filletoville.

"'As you may guess from what you have seen," said the young lady, "the party were prepared to murder me if I appealed to any one for assistance. If their accomplices find us here, we are lost. Two minutes hence may be too late. The mail!" With these words, overpowered by her feelings, and the exertion of sticking the young Marquess of Filletoville, she sank into my uncle's arms. My uncle caught her up, and bore her to the house door. There stood the mail, with four long-tailed, flowing-maned, black horses, ready harnessed; but no coachman, no guard, no hostler even, at the horses' heads.

'Gentlemen, I hope I do no injustice to my uncle's memory, when I express my opinion, that although he was a bachelor, he had held some ladies in his arms before this time; I believe, indeed, that he had rather a habit of kissing barmaids; and I know, that in one or two instances, he had been seen by credible witnesses, to hug a landlady in a very perceptible manner. I mention the circumstance, to show what a very uncommon sort of person this beautiful young lady must have been, to have affected my uncle in the way she did; he used to say, that as her long dark hair trailed over his arm, and her beautiful dark eyes fixed themselves upon his face when she recovered, he felt so strange and nervous that his legs trembled beneath him. But who can look in a sweet, soft pair of dark eyes, without feeling queer? I can't, gentlemen. I am afraid to look at some eyes I know, and that's the truth of it.

"'You will never leave me," murmured the young lady.

"'Never," said my uncle. And he meant it too.

"'My dear preserver!" exclaimed the young lady. "My dear, kind, brave preserver!"

"'Don't," said my uncle, interrupting her.

"'Why?" inquired the young lady.

"'Because your mouth looks so beautiful when you speak," rejoined my uncle, "that I'm afraid I shall be rude enough to kiss it."

'The young lady put up her hand as if to caution my uncle not to do so, and said—No, she didn't say anything—she smiled. When you are looking at a pair of the most delicious lips in the world, and see them gently break into a roguish smile—if you are very near them, and nobody else by—you cannot better testify your admiration of their beautiful form and colour than by kissing them at once. My uncle did so, and I honour him for it.

"'Hark!" cried the young lady, starting. "The noise of wheels, and horses!"

"'So it is," said my uncle, listening. He had a good ear for wheels, and the trampling of hoofs; but there appeared to be so many horses and carriages rattling towards them, from a distance, that it was impossible to form a guess at their number. The sound was like that of fifty brakes, with six blood cattle in each.

"'We are pursued!" cried the young lady, clasping her hands. "We are pursued. I have no hope but in you!"

'There was such an expression of terror in her beautiful face, that my uncle made up his mind at once. He lifted her into the coach, told her not to be frightened, pressed his lips to hers once more, and then advising her to draw up the window to keep the cold air out, mounted to the box.

"'Stay, love," cried the young lady.

"'What's the matter?" said my uncle, from the coach-box.

"'I want to speak to you," said the young lady; "only a word. Only one word, dearest."

"'Must I get down?" inquired my uncle. The lady made no answer, but she smiled again. Such a smile, gentlemen! It beat the other one, all to nothing. My uncle descended from his perch in a twinkling.

"'What is it, my dear?" said my uncle, looking in at the coach window. The lady happened to bend forward at the same time, and my uncle thought she looked more beautiful than she had done yet. He was very close to her just then, gentlemen, so he really ought to know.

"'What is it, my dear?" said my uncle.

"'Will you never love any one but me—never marry any one beside?" said the young lady.

'My uncle swore a great oath that he never would marry anybody else, and the young lady drew in her head, and pulled up the window. He jumped upon the box, squared his elbows, adjusted the ribands, seized the whip which lay on the roof, gave one flick to the off leader, and away went the four long-tailed, flowing-maned black horses, at fifteen good English miles an hour, with the old mail-coach behind them. Whew! How they tore along!

'The noise behind grew louder. The faster the old mail went, the faster came the pursuers—men, horses, dogs, were leagued in the pursuit. The noise was frightful, but, above all, rose the voice of the young lady, urging my uncle on, and shrieking, "Faster! Faster!"

'They whirled past the dark trees, as feathers would be swept before a hurricane. Houses, gates, churches, haystacks, objects of every kind they shot by, with a velocity and noise like roaring waters suddenly let loose. But still the noise of pursuit grew louder, and still my uncle could hear the young lady wildly screaming, "Faster! Faster!"

'My uncle plied whip and rein, and the horses flew onward till they were white with foam; and yet the noise behind increased; and yet the young lady cried, "Faster! Faster!" My uncle gave a loud stamp on the boot in the energy of the moment, and—found that it was gray morning, and he was sitting in the wheelwright's yard, on the box of an old Edinburgh mail, shivering with the cold and wet and stamping his feet to warm them! He got down, and looked eagerly inside for the beautiful young lady. Alas! There was neither door nor seat to the coach. It was a mere shell.

'Of course, my uncle knew very well that there was some mystery in the matter, and that everything had passed exactly as he used to relate it. He remained staunch to the great oath he had sworn to the beautiful young lady, refusing several eligible landladies on her account, and dying a bachelor at last. He always said what a curious thing it was that he should have found out, by such a mere accident as his clambering over the palings, that the ghosts of mail-coaches and horses, guards, coachmen, and passengers, were in the habit of making journeys regularly every night. He used to add, that he believed he was the only living person who had ever been taken as a passenger on one of these excursions. And I think he was right, gentlemen—at least I never heard of any other.'

'I wonder what these ghosts of mail-coaches carry in their bags,' said the landlord, who had listened to the whole story with profound attention.

'The dead letters, of course,' said the bagman.

'Oh, ah! To be sure,' rejoined the landlord. 'I never thought of that.'

AFTER reading this tale, most ghost story aficionados will naturally call to mind Amelia B. Edwards' classic "The Phantom Coach." The association is natural: Edwards' tale follows a wanderer who, becoming lost in a blizzard, is grateful to discover the post road, where he successfully hails and boards a passing mail coach. As the carriage rocks down the snowy pass, the narrator begins to note its horrendous disrepair: the rotten upholstery, the decayed blind shades, the mold encrusted walls. Looking up for the first time, he understands that his three fellow passengers are corpses, and that he has transcended the dimensions of time, becoming a passenger on the coach that was destroyed in a crash years ago. Dickens had no such intentions, and his specters are just as likely flights of fancy or drunken hallucinations, but the overall theme is the same: the barrier between past and present, hero and fool, living and dead, and monotony and adventure are thin things indeed. The uncle (very much indeed, it must be noted, like the grandfather in Irving's "Adventure of my Grandfather; or, the Bold Dragoon") may be chivalric romancer or a lazy ne'er-do-well – a Don Juan or a Don Quixote. Ultimately the truth is in perception: he believes the narrative of his spiriting away (whether he invented it, hallucinated it, dreamt it, or not), and he owns it. It becomes his identity, and causes a plain, ordinary, un-romantic man to be transformed in the eyes of others. Regardless of its veracity, its effect is entirely real, and the round, red-nosed clown is changed by the vision. Reality is only as real as far as we perceive it, and until we cling to the foundations of logic, perception, and fact, we may be utterly oblivious to the fact that the worthies our society idolizes are hideous idiots, that the untouchables we scorn are complex human souls, that the wealth we value is relatively worthless, and that a life dedicated blindly to hard, devoted work may be astronomically less satisfying than one shaped by indulgent passions and flights of fancy.

THE adherent of Edgar Allan Poe will immediately recognize the debt Poe owes to
this morbid tale. The immediate kinsman of "The Tell-Tale Heart," "The Cask of
Amontillado," "The Black Cat," "Berenice," and – to degrees – "Ligeia," "William
Wilson," and "Hop-Frog," it forged the program that Poe would later infuse into
these stories: a chilling sane madman recounts the history of his madness, his
increasing isolation from rational society, and the revolting exposure of his secret
lunacy through an act of violence. "A Madman's Manuscript" treads the line between
psychological thriller and speculative fiction in the same way that "Black Cat" and
"Tell-Tale Heart" do – by blurring the normally distinct boundaries between
fantasy/imagination and reality/sensation, between internality and externality. As
always, Dickens also manages to invest this parable with a degree of class criticism,
as his madman is apparently the only one who willing acknowledges the selfish
motives of the story's avaricious characters.

A Madman's Manuscript
EXCERPTED *from* THE PICKWICK PAPERS, CHAPTER *Eleven*
{1836}

"YES! -- a madman's! How that word would have struck to my heart, many years
ago! How it would have roused the terror that used to come upon me sometimes;
sending the blood hissing and tingling through my veins, till the cold dew of fear
stood in large drops upon my skin, and my knees knocked together with fright! I
like it now though. It's a fine name. Shew me the monarch whose angry frown was
ever feared like the glare of a madman's eye -- whose cord and axe were ever half
so sure as a madman's grip. Ho! ho! It's a grand thing to be mad! to be peeped at
like a wild lion through the iron bars -- to gnash one's teeth and howl, through the
long still night, to the merry ring of a heavy chain -- and to roll and twine among
the straw, transported with such brave music. Hurrah for the madhouse! Oh, it's a
rare place!

"I remember days when I was afraid of being mad; when I used to start from my
sleep, and fall upon my knees, and pray to be spared from the curse of my race;
when I rushed from the sight of merriment or happiness, to hide myself in
some lonely place, and spend the weary hours in watching the progress of the fever
that was to consume my brain. I knew that madness was mixed up with my very
blood, and the marrow of my bones; that one generation had passed away without
the pestilence appearing among them, and that I was the first in whom it would
revive. I knew it must be so: that so it always had been, and so it ever would be:
and when I cowered in some obscure corner of a crowded room, and saw men
whisper, and point, and turn their eyes towards me, I knew they were telling each
other of the doomed madman; and I slunk away again to mope in solitude.

"I did this for years; long, long years they were. The nights here are long
sometimes -- very long; but they are nothing to the restless nights, and dreadful

dreams I had at that time. It makes me cold to remember them. Large dusky forms with sly and jeering faces crouched in the corners of the room, and bent over my bed at night, tempting me to madness. They told me in low whispers, that the floor of the old house in which my father's father died, was stained with his own blood, shed by his own hand in raging madness. I drove my fingers into my ears, but they screamed into my head till the room rang with it, that in one generation before him the madness slumbered, but that his grandfather had lived for years with his hands fettered to the ground, to prevent his tearing himself to pieces. I knew they told the truth -- I knew it well. I had found it out years before, though they had tried to keep it from me. Ha! ha! I was too cunning for them, madman as they thought me.

"At last it came upon me, and I wondered how I could ever have feared it. I could go into the world now, and laugh and shout with the best among them. I knew I was mad, but they did not even suspect it. How I used to hug myself with delight, when I thought of the fine trick I was playing them after their old pointing and leering, when I was not mad, but only dreading that I might one day become so! And how I used to laugh for joy, when I was alone, and thought how well I kept my secret, and how quickly my kind friends would have fallen from me, if they had known the truth. I could have screamed with ecstasy when I dined alone with some fine roaring fellow, to think how pale he would have turned, and how fast he would have run, if he had known that the dear friend who sat close to him, sharpening a bright glittering knife, was a madman with all the power, and half the will, to plunge it in his heart. Oh, it was a merry life!

"Riches became mine, wealth poured in upon me, and I rioted in pleasures enhanced a thousandfold to me by the consciousness of my well-kept secret. I inherited an estate. The law -- the eagle-eyed law itself -- had been deceived, and had handed over disputed thousands to a madman's hands. Where was the wit of the sharp-sighted men of sound mind? Where the dexterity of the lawyers, eager to discover a flaw? The madman's cunning had over-reached them all.

"I had money. How I was courted! I spent it profusely. How I was praised! How those three proud overbearing brothers humbled themselves before me! The old white-headed father, too -- such deference -- such respect -- such devoted friendship -- he worshipped me! The old man had a daughter, and the young men a sister; and all the five were poor. I was rich; and when I married the girl, I saw a smile of triumph play upon the faces of her needy relatives, as they thought of their well-planned scheme, and their fine prize. It was for me to smile. To smile! To laugh outright, and tear my hair, and roll upon the ground with shrieks of merriment. They little thought they had married her to a madman.

"Stay. If they had known it, would they have saved her? A sister's happiness against her husband's gold. The lightest feather I blow into the air, against the gay chain that ornaments my body!

"In one thing I was deceived with all my cunning. If I had not been mad -- for though we madmen are sharp-witted enough, we get bewildered sometimes -- I should have known that the girl would rather have been placed, stiff and cold in a dull leaden coffin, than borne an envied bride to my rich, glittering house. I should have known that her heart was with the dark-eyed boy whose name I once heard her breathe in her troubled sleep; and that she had been sacrificed to me, to relieve the poverty of the old white-headed man, and the haughty brothers.

"I don't remember forms or faces now, but I know the girl was beautiful. I know she was; for in the bright moonlight nights, when I start from my sleep, and all is quiet about me, I see, standing still and motionless in one corner of this cell, a slight and wasted figure with long black hair, which streaming down her back, stirs with no earthly wind, and eyes that fix their gaze on me, and never wink or close. Hush! the blood chills at my heart as I write it down -- that form is hers; the face is very pale, and the eyes are glassy bright; but I know them well. That figure never moves; it never frowns and mouths as others do, that fill this place sometimes; but it is much more dreadful to me, even than the spirits that tempted me many years ago -- it comes fresh from the grave; and is so very death-like.

"For nearly a year I saw that face grow paler; for nearly a year I saw the tears steal down the mournful cheeks, and never knew the cause. I found it out at last though. They could not keep it from me long. She had never liked me; I had never thought she did: she despised my wealth, and hated the splendour in which she lived; -- I had not expected that. She loved another. This I had never thought of. Strange feelings came over me, and thoughts, forced upon me by some secret power, whirled round and round my brain. I did not hate her, though I hated the boy she still wept for. I pitied -- yes, I pitied -- the wretched life to which her cold and selfish relations had doomed her. I knew that she could not live long, but the thought that before her death she might give birth to some ill-fated being, destined to hand down madness to its offspring, determined me. I resolved to kill her.

"For many weeks I thought of poison, and then of drowning, and then of fire. A fine sight the grand house in flames, and the madman's wife smouldering away to cinders. Think of the jest of a large reward, too, and of some sane man swinging in the wind for a deed he never did, and all through a madman's cunning! I thought often of this, but I gave it up at last. Oh! the pleasure of stropping the razor day after day, feeling the sharp edge, and thinking of the gash one stroke of its thin bright edge would make!

At last the old spirits who had been with me so often before whispered in my ear that the time was come, and thrust the open razor into my hand. I grasped it firmly, rose softly from the bed, and leaned over my sleeping wife. Her face was buried in her hands. I withdrew them softly and they fell listlessly on her bosom. She had been weeping; for the traces of the tears were still wet upon her cheek. Her face was calm and placid; and even as I looked upon it, a tranquil smile lighted up her pale features. I laid my hand softly on her shoulder. She started -- it was only a passing dream. I leant forward again. She screamed, and woke.

"One motion of my hand, and she would never again have uttered cry or sound. But I was startled, and drew back. Her eyes were fixed on mine. I know not how it was, but they cowed and frightened me; and I quailed beneath them. She rose from the bed, still gazing fixedly and steadily on me. I trembled; the razor was in my hand, but I could not move. She made towards the door. As she neared it, she

turned, and withdrew her eyes from my face. The spell was broken. I bounded forward, and clutched her by the arm. Uttering shriek upon shriek, she sunk upon the ground.

"Now I could have killed her without a struggle; but the house was alarmed. I heard the tread of footsteps on the stairs. I replaced the razor in its usual drawer, unfastened the door, and called loudly for assistance.

"They came, and raised her, and placed her on the bed. She lay bereft of animation for hours; and when life, look, and speech returned, her senses had deserted her, and she raved wildly and furiously.

"Doctors were called in -- great men who rolled up to my door in easy carriages, with fine horses and gaudy servants. They were at her bed-side for weeks. They had a great meeting, and consulted together in low and solemn voices in another room. One, the cleverest and most celebrated among them, took me aside, and bidding me prepare for the worst, told me -- me, the madman! -- that my wife was mad. He stood close beside me at an open window, his eyes looking in my face, and his hand laid upon my arm. With one effort, I could have hurled him into the street beneath. It would have been rare sport to have done it; but my secret was at stake, and I let him go. A few days after, they told me I must place her under some restraint: I must provide a keeper for her. I! I went into the open fields where none could hear me, and laughed till the air resounded with my shouts!

"She died next day. The white-headed old man followed her to the grave, and the proud brothers dropped a tear over the insensible corpse of her whose sufferings they had regarded in her lifetime with muscles of iron. All this was food for my secret mirth, and I laughed behind the white handkerchief which I held up to my face, as we rode home, 'till the tears came into my eyes.

"But though I had carried my object and killed her, I was restless and disturbed, and I felt that before long my secret must be known. I could not hide the wild mirth and joy which boiled within me, and made me when I was alone, at home, jump and beat my hands together, and dance round and round, and roar aloud. When I went out, and saw the busy crowds hurrying about the streets; or to the theatre, and heard the sound of music, and beheld the people dancing, I felt such glee, that I could have rushed among them, and torn them to pieces limb from limb, and howled in transport. But I ground my teeth, and struck my feet upon the floor, and drove my sharp nails into my hands. I kept it down; and no one knew I was a madman yet.

"I remember -- though it's one of the last things I can remember: for now I mix up realities with my dreams, and having so much to do, and being always hurried here, have no time to separate the two, from some strange confusion in which they get involved -- I remember how I let it out at last. Ha! ha! I think I see their frightened looks now, and feel the ease with which I flung them from me, and dashed my clenched fist into their white faces, and then flew like the wind, and left them screaming and shouting far behind. The strength of a giant comes upon me when I think of it. There -- see how this iron bar bends beneath my furious wrench. I could snap it like a twig, only there are long galleries here with many doors -- I don't think I could find my way along them; and even if I could, I know there are iron gates below which they keep locked and barred. They know what a clever madman I have been, and they are proud to have me here, to show.

"Let me see; -- yes, I had been out. It was late at night when I reached home, and found the proudest of the three proud brothers waiting to see me -- urgent business he said: I recollect it well. I hated that man with all a madman's hate. Many and many a time had my fingers longed to tear him. They told me he was there. I ran swiftly up-stairs. He had a word to say to me. I dismissed the servants. It was late, and we were alone together --for the first time.

"I kept my eyes carefully from him at first, for I knew what he little thought -- and I gloried in the knowledge -- that the light of madness gleamed from them like fire. We sat in silence for a few minutes. He spoke at last. My recent dissipation, and strange remarks, made so soon after his sister's death, were an insult to her memory. Coupling together many circumstances which had at first escaped his observation, he thought I had not treated her well. He wished to know whether he was right in inferring that I meant to cast a reproach upon her memory, and a disrespect upon her family. It was due to the uniform he wore, to demand this explanation.

"This man had a commission in the army -- a commission, purchased with my money, and his sister's misery! This was the man who had been the foremost in the plot to ensnare me, and grasp my wealth. This was the man who had been the main instrument in forcing his sister to wed me; well knowing that her heart was given to that puling boy. Due to his uniform! The livery of his degradation! I turned my eyes upon him -- I could not help it -- but I spoke not a word.

"I saw the sudden change that came upon him beneath my gaze. He was a bold man, but the colour faded from his face, and he drew back his chair. I dragged mine nearer to him; and as I laughed -- I was very merry then -- I saw him shudder. I felt the madness rising within me. He was afraid of me.

"'You were very fond of your sister when she was alive' -- I said -- 'Very.'

"He looked uneasily round him, and I saw his hand grasp the back of his chair: but he said nothing.

"'You villain,' said I, 'I found you out; I discovered your hellish plots against me; I know her heart was fixed on some one else before you compelled her to marry me. I know it -- I know it.'

"He jumped suddenly from his chair, brandished it aloft, and bid me stand back -- for I took care to be getting closer to him all the time I spoke.

"I screamed rather than talked, for I felt tumultuous passions eddying through my veins, and the old spirits whispering and taunting me to tear his heart out.

"'Damn you,' said I, starting up, and rushing upon him; 'I killed her. I am a madman. Down with you. Blood, blood! I will have it!' "I turned aside with one blow the chair he hurled at me in his terror, and closed with him; and with a heavy crash we rolled upon the floor together.

"It was a fine struggle that; for he was a tall strong man, fighting for his life; and I, a powerful madman, thirsting to destroy him. I knew no strength could equal mine, and I was right. Right again, though a madman! His struggles grew fainter. I knelt upon his chest, and clasped his brawny throat firmly with both hands. His face grew purple; his eyes were starting from his head, and with protruded tongue, he seemed to mock me. I squeezed the tighter.

"The door was suddenly burst open with a loud noise, and a crowd of people rushed forward, crying aloud to each other to secure the madman.

"My secret was out; and my only struggle now was for liberty and freedom. I gained my feet before a hand was on me, threw myself among my assailants, and cleared my way with my strong arm, as if I bore a hatchet in my hand, and hewed them down before me. I gained the door, dropped over the banisters, and in an instant was in the street.

"Straight and swift I ran, and no one dared to stop me. I heard the noise of feet behind, and redoubled my speed. It grew fainter and fainter in the distance, and at length died away altogether: but on I bounded, through marsh and rivulet, over fence and wall, with a wild shout which was taken up by the strange beings that flocked around me on every side, and swelled the sound, till it pierced the air. I was borne upon the arms of demons who swept along upon the wind, and bore down bank and hedge before them, and spun me round and round with a rustle and a speed that made my head swim, until at last they threw me from them with a violent shock, and I fell heavily to the earth. When I woke I found myself here -- here in this gray cell where the sunlight seldom comes, and the moon steals in, in rays which only serve to show the dark shadows about me, and that silent figure in its old corner. When I lie awake, I can sometimes hear strange shrieks and cries from distant parts of this large place. What they are, I know not; but they neither come from that pale form, nor does it regard them. For from the first shades of dusk 'till the earliest light of morning, it still stands motionless in the same place, listening to the music of my iron chain, and watching my gambols on my straw bed."

LIKE "The Lawyer and the Ghost," this grisly episode derives its horror from the state of the human condition. It is a madman *who recognizes the evil of his wife's prostitutional marriage, while those who arranged it are by all appearances* sane. *The* madman *alone operates out of a sense of (albeit twisted) justice. The* madman – *like those of Poe – is deeply attuned to his motives, moods, and destiny, while the "sane" gatekeepers of culture and society (the insensible lawyers, self-important doctors, and delusional brothers) pass by in a reverie of self-importance, blind to reality. It is not until the madman is exposed and taken into custody by his oblivious society that he loses his powers of perception: once he awakens in his institutional cell he is divided into two men – the physical and the spiritual, the mental and the mortal – and one watches impotently as the other deteriorates in the custody of an irresponsible and negligent mankind. None of this is to take away from the horror of the situation: the lunatic is frothing with homicidal glee, and while he hopes to deliver his wife from her misery, his solution is not a divorce, or to flee in the night, or even suicide, but to slit her throat. He is an antihero if indeed a hero, and his ghostly gambols with the voices that rage in his head – are they hallucinations? Ancestral ghosts? Sadistic demons? – hold far more sway over his decisions and ethics than a genuine conscience. And yet, as the horror we experience demonstrates,* he *is the closest thing to a moral character that this story provides, and it is this moral impotence and blurred perspective between internality and externality that captivated Poe and led to some of his greatest works.*

IF the title of this story is familiar to you, it is probably due to the fact that it is often touted by editors and literature professors as the predecessor to A Christmas Carol – *and rightfully so. Like Dickens' most famous supernatural tale, this is a Christmas story which follows the reformation of a misanthropic curmudgeon through the agency of psychic visions administered by preternatural agents, resulting in a transformative comprehension of human suffering, beauty, and love. Like most of Dickens' early ghost stories, this one will not prevent you from falling to sleep from fear, but it is capable of lingering in the imagination for longer than you may at first suppose, and although it is a tremendously suitable tale for Christmas, this story of a gravedigger kidnapped by a grotesque goblin king and hauled into a cavern of telepathic visions is also highly fit for reading on a crisp Hallowe'en. As an aside, many devotees of Disney's vintage macabre shorts will recognize the pattern they borrowed from Dickens: that of a victim being momentarily dragged to hell by ghostly rascals, one which features in such disturbing cartoons as "Pluto's Judgment Day," "The Goddess of Spring," and – fittingly – "Mickey's Christmas Carol."*

The Story of the Goblins Who Stole a Sexton
EXCERPTED *from* THE PICKWICK PAPERS, CHAPTER *Twenty-Nine*
{1836}

IN an old abbey town, down in this part of the country, a long, long while ago—so long, that the story must be a true one, because our great-grandfathers implicitly believed it—there officiated as sexton and grave-digger in the churchyard, one Gabriel Grub. It by no means follows that because a man is a sexton, and constantly surrounded by the emblems of mortality, therefore he should be a morose and melancholy man; your undertakers are the merriest fellows in the world; and I once had the honour of being on intimate terms with a mute, who in private life, and off duty, was as comical and jocose a little fellow as ever chirped out a devil-may-care song, without a hitch in his memory, or drained off a good stiff glass without stopping for breath. But notwithstanding these precedents to the contrary, Gabriel Grub was an ill-conditioned, cross-grained, surly fellow—a morose and lonely man, who consorted with nobody but himself, and an old wicker bottle which fitted into his large deep waistcoat pocket—and who eyed each merry face, as it passed him by, with such a deep scowl of malice and ill-humour, as it was difficult to meet without feeling something the worse for.

'A little before twilight, one Christmas Eve, Gabriel shouldered his spade, lighted his lantern, and betook himself towards the old churchyard; for he had got a grave to finish by next morning, and, feeling very low, he thought it might raise his spirits, perhaps, if he went on with his work at once. As he went his way, up the ancient street, he saw the cheerful light of the blazing fires gleam through the old casements, and heard the loud laugh and the cheerful shouts of those who were assembled around them; he marked the bustling preparations for next day's cheer, and smelled the numerous savoury odours consequent thereupon, as they steamed up from the kitchen window in clouds. All this was gall and wormwood to the heart of Gabriel Grub; and when groups of children bounded out of the houses, tripped across the road, and were met, before they could knock at the opposite door, by half a dozen curly-headed little rascals who crowded round them as they flocked upstairs to spend the evening in their Christmas games, Gabriel smiled grimly, and clutched the handle of his spade with a firmer grasp, as he thought of measles, scarlet fever, thrush, whooping-cough, and a good many other sources of consolation besides.

'In this happy frame of mind, Gabriel strode along, returning a short, sullen growl to the good-humoured greetings of such of his neighbours as now and then passed him, until he turned into the dark lane which led to the churchyard. Now, Gabriel had been looking forward to reaching the dark lane, because it was, generally speaking, a nice, gloomy, mournful place, into which the townspeople did not much care to go, except in broad daylight, and when the sun was shining; consequently, he was not a little indignant to hear a young urchin roaring out some jolly song about a merry Christmas, in this very sanctuary which had been called Coffin Lane ever since the days of the old abbey, and the time of the shaven-headed monks. As Gabriel walked on, and the voice drew nearer, he found it proceeded from a small boy, who was hurrying along, to join one of the little parties in the old street, and who, partly to keep himself company, and partly to prepare himself for the occasion, was shouting out the song at the highest pitch of his lungs. So Gabriel waited until the boy came up, and then dodged him into a corner, and rapped him over the head with his lantern five or six times, just to teach him to modulate his voice. And as the boy hurried away with his hand to his head, singing quite a different sort of tune, Gabriel Grub chuckled very heartily to himself, and entered the churchyard, locking the gate behind him.

'He took off his coat, set down his lantern, and getting into the unfinished grave, worked at it for an hour or so with right good-will. But the earth was hardened with the frost, and it was no very easy matter to break it up, and shovel it out; and although there was a moon, it was a very young one, and shed little light upon the grave, which was in the shadow of the church. At any other time, these obstacles would have made Gabriel Grub very moody and miserable, but he was so well pleased with having stopped the small boy's singing, that he took little heed of the scanty progress he had made, and looked down into the grave, when he had finished work for the night, with grim satisfaction, murmuring as he gathered up his things—

Brave lodgings for one, brave lodgings for one,
A few feet of cold earth, when life is done;
A stone at the head, a stone at the feet,
A rich, juicy meal for the worms to eat;
Rank grass overhead, and damp clay around,
Brave lodgings for one, these, in holy ground!

"'Ho! ho!" laughed Gabriel Grub, as he sat himself down on a flat tombstone which was a favourite resting-place of his, and drew forth his wicker bottle. "A coffin at Christmas! A Christmas box! Ho! ho! ho!"

"'Ho! ho! ho!" repeated a voice which sounded close behind him.

'Gabriel paused, in some alarm, in the act of raising the wicker bottle to his lips, and looked round. The bottom of the oldest grave about him was not more still and quiet than the churchyard in the pale moonlight. The cold hoar frost glistened on the tombstones, and sparkled like rows of gems, among the stone carvings of the old church. The snow lay hard and crisp upon the ground; and spread over the thickly-strewn mounds of earth, so white and smooth a cover that it seemed as if corpses lay there, hidden only by their winding sheets. Not the faintest rustle broke the profound tranquillity of the solemn scene. Sound itself appeared to be frozen up, all was so cold and still.

"'It was the echoes," said Gabriel Grub, raising the bottle to his lips again.

"'It was NOT," said a deep voice.

'Gabriel started up, and stood rooted to the spot with astonishment and terror; for his eyes rested on a form that made his blood run cold.

'Seated on an upright tombstone, close to him, was a strange, unearthly figure, whom Gabriel felt at once, was no being of this world. His long, fantastic legs which might have reached the ground, were cocked up, and crossed after a quaint, fantastic fashion; his sinewy arms were bare; and his hands rested on his knees. On his short, round body, he wore a close covering, ornamented with small slashes; a short cloak dangled at his back; the collar was cut into curious peaks, which served the goblin in lieu of ruff or neckerchief; and his shoes curled up at his toes into long points. On his head, he wore a broad-brimmed sugar-loaf hat, garnished with a single feather. The hat was covered with the white frost; and the goblin looked as if he had sat on the same tombstone very comfortably, for two or three hundred years. He was sitting perfectly still; his tongue was put out, as if in derision; and he was grinning at Gabriel Grub with such a grin as only a goblin could call up.

"'It was NOT the echoes," said the goblin.

'Gabriel Grub was paralysed, and could make no reply.

"'What do you do here on Christmas Eve?" said the goblin sternly. "'I came to dig a grave, Sir," stammered Gabriel Grub.

"'What man wanders among graves and churchyards on such a night as this?" cried the goblin.

"'Gabriel Grub! Gabriel Grub!" screamed a wild chorus of voices that seemed to fill the churchyard. Gabriel looked fearfully round—nothing was to be seen.

"'What have you got in that bottle?" said the goblin.

"'Hollands, sir," replied the sexton, trembling more than ever; for he had bought it of the smugglers, and he thought that perhaps his questioner might be in the excise department of the goblins.

"'Who drinks Hollands alone, and in a churchyard, on such a night as this?" said the goblin.

"'Gabriel Grub! Gabriel Grub!" exclaimed the wild voices again.

'The goblin leered maliciously at the terrified sexton, and then raising his voice, exclaimed—

"'And who, then, is our fair and lawful prize?'"

'To this inquiry the invisible chorus replied, in a strain that sounded like the voices of many choristers singing to the mighty swell of the old church organ—a strain that seemed borne to the sexton's ears upon a wild wind, and to die away as it passed onward; but the burden of the reply was still the same, "Gabriel Grub! Gabriel Grub!"

'The goblin grinned a broader grin than before, as he said, "Well, Gabriel, what do you say to this?"

'The sexton gasped for breath. "'What do you think of this, Gabriel?" said the goblin, kicking up his feet in the air on either side of the tombstone, and looking at the turned-up points with as much complacency as if he had been contemplating the most fashionable pair of Wellingtons in all Bond Street.

"'It's—it's—very curious, Sir," replied the sexton, half dead with fright; "very curious, and very pretty, but I think I'll go back and finish my work, Sir, if you please."

"'Work!" said the goblin, "what work?"

"'The grave, Sir; making the grave," stammered the sexton.

"'Oh, the grave, eh?" said the goblin; "who makes graves at a time when all other men are merry, and takes a pleasure in it?"

'Again the mysterious voices replied, "Gabriel Grub! Gabriel Grub!"

"'I am afraid my friends want you, Gabriel," said the goblin, thrusting his tongue farther into his cheek than ever—and a most astonishing tongue it was—"I'm afraid my friends want you, Gabriel," said the goblin.

"'Under favour, Sir," replied the horror-stricken sexton, "I don't think they can, Sir; they don't know me, Sir; I don't think the gentlemen have ever seen me, Sir."

"'Oh, yes, they have," replied the goblin; "we know the man with the sulky face and grim scowl, that came down the street to-night, throwing his evil looks at the children, and grasping his burying-spade the tighter. We know the man who struck the boy in the envious malice of his heart, because the boy could be merry, and he could not. We know him, we know him."

'Here, the goblin gave a loud, shrill laugh, which the echoes returned twentyfold; and throwing his legs up in the air, stood upon his head, or rather upon the very point of his sugar-loaf hat, on the narrow edge of the tombstone, whence he threw a Somerset with extraordinary agility, right to the sexton's feet, at which he planted himself in the attitude in which tailors generally sit upon the shop-board.

"'I—I—am afraid I must leave you, Sir," said the sexton, making an effort to move.

"'Leave us!" said the goblin, "Gabriel Grub going to leave us. Ho! ho! ho!"

'As the goblin laughed, the sexton observed, for one instant, a brilliant illumination within the windows of the church, as if the whole building were lighted up; it disappeared, the organ pealed forth a lively air, and whole troops of goblins, the very counterpart of the first one, poured into the churchyard, and began playing at leap-frog with the tombstones, never stopping for an instant to take breath, but "overing" the highest among them, one after the other, with the most marvellous dexterity. The first goblin was a most astonishing leaper, and none of the others could come near him; even in the extremity of his terror the sexton could not help observing, that while his friends were content to leap over the common-sized gravestones, the first one took the family vaults, iron railings and all, with as much ease as if they had been so many street-posts.

'At last the game reached to a most exciting pitch; the organ played quicker and quicker, and the goblins leaped faster and faster, coiling themselves up, rolling head over heels upon the ground, and bounding over the tombstones like footballs. The sexton's brain whirled round with the rapidity of the motion he beheld, and his legs reeled beneath him, as the spirits flew before his eyes; when the goblin king, suddenly darting towards him, laid his hand upon his collar, and sank with him through the earth.

'When Gabriel Grub had had time to fetch his breath, which the rapidity of his descent had for the moment taken away, he found himself in what appeared to be a large cavern, surrounded on all sides by crowds of goblins, ugly and grim; in the centre of the room, on an elevated seat, was stationed his friend of the churchyard; and close behind him stood Gabriel Grub himself, without power of motion.

'"Cold to-night," said the king of the goblins, "very cold. A glass of something warm here!"

'At this command, half a dozen officious goblins, with a perpetual smile upon their faces, whom Gabriel Grub imagined to be courtiers, on that account, hastily disappeared, and presently returned with a goblet of liquid fire, which they presented to the king.

'"Ah!" cried the goblin, whose cheeks and throat were transparent, as he tossed down the flame, "this warms one, indeed! Bring a bumper of the same, for Mr. Grub."

'It was in vain for the unfortunate sexton to protest that he was not in the habit of taking anything warm at night; one of the goblins held him while another poured the blazing liquid down his throat; the whole assembly screeched with laughter, as he coughed and choked, and wiped away the tears which gushed plentifully from his eyes, after swallowing the burning draught.

'"And now," said the king, fantastically poking the taper corner of his sugar-loaf hat into the sexton's eye, and thereby occasioning him the most exquisite pain; "and now, show the man of misery and gloom, a few of the pictures from our own great storehouse!"

'As the goblin said this, a thick cloud which obscured the remoter end of the cavern rolled gradually away, and disclosed, apparently at a great distance, a small and scantily furnished, but neat and clean apartment. A crowd of little children were gathered round a bright fire, clinging to their mother's gown, and gambolling around her chair. The mother occasionally rose, and drew aside the window-curtain, as if to look for some expected object; a frugal meal was ready spread upon the table; and an elbow chair was placed near the fire. A knock was heard at the door; the mother opened it, and the children crowded round her, and clapped their hands for joy, as their father entered. He was wet and weary, and shook the snow from his garments, as the children crowded round him, and seizing his cloak, hat, stick, and gloves, with busy zeal, ran with them from the room. Then, as he sat down to his meal before the fire, the children climbed about his knee, and the mother sat by his side, and all seemed happiness and comfort.

'But a change came upon the view, almost imperceptibly. The scene was altered to a small bedroom, where the fairest and youngest child lay dying; the roses had fled from his cheek, and the light from his eye; and even as the sexton looked upon him with an interest he had never felt or known before, he died. His young brothers and sisters crowded round his little bed, and seized his tiny hand, so cold and heavy; but they shrank back from its touch, and looked with awe on his infant face; for calm and tranquil as it was, and sleeping in rest and peace as the beautiful child seemed to be, they saw that he was dead, and they knew that he was an angel looking down upon, and blessing them, from a bright and happy Heaven.

'Again the light cloud passed across the picture, and again the subject changed. The father and mother were old and helpless now, and the number of those about them was diminished more than half; but content and cheerfulness sat on every face, and beamed in every eye, as they crowded round the fireside, and told and listened to old stories of earlier and bygone days. Slowly and peacefully, the father sank into the grave, and, soon after, the sharer of all his cares and troubles followed him to a place of rest. The few who yet survived them, kneeled by their tomb, and watered the green turf which covered it with their tears; then rose, and turned away, sadly and mournfully, but not with bitter cries, or despairing lamentations, for they knew that they should one day meet again; and once more they mixed with the busy world, and their content and cheerfulness were restored. The cloud settled upon the picture, and concealed it from the sexton's view.

'"What do you think of THAT?" said the goblin, turning his large face towards Gabriel Grub.

'Gabriel murmured out something about its being very pretty, and looked somewhat ashamed, as the goblin bent his fiery eyes upon him.

'"You miserable man!" said the goblin, in a tone of excessive contempt. "You!" He appeared disposed to add more, but indignation choked his utterance, so he lifted up one of his very pliable legs, and, flourishing it above his head a little, to insure his aim, administered a good sound kick to Gabriel Grub; immediately after which, all the goblins in waiting crowded round the wretched sexton, and kicked him without mercy, according to the established and invariable custom of courtiers upon earth, who kick whom royalty kicks, and hug whom royalty hugs.

'"Show him some more!" said the king of the goblins.

'At these words, the cloud was dispelled, and a rich and beautiful landscape was disclosed to view—there is just such another, to this day, within half a mile of the old abbey town. The sun shone from out the clear blue sky, the water sparkled beneath his rays, and the trees looked greener, and the flowers more gay, beneath its cheering influence. The water rippled on with a pleasant sound, the trees rustled in the light wind that murmured among their leaves, the birds sang upon the boughs, and the lark carolled on high her welcome to the morning. Yes, it was morning; the bright, balmy morning of summer; the minutest leaf, the smallest blade of grass, was instinct with life. The ant crept forth to her daily toil, the butterfly fluttered and basked in the warm rays of the sun; myriads of insects spread their transparent wings, and revelled in their brief but happy existence. Man walked forth, elated with the scene; and all was brightness and splendour.

'"YOU a miserable man!" said the king of the goblins, in a more contemptuous tone than before. And again the king of the goblins gave his leg a flourish; again it descended on the shoulders of the sexton; and again the attendant goblins imitated the example of their chief.

'Many a time the cloud went and came, and many a lesson it taught to Gabriel Grub, who, although his shoulders smarted with pain from the frequent applications of the goblins' feet thereunto, looked on with an interest that nothing could diminish. He saw that men who worked hard, and earned their scanty bread with lives of labour, were cheerful and happy; and that to the most ignorant, the sweet face of Nature was a never-failing source of cheerfulness and joy. He saw those who had been delicately nurtured, and tenderly brought up, cheerful under privations, and superior to suffering, that would have crushed many of a rougher grain, because they bore within their own bosoms the materials of happiness, contentment, and peace. He saw that women, the tenderest and most fragile of all God's creatures, were the oftenest superior to sorrow, adversity, and distress; and he saw that it was because they bore, in their own hearts, an inexhaustible well-spring of affection and devotion. Above all, he saw that men like himself, who snarled at the mirth and cheerfulness of others, were the foulest weeds on the fair surface of the earth; and setting all the good of the world against the evil, he came to the conclusion that it was a very decent and respectable sort of world after all. No sooner had he formed it, than the cloud which had closed over the last picture, seemed to settle on his senses, and lull him to repose. One by one, the goblins faded from his sight; and, as the last one disappeared, he sank to sleep.

'The day had broken when Gabriel Grub awoke, and found himself lying at full length on the flat gravestone in the churchyard, with the wicker bottle lying empty by his side, and his coat, spade, and lantern, all well whitened by the last night's frost, scattered on the ground. The stone on which he had first seen the goblin seated, stood bolt upright before him, and the grave at which he had worked, the night before, was not far off. At first, he began to doubt the reality of his adventures, but the acute pain in his shoulders when he attempted to rise, assured him that the kicking of the goblins was certainly not ideal. He was staggered again, by observing no traces of footsteps in the snow on which the goblins had played at leap-frog with the gravestones, but he speedily accounted for this circumstance when he remembered that, being spirits, they would leave no visible impression behind them. So, Gabriel Grub got on his feet as well as he could, for the pain in his back; and, brushing the frost off his coat, put it on, and turned his face towards the town.

'But he was an altered man, and he could not bear the thought of returning to a place where his repentance would be scoffed at, and his reformation disbelieved. He hesitated for a few moments; and then turned away to wander where he might, and seek his bread elsewhere.

'The lantern, the spade, and the wicker bottle were found, that day, in the churchyard. There were a great many speculations about the sexton's fate, at first, but it was speedily determined that he had been carried away by the goblins; and there were not wanting some very credible witnesses who had distinctly seen him whisked through the air on the back of a chestnut horse blind of one eye, with the hind-quarters of a lion, and the tail of a bear. At length all this was devoutly believed; and the new sexton used to exhibit to the curious, for a trifling emolument, a good-sized piece of the church weathercock which had been accidentally kicked off by the aforesaid horse in his aerial flight, and picked up by himself in the churchyard, a year or two afterwards.

'Unfortunately, these stories were somewhat disturbed by the unlooked-for reappearance of Gabriel Grub himself, some ten years afterwards, a ragged, contented, rheumatic old man. He told his story to the clergyman, and also to the mayor; and in course of time it began to be received as a matter of history, in which form it has continued down to this very day. The believers in the weathercock tale, having misplaced their confidence once, were not easily prevailed upon to part with it again, so they looked as wise as they could, shrugged their shoulders, touched their foreheads, and murmured something about Gabriel Grub having drunk all the Hollands, and then fallen asleep on the flat tombstone; and they affected to explain what he supposed he had witnessed in the goblin's cavern, by saying that he had seen the world, and grown wiser. But this opinion, which was by no means a popular one at any time, gradually died off; and be the matter how it may, as Gabriel Grub was afflicted with rheumatism to the end of his days, this story has at least one moral, if it teach no better one—and that is, that if a man turn sulky and drink by himself at Christmas time, he may make up his mind to be not a bit the better for it: let the spirits be never so good, or let them be even as many degrees beyond proof, as those which Gabriel Grub saw in the goblin's cavern.'

"SEXTON" is understandably lauded for its prefiguration of A Christmas Carol, and this is a justifiable legacy. Just as interesting as its influence, however, are its influences, namely, the supernatural literature of America's first professional man of letters, Washington Irving. Irving was unquestionably the most influential writer to Dickens, who adored and emulated his command of whit, satire, prose, and character. Irving's Christmastime festivities in Bracebridge Hall and The Sketch-Book were the authoritative inspiration for Dickens' own yuletide literature (before Irving, Christmas was a mere business holiday in Britain, having lost traction during the puritanical Civil War. Irving along with Dickens and Prince Albert reignited Britons' appetite for Christmastime). But aside from the Christmas setting – a favorite of the nostalgic Irving – the supernatural activity is uncannily similar to that in Irving's two most beloved stories: "The Legend of Sleepy Hollow" and "Rip Van Winkle." Featuring a group of dwarfish spirits who mischievously steal a man away only to awaken transformed forever, and an aftermath in which his discarded personal artifacts fuel the false rumors (or shall I say "legend") of his being "spirited away" by a vindictive hellion, the story is a deep homage to the man whose use of the supernatural – like Dickens' – was always a roundabout pursuit of something impishly hidden if the reader only look past the paper-dry humor and the farcical characters.

HERE we begin to approach a turning point in Dickens' writing. This is redolent with humor, thick with color, and brimming with opaque symbolism like that of the previous tales ("Madman's Manuscript" being an obvious exception), but here we begin to see a darkness steal into his tales. They shift from social satires to existential ponderings – from moralistic parables to darker musings on the very essence and worth of life, and while he does not yet fall deeply into the dark tunnels that await us in "The Signal-Man," we begin to sense shadows stealing from his pen. In this comical episode, the alcohol loving baron of Grogzwig (read: swigs grog) is haunted by the genius, or physical manifestation (the Grim Reaper and Father Time are geniuses of death and time respectively) of Suicide. The tale, which plays humorously off of the Gothic conventions of a cursed German baron pairs nicely with the similarly themed (and almost certainly influential) stories of two American contemporaries: Washington Irving's "The Spectre Bridegrom," and Edgar Allan Poe's "Metzengerstein." Both are lovely little ghost stories in their own rights. This particular tale would also have some influence of its own on Dickens' later work: just as Grub was a premonition of Scrooge, this clanging specter foretells Jacob Marley – but it is a far, far grimmer shade than Marley.

Baron Koeldwethout's Apparition
Or, The Baron of Grogzwig
EXCERPTED *from* NICHOLAS NICKLEBY, CHAPTER *Six*
{1838}

'THE Baron Von Koeldwethout, of Grogzwig in Germany, was as likely a young baron as you would wish to see. I needn't say that he lived in a castle, because that's of course; neither need I say that he lived in an old castle; for what German baron ever lived in a new one? There were many strange circumstances connected with this venerable building, among which, not the least startling and mysterious were, that when the wind blew, it rumbled in the chimneys, or even howled among the trees in the neighbouring forest; and that when the moon shone, she found her way through certain small loopholes in the wall, and actually made some parts of the wide halls and galleries quite light, while she left others in gloomy shadow. I believe that one of the baron's ancestors, being short of money, had inserted a dagger in a gentleman who called one night to ask his way, and it WAS supposed that these miraculous occurrences took place in consequence. And yet I hardly know how that could have been, either, because the baron's ancestor, who was an amiable man, felt very sorry afterwards for having been so rash, and laying violent hands upon a quantity of stone and timber which belonged to a weaker baron, built a chapel as an apology, and so took a receipt from Heaven, in full of all demands.

'Talking of the baron's ancestor puts me in mind of the baron's great claims to respect, on the score of his pedigree. I am afraid to say, I am sure, how many ancestors the baron had; but I know that he had a great many more than any other man of his time; and I only wish that he had lived in these latter days, that he might have had more. It is a very hard thing upon the great men of past centuries, that they should have come into the world so soon, because a man who was born three or four hundred years ago, cannot reasonably be expected to have had as many relations before him, as a man who is born now. The last man, whoever he is--and he may be a cobbler or some low vulgar dog for aught we know--will have a longer pedigree than the greatest nobleman now alive; and I contend that this is not fair.

'Well, but the Baron Von Koeldwethout of Grogzwig! He was a fine swarthy fellow, with dark hair and large moustachios, who rode a-hunting in clothes of Lincoln green, with russet boots on his feet, and a bugle slung over his shoulder like the guard of a long stage. When he blew this bugle, four-and-twenty other gentlemen of inferior rank, in Lincoln green a little coarser, and russet boots with a little thicker soles, turned out directly: and away galloped the whole train, with spears in their hands like lacquered area railings, to hunt down the boars, or perhaps encounter a bear: in which latter case the baron killed him first, and greased his whiskers with him afterwards.

'This was a merry life for the Baron of Grogzwig, and a merrier still for the baron's retainers, who drank Rhine wine every night till they fell under the table, and then had the bottles on the floor, and called for pipes. Never were such jolly, roystering, rollicking, merry-making blades, as the jovial crew of Grogzwig.

'But the pleasures of the table, or the pleasures of under the table, require a little variety; especially when the same five-and- twenty people sit daily down to the same board, to discuss the same subjects, and tell the same stories. The baron grew weary, and wanted excitement. He took to quarrelling with his gentlemen, and tried kicking two or three of them every day after dinner. This was a pleasant change at first; but it became monotonous after a week or so, and the baron felt quite out of sorts, and cast about, in despair, for some new amusement.

'One night, after a day's sport in which he had outdone Nimrod or Gillingwater, and slaughtered "another fine bear," and brought him home in triumph, the Baron Von Koeldwethout sat moodily at the head of his table, eyeing the smoky roof of the hall with a discontended aspect. He swallowed huge bumpers of wine, but the more he swallowed, the more he frowned. The gentlemen who had been honoured with the dangerous distinction of sitting on his right and left, imitated him to a miracle in the drinking, and frowned at each other.

'"I will!" cried the baron suddenly, smiting the table with his right hand, and twirling his moustache with his left. "Fill to the Lady of Grogzwig!"

'The four-and-twenty Lincoln greens turned pale, with the exception of their four-and-twenty noses, which were unchangeable.

'"I said to the Lady of Grogzwig," repeated the baron, looking round the board.

'"To the Lady of Grogzwig!" shouted the Lincoln greens; and down their four-and-twenty throats went four-and-twenty imperial pints of such rare old hock, that they smacked their eight-and-forty lips, and winked again.

'"The fair daughter of the Baron Von Swillenhausen," said Koeldwethout, condescending to explain. "We will demand her in marriage of her father, ere the sun goes down tomorrow. If he refuse our suit, we will cut off his nose."

'A hoarse murmur arose from the company; every man touched, first the hilt of his sword, and then the tip of his nose, with appalling significance.

'What a pleasant thing filial piety is to contemplate! If the daughter of the Baron Von Swillenhausen had pleaded a preoccupied heart, or fallen at her father's feet and corned them in salt tears, or only fainted away, and complimented the old gentleman in frantic ejaculations, the odds are a hundred to one but Swillenhausen Castle would have been turned out at window, or rather the baron turned out at window, and the castle demolished. The damsel held her peace, however, when an early messenger bore the request of Von Koeldwethout next morning, and modestly retired to her chamber, from the casement of which she watched the coming of the suitor and his retinue. She was no sooner assured that the horseman with the large moustachios was her proffered husband, than she hastened to her father's presence, and expressed her readiness to sacrifice herself to secure his peace. The venerable baron caught his child to his arms, and shed a wink of joy.

'There was great feasting at the castle, that day. The four-and- twenty Lincoln greens of Von Koeldwethout exchanged vows of eternal friendship with twelve Lincoln greens of Von Swillenhausen, and promised the old baron that they would drink his wine "Till all was blue"--meaning probably until their whole countenances had acquired the same tint as their noses. Everybody slapped everybody else's back, when the time for parting came; and the Baron Von Koeldwethout and his followers rode gaily home.

'For six mortal weeks, the bears and boars had a holiday. The houses of Koeldwethout and Swillenhausen were united; the spears rusted; and the baron's bugle grew hoarse for lack of blowing.

'Those were great times for the four-and-twenty; but, alas! their high and palmy days had taken boots to themselves, and were already walking off.

'"My dear," said the baroness.

'"My love," said the baron.

'"Those coarse, noisy men--"

'"Which, ma'am?" said the baron, starting.

'The baroness pointed, from the window at which they stood, to the courtyard beneath, where the unconscious Lincoln greens were taking a copious stirrup-cup, preparatory to issuing forth after a boar or two.

'"My hunting train, ma'am," said the baron.

'"Disband them, love," murmured the baroness.

'"Disband them!" cried the baron, in amazement.

'"To please me, love," replied the baroness.

'"To please the devil, ma'am," answered the baron.

'Whereupon the baroness uttered a great cry, and swooned away at the baron's feet.

'What could the baron do? He called for the lady's maid, and roared for the doctor; and then, rushing into the yard, kicked the two Lincoln greens who were the most used to it, and cursing the others all round, bade them go--but never mind where. I don't know the German for it, or I would put it delicately that way.

'It is not for me to say by what means, or by what degrees, some wives manage to keep down some husbands as they do, although I may have my private opinion on the subject, and may think that no Member of Parliament ought to be married, inasmuch as three married members out of every four, must vote according to their wives' consciences (if there be such things), and not according to their own. All I need say, just now, is, that the Baroness Von Koeldwethout somehow or other acquired great control over the Baron Von Koeldwethout, and that, little by little, and bit by bit, and day by day, and year by year, the baron got the worst of some disputed question, or was slyly unhorsed from some old hobby; and that by the time he was a fat hearty fellow of forty-eight or thereabouts, he had no feasting, no revelry, no hunting train, and no hunting--nothing in short that he liked, or used to have; and that, although he was as fierce as a lion, and as bold as brass, he was decidedly snubbed and put down, by his own lady, in his own castle of Grogzwig.

'Nor was this the whole extent of the baron's misfortunes. About a year after his nuptials, there came into the world a lusty young baron, in whose honour a great many fireworks were let off, and a great many dozens of wine drunk; but next year there came a young baroness, and next year another young baron, and so on, every year, either a baron or baroness (and one year both together), until the baron found himself the father of a small family of twelve. Upon every one of these anniversaries, the venerable Baroness Von Swillenhausen was nervously sensitive for the well-being of her child the Baroness Von Koeldwethout; and although it was not found that the good lady ever did anything material towards contributing to her child's recovery, still she made it a point of duty to be as nervous as possible at the castle of Grogzwig, and to divide her time between moral observations on the baron's housekeeping, and bewailing the hard lot of her unhappy daughter. And if the Baron of Grogzwig, a little hurt and irritated at this, took heart, and ventured to suggest that his wife was at least no worse off than the wives of other barons, the Baroness Von Swillenhausen begged all persons to take notice, that nobody but she, sympathised with her dear daughter's sufferings; upon which, her relations and friends remarked, that to be sure she did cry a great deal more than her son-in-law, and that if there were a hard-hearted brute alive, it was that Baron of Grogzwig.

'The poor baron bore it all as long as he could, and when he could bear it no longer lost his appetite and his spirits, and sat himself gloomily and dejectedly down. But there were worse troubles yet in store for him, and as they came on, his melancholy and sadness increased. Times changed. He got into debt. The Grogzwig coffers ran low, though the Swillenhausen family had looked upon them as inexhaustible; and just when the baroness was on the point of making a thirteenth addition to the family pedigree, Von Koeldwethout discovered that he had no means of replenishing them.

'"I don't see what is to be done," said the baron. "I think I'll kill myself."

'This was a bright idea. The baron took an old hunting-knife from a cupboard hard by, and having sharpened it on his boot, made what boys call "an offer" at his throat.

'"Hem!" said the baron, stopping short. "Perhaps it's not sharp enough."

'The baron sharpened it again, and made another offer, when his hand was arrested by a loud screaming among the young barons and baronesses, who had a nursery in an upstairs tower with iron bars outside the window, to prevent their tumbling out into the moat.

'"If I had been a bachelor," said the baron sighing, "I might have done it fifty times over, without being interrupted. Hallo! Put a flask of wine and the largest pipe in the little vaulted room behind the hall."

'One of the domestics, in a very kind manner, executed the baron's order in the course of half an hour or so, and Von Koeldwethout being apprised thereof, strode to the vaulted room, the walls of which, being of dark shining wood, gleamed in the light of the blazing logs which were piled upon the hearth. The bottle and pipe were ready, and, upon the whole, the place looked very comfortable.

'"Leave the lamp," said the baron.

'"Anything else, my lord?" inquired the domestic.

'"The room," replied the baron. The domestic obeyed, and the baron locked the door.

'"I'll smoke a last pipe," said the baron, "and then I'll be off." So, putting the knife upon the table till he wanted it, and tossing off a goodly measure of wine, the Lord of Grogzwig threw himself back in his chair, stretched his legs out before the fire, and puffed away.

'He thought about a great many things--about his present troubles and past days of bachelorship, and about the Lincoln greens, long since dispersed up and down the country, no one knew whither: with the exception of two who had been unfortunately beheaded, and four who had killed themselves with drinking. His mind was running upon bears and boars, when, in the process of draining his glass to the bottom, he raised his eyes, and saw, for the first time and with unbounded astonishment, that he was not alone.

'No, he was not; for, on the opposite side of the fire, there sat with folded arms a wrinkled hideous figure, with deeply sunk and bloodshot eyes, and an immensely long cadaverous face, shadowed by jagged and matted locks of coarse black hair. He wore a kind of tunic of a dull bluish colour, which, the baron observed, on regarding it attentively, was clasped or ornamented down the front with coffin handles. His legs, too, were encased in coffin plates as though in armour; and over his left shoulder he wore a short dusky cloak, which seemed made of a remnant of some pall. He took no notice of the baron, but was intently eyeing the fire.

'"Halloa!" said the baron, stamping his foot to attract attention.

'"Halloa!" replied the stranger, moving his eyes towards the baron, but not his face or himself "What now?"

'"What now!" replied the baron, nothing daunted by his hollow voice and lustreless eyes. "I should ask that question. How did you get here?"

'"Through the door," replied the figure.

'"What are you?" says the baron.

'"A man," replied the figure.

'"I don't believe it," says the baron.

'"Disbelieve it then," says the figure.

"'I will," rejoined the baron.

'The figure looked at the bold Baron of Grogzwig for some time, and then said familiarly,

"'There's no coming over you, I see. I'm not a man!"

"'What are you then?" asked the baron.

"'A genius," replied the figure.

"'You don't look much like one," returned the baron scornfully.

"'I am the Genius of Despair and Suicide," said the apparition. "Now you know me."

'With these words the apparition turned towards the baron, as if composing himself for a talk--and, what was very remarkable, was, that he threw his cloak aside, and displaying a stake, which was run through the centre of his body, pulled it out with a jerk, and laid it on the table, as composedly as if it had been a walking-stick.

"'Now," said the figure, glancing at the hunting-knife, "are you ready for me?"

"'Not quite," rejoined the baron; "I must finish this pipe first."

"'Look sharp then," said the figure.

"'You seem in a hurry," said the baron.

"'Why, yes, I am," answered the figure; "they're doing a pretty brisk business in my way, over in England and France just now, and my time is a good deal taken up."

"'Do you drink?" said the baron, touching the bottle with the bowl of his pipe.

"'Nine times out of ten, and then very hard," rejoined the figure, drily.

"'Never in moderation?" asked the baron.

"'Never," replied the figure, with a shudder, "that breeds cheerfulness."

'The baron took another look at his new friend, whom he thought an uncommonly queer customer, and at length inquired whether he took any active part in such little proceedings as that which he had in contemplation.

"'No," replied the figure evasively; "but I am always present."

"'Just to see fair, I suppose?" said the baron.

"'Just that," replied the figure, playing with his stake, and examining the ferule. "Be as quick as you can, will you, for there's a young gentleman who is afflicted with too much money and leisure wanting me now, I find."

"'Going to kill himself because he has too much money!" exclaimed the baron, quite tickled. "Ha! ha! that's a good one." (This was the first time the baron had laughed for many a long day.)

"'I say," expostulated the figure, looking very much scared; "don't do that again."

"'Why not?" demanded the baron.

"'Because it gives me pain all over," replied the figure. "Sigh as much as you please: that does me good."

'The baron sighed mechanically at the mention of the word; the figure, brightening up again, handed him the hunting-knife with most winning politeness.

"'It's not a bad idea though," said the baron, feeling the edge of the weapon; "a man killing himself because he has too much money."

'"Pooh!" said the apparition, petulantly, "no better than a man's killing himself because he has none or little."

'Whether the genius unintentionally committed himself in saying this, or whether he thought the baron's mind was so thoroughly made up that it didn't matter what he said, I have no means of knowing. I only know that the baron stopped his hand, all of a sudden, opened his eyes wide, and looked as if quite a new light had come upon him for the first time.

'"Why, certainly," said Von Koeldwethout, "nothing is too bad to be retrieved."

'"Except empty coffers," cried the genius.

'"Well; but they may be one day filled again," said the baron.

'"Scolding wives," snarled the genius.

'"Oh! They may be made quiet," said the baron.

'"Thirteen children," shouted the genius.

'"Can't all go wrong, surely," said the baron.

'The genius was evidently growing very savage with the baron, for holding these opinions all at once; but he tried to laugh it off, and said if he would let him know when he had left off joking he should feel obliged to him.

'"But I am not joking; I was never farther from it," remonstrated the baron.

'"Well, I am glad to hear that," said the genius, looking very grim, "because a joke, without any figure of speech, IS the death of me. Come! Quit this dreary world at once."

'"I don't know," said the baron, playing with the knife; "it's a dreary one certainly, but I don't think yours is much better, for you have not the appearance of being particularly comfortable. That puts me in mind--what security have I, that I shall be any the better for going out of the world after all!" he cried, starting up; "I never thought of that."

'"Dispatch," cried the figure, gnashing his teeth.

'"Keep off!" said the baron. 'I'll brood over miseries no longer, but put a good face on the matter, and try the fresh air and the bears again; and if that don't do, I'll talk to the baroness soundly, and cut the Von Swillenhausens dead.' With this the baron fell into his chair, and laughed so loud and boisterously, that the room rang with it.

'The figure fell back a pace or two, regarding the baron meanwhile with a look of intense terror, and when he had ceased, caught up the stake, plunged it violently into its body, uttered a frightful howl, and disappeared.

'Von Koeldwethout never saw it again. Having once made up his mind to action, he soon brought the baroness and the Von Swillenhausens to reason, and died many years afterwards: not a rich man that I am aware of, but certainly a happy one: leaving behind him a numerous family, who had been carefully educated in bear and boar-hunting under his own personal eye. And my advice to all men is, that if ever they become hipped and melancholy from similar causes (as very many men do), they look at both sides of the question, applying a magnifying-glass to the best one; and if they still feel tempted to retire without leave, that they smoke a large pipe and drink a full bottle first, and profit by the laudable example of the Baron of Grogzwig.'

As with "The Signal-Man," there is a grim kernel of autobiography in this parable. Dickens, too, was a newly-wed, having two years previously entered into matrimony with Catherine Hogarth – a marriage which was only doomed to grow increasingly strained and disastrous. While the Dickenses were still relatively happy at this point – long before his mistresses, her sister's domestic coup d'état, and their miserably public separation – the author was already becoming aware of the constraints of married life. The specter of suicide does not seem to have haunted Dickens, and certainly not at this early point in his marriage, but a heavy shadow did begin to descend on his moods and perspective after wedding Kate, and with it came a personal depression that – like Saint Paul's thorn in the flesh, and unlike the Baron of Grogzwig's slain apparition – truly did haunt him inextricably. Depression hounded Dickens both artistically and interpersonally, commencing reliably at the start of each new novel (before tapering into mania) and wedging its way into his relationships, causing him to become – at times – nearly as "mercurial" as his moody Ghost of Christmas Yet to Come. In time the flows overpowered the ebbs, and after the train accident that so horrendously shook him, it finally crushed his muse: "his depression worsened with age ... four years before his death ... [it] seems to have finally staunched his creativity, and his previously prolific output virtually ceased." Koeldwethout managed to slay his leering tormentor. Dickens was not so fortunate as his comic creation.

Just as "A Madman's Manuscript" so undoubtedly fueled the fires of Poe's imagination, so too did "The Mother's Eyes." In it can be found the genesis of "The Black Cat," "William Wilson," "The Imp of the Perverse," but most especially – almost outrageously – "The Tell-Tale Heart," which is a virtual offspring of Dickens' tale, written a mere three years prior. In the same way that "Tell-Tale" is infused with a pseudo-supernatural power that flushes out confession with hot jets of guilt and self-exposure, and in the same way that it explores the interplay between behavioral integrity, psychological multiplicity, and both figurative and literal schizoid psychosis, "The Mother's Eyes" probes the relationship between the spirit of a man – the id and superego that battle for dominance – and his actions – sin and repentance, perversity and piety, concealment and confession.

The Mother's Eyes
Or, A Confession Found in Prison at the Time of Charles II
EXCERPTED *from* MASTER HUMPHREY'S CLOCK, CHAPTER *Two*
{1841}

I held a lieutenant's commission in his Majesty's army, and served abroad in the campaigns of 1677 and 1678. The treaty of Nimeguen being concluded, I returned home, and retiring from the service, withdrew to a small estate lying a few miles east of London, which I had recently acquired in right of my wife.

This is the last night I have to live, and I will set down the naked truth without disguise. I was never a brave man, and had always been from my childhood of a secret, sullen, distrustful nature. I speak of myself as if I had passed from the world; for while I write this, my grave is digging, and my name is written in the black-book of death.

Soon after my return to England, my only brother was seized with mortal illness. This circumstance gave me slight or no pain; for since we had been men, we had associated but very little together. He was open-hearted and generous, handsomer than I, more accomplished, and generally beloved. Those who sought my acquaintance abroad or at home, because they were friends of his, seldom attached themselves to me long, and would usually say, in our first conversation, that they were surprised to find two brothers so unlike in their manners and appearance. It was my habit to lead them on to this avowal; for I knew what comparisons they must draw between us; and having a rankling envy in my heart, I sought to justify it to myself.

We had married two sisters. This additional tie between us, as it may appear to some, only estranged us the more. His wife knew me well. I never struggled with any secret jealousy or gall when she was present but that woman knew it as well as I did. I never raised my eyes at such times but I found hers fixed upon me; I never bent them on the ground or looked another way but I felt that she overlooked me always. It was an inexpressible relief to me when we quarrelled, and a greater relief still when I heard abroad that she was dead. It seems to me now as if some strange and terrible foreshadowing of what has happened since must have hung over us then. I was afraid of her; she haunted me; her fixed and steady look comes back upon me now, like the memory of a dark dream, and makes my blood run cold.

She died shortly after giving birth to a child - a boy. When my brother knew that all hope of his own recovery was past, he called my wife to his bedside, and confided this orphan, a child of four years old, to her protection. He bequeathed to him all the property he had, and willed that, in case of his child's death, it should pass to my wife, as the only acknowledgment he could make her for her care and love. He exchanged a few brotherly words with me, deploring our long separation; and being exhausted, fell into a slumber, from which he never awoke.

We had no children; and as there had been a strong affection between the sisters, and my wife had almost supplied the place of a mother to this boy, she loved him as if he had been her own. The child was ardently attached to her; but he was his mother's image in face and spirit, and always mistrusted me.

I can scarcely fix the date when the feeling first came upon me; but I soon began to be uneasy when this child was by. I never roused myself from some moody train of thought but I marked him looking at me; not with mere childish wonder, but with something of the purpose and meaning that I had so often noted in his mother. It was no effort of my fancy, founded on close resemblance of feature and expression. I never could look the boy down. He feared me, but seemed by some instinct to despise me while he did so; and even when he drew back beneath my gaze - as he would when we were alone, to get nearer to the door - he would keep his bright eyes upon me still.

Perhaps I hide the truth from myself, but I do not think that, when this began, I meditated to do him any wrong. I may have thought how serviceable his inheritance would be to us, and may have wished him dead; but I believe I had no thought of compassing his death. Neither did the idea come upon me at once, but by very slow degrees, presenting itself at first in dim shapes at a very great distance, as men may think of an earthquake or the last day; then drawing nearer and nearer, and losing something of its horror and improbability; then coming to be part and parcel - nay nearly the whole sum and substance - of my daily thoughts, and resolving itself into a question of means and safety; not of doing or abstaining from the deed.

While this was going on within me, I never could bear that the child should see me looking at him, and yet I was under a fascination which made it a kind of business with me to contemplate his slight and fragile figure and think how easily it might be done. Sometimes I would steal up-stairs and watch him as he slept; but usually I hovered in the garden near the window of the room in which he learnt his little tasks; and there, as he sat upon a low seat beside my wife, I would peer at him for hours together from behind a tree; starting, like the guilty wretch I was, at every rustling of a leaf, and still gliding back to look and start again.

Hard by our cottage, but quite out of sight, and (if there were any wind astir) of hearing too, was a deep sheet of water. I spent days in shaping with my pocket-knife a rough model of a boat, which I finished at last and dropped in the child's way. Then I withdrew to a secret place, which he must pass if he stole away alone

to swim this bauble, and lurked there for his coming. He came neither that day nor the next, though I waited from noon till nightfall. I was sure that I had him in my net, for I had heard him prattling of the toy, and knew that in his infant pleasure he kept it by his side in bed. I felt no weariness or fatigue, but waited patiently, and on the third day he passed me, running joyously along, with his silken hair streaming in the wind, and he singing - God have mercy upon me! - singing a merry ballad, - who could hardly lisp the words.

I stole down after him, creeping under certain shrubs which grow in that place, and none but devils know with what terror I, a strong, full-grown man, tracked the footsteps of that baby as he approached the water's brink. I was close upon him, had sunk upon my knee and raised my hand to thrust him in, when he saw my shadow in the stream and turned him round.

His mother's ghost was looking from his eyes. The sun burst forth from behind a cloud; it shone in the bright sky, the glistening earth, the clear water, the sparkling drops of rain upon the leaves. There were eyes in everything. The whole great universe of light was there to see the murder done. I know not what he said; he came of bold and manly blood, and, child as he was, he did not crouch or fawn upon me. I heard him cry that he would try to love me, - not that he did, - and then I saw him running back towards the house. The next I saw was my own sword naked in my hand, and he lying at my feet stark dead, - dabbled here and there with blood, but otherwise no different from what I had seen him in his sleep - in the same attitude too, with his cheek resting upon his little hand.

I took him in my arms and laid him - very gently now that he was dead - in a thicket. My wife was from home that day, and would not return until the next. Our bedroom window, the only sleeping-room on that side of the house, was but a few feet from the ground, and I resolved to descend from it at night and bury him in the garden. I had no thought that I had failed in my design, no thought that the water would be dragged and nothing found, that the money must now lie waste, since I must encourage the idea that the child was lost or stolen. All my thoughts were bound up and knotted together in the one absorbing necessity of hiding what I had done.

How I felt when they came to tell me that the child was missing, when I ordered scouts in all directions, when I gasped and trembled at every one's approach, no tongue can tell or mind of man conceive. I buried him that night. When I parted the boughs and looked into the dark thicket, there was a glow-worm shining like the visible spirit of God upon the murdered child. I glanced down into his grave when I had placed him there, and still it gleamed upon his breast; an eye of fire looking up to Heaven in supplication to the stars that watched me at my work.

I had to meet my wife, and break the news, and give her hope that the child would soon be found. All this I did, - with some appearance, I suppose, of being sincere, for I was the object of no suspicion. This done, I sat at the bedroom window all day long, and watched the spot where the dreadful secret lay.

It was in a piece of ground which had been dug up to be newly turfed, and which I had chosen on that account, as the traces of my spade were less likely to attract attention. The men who laid down the grass must have thought me mad. I called to them continually to expedite their work, ran out and worked beside them, trod down the earth with my feet, and hurried them with frantic eagerness. They had finished their task before night, and then I thought myself comparatively safe.

I slept, - not as men do who awake refreshed and cheerful, but I did sleep, passing from vague and shadowy dreams of being hunted down, to visions of the plot of grass, through which now a hand, and now a foot, and now the head itself was starting out. At this point I always woke and stole to the window, to make sure that it was not really so. That done, I crept to bed again; and thus I spent the night in fits and starts, getting up and lying down full twenty times, and dreaming the same dream over and over again, - which was far worse than lying awake, for every dream had a whole night's suffering of its own. Once I thought the child was alive, and that I had never tried to kill him. To wake from that dream was the most dreadful agony of all.

The next day I sat at the window again, never once taking my eyes from the place, which, although it was covered by the grass, was as plain to me - its shape, its size, its depth, its jagged sides, and all - as if it had been open to the light of day. When a servant walked across it, I felt as if he must sink in; when he had passed, I looked to see that his feet had not worn the edges. If a bird lighted there, I was in terror lest by some tremendous interposition it should be instrumental in the discovery; if a breath of air sighed across it, to me it whispered murder. There was not a sight or a sound - how ordinary, mean, or unimportant soever - but was fraught with fear. And in this state of ceaseless watching I spent three days.

On the fourth there came to the gate one who had served with me abroad, accompanied by a brother officer of his whom I had never seen. I felt that I could not bear to be out of sight of the place. It was a summer evening, and I bade my people take a table and a flask of wine into the garden. Then I sat down WITH MY CHAIR UPON THE GRAVE, and being assured that nobody could disturb it now without my knowledge, tried to drink and talk.

They hoped that my wife was well, - that she was not obliged to keep her chamber, - that they had not frightened her away. What could I do but tell them with a faltering tongue about the child? The officer whom I did not know was a down-looking man, and kept his eyes upon the ground while I was speaking. Even that terrified me. I could not divest myself of the idea that he saw something there which caused him to suspect the truth. I asked him hurriedly if he supposed that - and stopped. 'That the child has been murdered?' said he, looking mildly at me: 'O no! what could a man gain by murdering a poor child?' I could have told him what a man gained by such a deed, no one better: but I held my peace and shivered as with an ague.

Mistaking my emotion, they were endeavouring to cheer me with the hope that the boy would certainly be found, - great cheer that was for me! - when we heard a low deep howl, and presently there sprung over the wall two great dogs, who, bounding into the garden, repeated the baying sound we had heard before.

'Bloodhounds!' cried my visitors.

What need to tell me that! I had never seen one of that kind in all my life, but I knew what they were and for what purpose they had come. I grasped the elbows of my chair, and neither spoke nor moved.

'They are of the genuine breed,' said the man whom I had known abroad, 'and being out for exercise have no doubt escaped from their keeper.'

Both he and his friend turned to look at the dogs, who with their noses to the ground moved restlessly about, running to and fro, and up and down, and across, and round in circles, careering about like wild things, and all this time taking no notice of us, but ever and again repeating the yell we had heard already, then dropping their noses to the ground again and tracking earnestly here and there. They now began to snuff the earth more eagerly than they had done yet, and although they were still very restless, no longer beat about in such wide circuits, but kept near to one spot, and constantly diminished the distance between themselves and me.

At last they came up close to the great chair on which I sat, and raising their frightful howl once more, tried to tear away the wooden rails that kept them from the ground beneath. I saw how I looked, in the faces of the two who were with me.

'They scent some prey,' said they, both together.

'They scent no prey!' cried I.

'In Heaven's name, move!' said the one I knew, very earnestly, 'or you will be torn to pieces.'

'Let them tear me from limb to limb, I'll never leave this place!' cried I. 'Are dogs to hurry men to shameful deaths? Hew them down, cut them in pieces.'

'There is some foul mystery here!' said the officer whom I did not know, drawing his sword. 'In King Charles's name, assist me to secure this man.'

They both set upon me and forced me away, though I fought and bit and caught at them like a madman. After a struggle, they got me quietly between them; and then, my God! I saw the angry dogs tearing at the earth and throwing it up into the air like water.

What more have I to tell? That I fell upon my knees, and with chattering teeth confessed the truth, and prayed to be forgiven. That I have since denied, and now confess to it again. That I have been tried for the crime, found guilty, and sentenced. That I have not the courage to anticipate my doom, or to bear up manfully against it. That I have no compassion, no consolation, no hope, no friend. That my wife has happily lost for the time those faculties which would enable her to know my misery or hers. That I am alone in this stone dungeon with my evil spirit, and that I die tomorrow.

ALTHOUGH perhaps not a thoroughly grim as "A Madman's Manuscript," this descendent is a very clear and obvious return to the themes that compose the best of Dickens' supernatural tales: the struggle between corruption and virtue, inherited sin, the moral corrosion of society, the chaos and childishness of human psychology, and a universe without heroes or redemption – one more composed of cosmic questions than providential responses. The criminal is captured, it is true, and – like the eponymous "Madman" and the killer in "The Trial for Murder" – will suffer under the rules of society, but the spiritual problem of his murder is never solved, never entirely understood, never as exposed and apparent as the rotting corpse that the bloodhounds so inescapably brought to human attention. The protagonist will pay with his body for a sin bred in his soul, a soul which will ostensibly escape exposure: unlike his flesh, which will be wrung to death on a gibbet, his spirit and the motives for his murder flee into the obscurity of a dark and sinister universe. These themes are being slowly stropped in "Madman's" and "Mother's," and will arrive at a keen, cutthroat edge by the time we dip into Dickens' three supernatural masterpieces – stories which dwell unwaveringly with the darkness that so evidently lurks behind our great societies and progress and wealth: cheap facades that distract us from a cosmos teeming with moral confusion and existential turmoil.

MOST famous of all Dickens' specters, Marley's Ghost is the culmination of his early ghost stories – merging the medium of Baron Koeldwethout's iron-clad phantom with the plot of "The Goblins Who Stole a Sexton," with the whimsy and caustic social conscience of "The Lawyer and the Ghost," with the charming characterizations and adventure of "The Ghosts of the Mail." A Christmas Carol is most accurately cataloged as a moral parable, but in its first stave lurk all the hallmarks of a classic English ghost story in the manner of Le Fanu, Blackwood, Onions, Collins, or James: a brooding, living natural atmosphere that reflects the moral condition of the characters that inhabit it; a visceral sense of approaching comeuppance or just desserts on the part of its protagonist; a slow-burning journey from arrogance to confusion to denial to dread to horror; and a haunted house, haunting, and haunt which are each truly original yet beholden to the conventions of Gothic horror for their eerie structure. Indeed, Marley suffers from oversaturation, for we have seen too many movies, cartoons, and musicals which depress his pathos and familiarize his hideousness. Try to detach yourself from the tale you are so familiar with and experience the genuine horror of discovering a successful businessman and member of posh society lurking in the vacant cellar of his partner's apartment, crawling up to him weighed down with the damnation that he assures will befall his successor if his life does not change. It is shocking, ghoulish, and pitiable, achieving what the impish Goblin King could not: a vision of human misery and regret, one which sears the heart and troubles the conscience.

Marley's Ghost
EXCERPTED *from* A CHRISTMAS CAROL, STAVE *One*
{1843}

MARLEY[1] was dead: to begin with. There is no doubt whatever about that. The register of his burial was signed by the clergyman, the clerk, the undertaker, and the chief mourner. Scrooge signed it: and Scrooge's name[2] was good upon

---

[1] Unlike some of Dickens' characters, this name has no implications. The story is that Dickens was at a St. Patrick's Day party, where he was guest of the Irish physician Dr. Miles Marley. Marley mentioned in passing (probably in reference to the unusual and playful surnames of many Dickens characters) that he thought his own surname was somewhat unique. Dickens pledged to him "your name shall be a household word before the year is out"

[2] Speaking of which: the name derives from a defunct English verb – "scrouge," meaning to squeeze or crush. It also has homophonic relations to "screw" (as in to tighten the screws in torture scenarios) and "gouge," as in to overcharge or swindle

'Change[1], for anything he chose to put his hand to. Old Marley was as dead as a door-nail[2].

Mind! I don't mean to say that I know, of my own knowledge, what there is particularly dead about a door-nail. I might have been inclined, myself, to regard a coffin-nail as the deadest piece of ironmongery in the trade. But the wisdom of our ancestors is in the simile[3]; and my unhallowed hands shall not disturb it, or the Country's done for. You will therefore permit me to repeat, emphatically, that Marley was as dead as a door-nail[4].

---

[1] That is, the London Stock Exchange. Dickens immediately associates Scrooge with commerce, simultaneously informing us that he is wealthy enough to have stupendous credit with the stock brokers

[2] A doornail is not what you may think, and it actually has an interesting connection to Marley: a doornail is the plate which a doorknocker strikes when knocked (originally this was simply a large-headed nail) – which is of course what Marley fists manifests as. The meaning is simply that a doornail endures a great deal of punishment – being struck on the head regularly – and thus must be quite dead indeed. The simile dates back at least to 1362 when it appeared in *The Vision of Piers Plowman,* though it was popularized by Shakespeare in Henry IV 2

[3] Another of his greatest ghost stories begins with the narrator meditating on a simile which will be important to understanding the philosophical plot: "To Be Read at Dusk," which compares a sunset in the Alps to watching wine spill over a table cloth, then comparing the wine to blood, drawing attention to the dozens of bodies hidden under the unforgiving snow

[4] This witty tangent is typical of Dickens, even in his more serious works. However, there is more than wit to this idiomatic thesis. "A Christmas Carol" will go on to celebrate a season that had – by Dickens' youth – fallen into extreme neglect. Christmas was seen as a somewhat Popish celebration that smacked of debauched Catholic feast days, pagan rituals, and the sort of indulgent frivolity that the English stereotyped the French and Italians with. By the 1820s it was little more than a Bank holiday with very strong religious (rather than social) overtones. Giving, charity, and human fellowship were not associated with the holiday in the way they are today before Dickens' novella was published. The pathos, brotherhood, and humanity portrayed in the story are largely drawn from Washington Irving's own nostalgic portrayal of backwoods English country Christmases in his 1819 *Sketch-Book*. The countryside was where Royalists, conservatives, and Catholics flourished during the Civil War and after, and as a result, the Puritan defamation of Christmas had little effect on their traditions, leaving old, rustic, out-of-the-way English manors (particularly in the north and west) as figurative time capsules where the Elizabethan traditions of Yuletide were preserved. Irving happened upon some of these homespun festivities during his tenure in Britain (particularly at Aston Hall in Birmingham), and described them (dressing them up with the romantic flair, quaint affectations, and humorous overtones that Dickens so adored) in his series of Bracebridge Hall tales in both *The Sketch-Book* and *Bracebridge Hall* (1821). Dickens begins the story by meditating on English traditions which might be

Scrooge knew he was dead? Of course he did. How could it be otherwise? Scrooge and he were partners for I don't know how many years. Scrooge was his sole executor, his sole administrator, his sole assign, his sole residuary legatee[1], his sole friend, and sole mourner[2]. And even Scrooge was not so dreadfully cut up by the sad event, but that he was an excellent man of business on the very day of the funeral, and solemnised it with an undoubted bargain.

The mention of Marley's funeral brings me back to the point I started from. There is no doubt that Marley was dead. This must be distinctly understood, or nothing wonderful can come of the story I am going to relate. If we were not perfectly convinced that Hamlet's Father died before the play began[3], there would be nothing more remarkable in his taking a stroll at night, in an easterly wind, upon his own ramparts, than there would be in any other middle-aged gentleman rashly turning out after dark in a breezy spot—say Saint Paul's Churchyard[4] for instance—literally to astonish his son's weak mind.

Scrooge never painted out Old Marley's name. There it stood, years afterwards, above the warehouse door: Scrooge and Marley. The firm[5] was known as Scrooge and Marley. Sometimes people new to the business called Scrooge Scrooge, and sometimes Marley, but he answered to both names. It was all the same to him[6].

Oh! But he was a tight-fisted hand at the grindstone, Scrooge! a squeezing, wrenching, grasping, scraping, clutching, covetous, old sinner[7]! Hard and sharp as

---

quaint and out-of-date, but which nevertheless deserve a certain hallowed-ness and reverence. Let it not be mistaken, he is telling us: this story is a celebration – not a mockery – of old English values and traditions

[1] An heir who receives the residual of an estate once debts have been extracted

[2] Dickens mirrors the litany of the first paragraph – the list of those present at the funeral

[3] For the uninitiated, *Hamlet,* which many consider to be Shakespeare's greatest tragic play, if not his magnum opus, begins with rumors of his dead father's ghost wandering around the castle walls. Troubled by these stories, Hamlet sets out to meet the ghost, which he does. There is no question at the beginning of the play, like Marley, that King Hamlet is dead

[4] Not a churchyard in the cemetery sense, but a literal commons yard on the church grounds. St Paul's churchyard would be a busy place even after dark in Victorian London

[5] While Dickens never specifies what the firm is, it has been traditional for portrayals to hint that he is a moneylender who deals in mortgages, business loans, and investments, an interpretation strongly supported by the text's few clues

[6] Scrooge has no concern for personal identity, personal respect, or personal humanity. To him a name is not a record of selfhood and personality; it is something to wear like a used overcoat

[7] While Scrooge bears an obvious resemblance to his miserly forefather in "The Goblins who Stole a Sexton," he also owes his character to several real-life penny-pinchers: the Dutchman Gabriel de Graaf (who lent Gabriel Grub his name), the economist Thomas

flint, from which no steel had ever struck out generous fire[1]; secret, and self-contained, and solitary as an oyster. The cold within him froze his old features, nipped his pointed nose, shrivelled his cheek, stiffened his gait; made his eyes red, his thin lips blue; and spoke out shrewdly in his grating voice. A frosty rime[2] was on his head, and on his eyebrows, and his wiry chin. He carried his own low temperature always about with him; he iced his office in the dog-days[3]; and didn't thaw it one degree at Christmas.

External heat and cold had little influence on Scrooge. No warmth could warm, no wintry weather chill him. No wind that blew was bitterer than he, no falling snow was more intent upon its purpose, no pelting rain less open to entreaty. Foul weather didn't know where to have him[4]. The heaviest rain, and snow, and hail, and sleet, could boast of the advantage over him in only one respect. They often "came down" handsomely[5], and Scrooge never did.

Nobody ever stopped him in the street to say, with gladsome looks, "My dear Scrooge, how are you? When will you come to see me?" No beggars implored him to bestow a trifle, no children asked him what it was o'clock[6], no man or woman ever once in all his life inquired the way to such and such a place, of Scrooge. Even the blind men's dogs appeared to know him; and when they saw him coming on, would tug their owners into doorways and up courts; and then would wag their tails as though they said, "No eye at all is better than an evil eye[7], dark master!"

Malthus, Britain's first millionaire – Jemmy Wood, and the likeliest candidate (whom Dickens mentions in letters, and after whom John Leech fashioned his illustrations of Scrooge) the hoarder and miser John Elwes. This 18th century moneylender dressed like a beggar, ate like a prisoner, and suffered the pain of untreated wounds rather than pay for a doctor, and very nearly died the lonely death predicted of Scrooge

[1] Flint is notoriously hard and sharp, and has been used for centuries to start fires by striking it with steel: the flint is so hard that a small sliver of the steel is shorn off, flying away in the form of a spark or sparks, which – if landing in dry tender – can be coaxed into giving off life-giving heat

[2] Frost formed on a cold object by the rapid freezing of water vapor – such as on a window pane

[3] The hottest days of July and August, so-called because Sirius – the dog star – would rise with the sun during that time of the year

[4] A quote from *Henry IV 1*,: "She's neither fish nor flesh: a man knows not where to have her"

[5] To "come down handsomely" could mean meteorologically (for rain to pour excessively) or philanthropically (for a man to be generous)

[6] That is, "what time is it?"

[7] A complicated piece of folklore that manifests in a vast number of cultural traditions, the "evil eye" is generally thought to belong to a person who has the ability to curse with a mere glance

But what did Scrooge care! It was the very thing he liked. To edge his way along the crowded paths of life, warning all human sympathy to keep its distance, was what the knowing ones call "nuts[1]" to Scrooge.

Once upon a time[2]—of all the good days in the year, on Christmas Eve—old Scrooge sat busy in his counting-house. It was cold, bleak, biting weather: foggy withal: and he could hear the people in the court outside, go wheezing up and down, beating their hands upon their breasts, and stamping their feet upon the pavement stones to warm them[3]. The city clocks had only just gone three, but it was quite dark already—it had not been light all day[4]—and candles were flaring in the windows of the neighbouring offices, like ruddy smears upon the palpable

---

[1] Not remotely similar to any colloquial uses that the word "nuts" is given today: it meant "good luck," signifying something which was gratifying and pleasant. Dickens patronizes the slang term by referring to its foppish users as "knowing ones." It would be similar to saying "what the knowing ones call wicked sick"

[2] Dickens moves forward from his exposition and sets up the parable-like nature of his tale by employing the infamous fairy tale opener "once upon a time." In use in several manifestations since 1380, the phrase (or some variation) is employed in most languages (the French say "There was one time"; the Chinese: "A very, very long time ago"; the Swedish: "Once, long ago"; and the Germans either say "Once there was" or "Back in the days when it was still of help to wish for a thing." In any case, Dickens creates a pleasant juxtaposition between the fairy tales which are remote and fanciful – as the Estonians say in their opening phrase, "behind seven lands and seas" – and the very real, very harsh coal-stained cobbles of Victorian London

[3] As I will point out in the following note, the struggle to stave off frost and to generate warmth is a recurring theme that repeats through the novella, symbolizing the presence of Want and the absence of Charity

[4] Throughout the text Dickens employs two recurring motifs of natural dichotomies to symbolize the two ghouls that most haunt Scrooge: Ignorance and Want. The first – ignorance – is indicated by the presence of darkness or the struggle between darkness and light. The darkness is both symbolized by a literal lack of light, and by the obscuring, omnipresent fog. In some cases (like the ruddy smears of candles in the street which are all but strangled by the fog and murk) the light is faint and cowed by the tremendous power of metaphorical ignorance, while in others (the eye-searing Ghost of Christmas Past) the balance is entirely tipped in favor of Truth and Reality. The second is the struggle between cold and warmth, which represent the clash between Want and Charity. Frost, icy temperatures, and low fires – both in Scrooge's quarters and in those of the poor whom he witnesses in the Present and Future – symbolize material poverty and the absence of generosity, while heat, fire, and liquor represent spiritual wealth and the presence of generosity – seen in the company of Fezziwig, Fred, and others, eventually including Scrooge himself

brown air[1]. The fog came pouring in at every chink and keyhole, and was so dense without[2], that although the court was of the narrowest, the houses opposite were mere phantoms[3]. To see the dingy cloud come drooping down, obscuring everything, one might have thought that Nature lived hard by, and was brewing on a large scale[4].

The door of Scrooge's counting-house was open that he might keep his eye upon his clerk[5], who in a dismal little cell beyond, a sort of tank, was copying

---

[1] Symbolically we may take this to represent a higher level of employer/employee Charity existing in these neighboring offices than that in Scrooge's counting house. The fog (read: Scrooge's ignorance), however, reduces the light of understanding to a red stain on the brown sea of smog

[2] The level of Ignorance in Scrooge's world (for this office far more than his quarters constitute his world) is extreme, permeating everything, blocking him from even his closest neighbors, and crawling through each keyhole and kink like a parasitic miasma that has aggressively infected his mind and warped his worldview

[3] Besides foreshadowing (literally), this introduces us to the motif of "phantom," causing us to have a clearer view of what exactly a "phantom" is to Dickens. Phantoms are shadows of reality, suggesting what is real without being what is real; they are representations of the truth, just as the blank shadows of the adjacent houses are mere "phantoms" of their real selves – they point out the truth when the truth is avoided, calling attention to reality when mankind sees fit to ignore it

[4] To begin with, this is a phrase pulled right out of Washington Irving's playbook, and it is a testament to Dickens' admiration of the American Romantic. The phrase implies several things: first, it reinforces the symbolism of the murk by using the phrase "obscuring everything" – for everything truly is obscured from Scrooge's vantage point, and twisted into a false perception of reality that weighs commerce over human lives. Second, it insinuates Nature into the context of human industry (viz. London in all of its stony, sooty, industrial grandeur). This is ironic since Victorian London was the farthest thing from the throne of Nature, but it suggests that mankind and all of his ambitions are mortal and inferior to the constant onslaught of Nature, who can be just at home is smog-choked London as the loneliest shores of the Hebrides. The takeaway from this: Scrooge is invested in a manmade world of money and sales, but this is merely a passing fad in the path of omnipresent Nature which is responsible for human love, sentiment, and spirit, and Nature will – as we see in the end – win out. Lastly, it implies that a change is being brewed, or at least some form of catalyst. What is Nature cooking up? A potion for transformation

[5] Dickens' father was himself a clerk (pronounced "clark") for the Royal Navy Pay Office in Portsmouth, and is said to bear some resemblances to Bob Cratchit and the optimistic pauper Micawber, an impoverished clerk in *David Copperfield*. Clerks like Cratchit were copyists – or scriveners – who would today be considered members of the data entry profession. Clerks had a poor (that is to say pitiable) reputation in British society, being

letters. Scrooge had a very small fire, but the clerk's fire was so very much smaller that it looked like one coal. But he couldn't replenish it, for Scrooge kept the coal-box in his own room; and so surely as the clerk came in with the shovel, the master predicted that it would be necessary for them to part. Wherefore the clerk put on his white comforter, and tried to warm himself at the candle; in which effort, not being a man of a strong imagination, he failed.

"A merry Christmas, uncle! God save you!" cried a cheerful voice. It was the voice of Scrooge's nephew, who came upon him so quickly that this was the first intimation he had of his approach.

"Bah!" said Scrooge, "Humbug[1]!"

He had so heated himself with rapid walking in the fog and frost, this nephew of Scrooge's, that he was all in a glow; his face was ruddy and handsome[2]; his eyes sparkled, and his breath smoked again[3].

"Christmas a humbug, uncle!" said Scrooge's nephew. "You don't mean that, I am sure?"

"I do," said Scrooge. "Merry Christmas! What right have you to be merry? What reason have you to be merry? You're poor enough."

"Come, then," returned the nephew gaily. "What right have you to be dismal? What reason have you to be morose? You're rich enough."

Scrooge having no better answer ready on the spur of the moment, said, "Bah!" again; and followed it up with "Humbug."

"Don't be cross, uncle!" said the nephew.

"What else can I be," returned the uncle, "when I live in such a world of fools as this? Merry Christmas! Out upon merry Christmas! What's Christmas time to you but a time for paying bills without money; a time for finding yourself a year older, but not an hour richer; a time for balancing your books and having every item in 'em through a round dozen of months presented dead against you? If I could work my will," said Scrooge indignantly, "every idiot who goes about with 'Merry

---

stereotyped as middle-aged men burdened by large, squalling families, known for their unvaryingly threadbare wardrobes, and given to walking alcoholism

[1] Humbug means a deceit, a hypocrisy, a staged act. Scrooge implies that those who wish others a happy Christmas are covering a hidden agenda (ostensibly a financial agenda)

[2] This quotation from the Bible is in reference to David – another warm and passionate young man who saw fit to turn the tables on his elder (in his case the paranoid tyrant Saul)

[3] With his sparking eyes, smoking breath, and handsome red cheeks, Fred is coded as a veritable flashpoint of warmth and human generosity – the antithesis of Want which is symbolized by frost and lack of heat. He is a walking boiler of humanitarianism, benevolence, and good spirit

Christmas' on his lips, should be boiled with his own pudding[1], and buried with a stake of holly through his heart[2]. He should!"

"Uncle!" pleaded the nephew.

"Nephew!" returned the uncle sternly, "keep Christmas in your own way, and let me keep it in mine."

"Keep it!" repeated Scrooge's nephew. "But you don't keep it."

"Let me leave it alone, then," said Scrooge. "Much good may it do you! Much good it has ever done you!"

"There are many things from which I might have derived good, by which I have not profited, I dare say," returned the nephew. "Christmas among the rest. But I am sure I have always thought of Christmas time, when it has come round—apart from the veneration due to its sacred name and origin[3], if anything belonging to it can be apart from that—as a good time; a kind, forgiving, charitable, pleasant time; the only time I know of, in the long calendar of the year, when men and women seem by one consent to open their shut-up hearts freely, and to think of people below them as if they really were fellow-passengers to the grave[4], and not another

---

[1] Christmas puddings were fruit cakes made of dried fruits, nuts, and spices mixed in with eggs and suet, and boiled in a bag. After boiling, the bag is left to dry for several days or even longer. After being allowed to set, it is soaked in rum or brandy, lit on fire, and served

[2] Traditionally (as is depicted in *The Old Curiosity Shop*) murderers, suicides, and suspected cannibals were buried at a crossroads with stakes pounded through them into the earth. This was standard practice (for suicides at least) in Britain until 1826 – if you can believe it or not. The theory behind the practice was that these criminals were liable to return from the dead as vampires, or other revenants. In this sense, Scrooge is accusing Christmas well-wishers of being little more than sycophantic vampires eager to drain his bank account

[3] Christmas experienced several transformations before and after the English Revolution. Before the ousting of Charles II Christmas was a thoroughly religious holiday, as orthodox in tone as Easter, Good Friday, or Passover are to some Christians and Jews today. But after Charles' execution, the holiday was banned for being too Catholic in its nature, and for its relationship to Roman, Druidic, and Gothic pagan celebrations. After its return with the Restoration, the holiday had been stripped of its shine, and by the ascension of William of Orange – and well into the Georgian Period – the day was little more than a bank holiday (akin to Labor Day in the United States: a holiday with no popular sentiment seen as an excuse to take off work). Dickens is trying to strike a balance: he wants to remind his readers that Christmas (literally, Christ's Mass, or Christ's Day) was a holiday of religious and spiritual significance, but he wanted to stop short of the purely orthodox Mass of the Stewart monarchs, that is, he wanted to take Christmas out of the church and into the streets, out of the structured enclosure of organized religion and into the teeming mess of social life

[4] Marley is certainly pained by this truth, and reminds Scrooge that death is rapidly approaching all living men, and that after death the choices made to engage in either

race of creatures bound on other journeys. And therefore, uncle, though it has never put a scrap of gold or silver in my pocket[1], I believe that it has done me good, and will do me good; and I say, God bless it!"

The clerk in the Tank involuntarily applauded. Becoming immediately sensible of the impropriety, he poked the fire, and extinguished the last frail spark for ever[2].

"Let me hear another sound from you," said Scrooge, "and you'll keep your Christmas by losing your situation! You're quite a powerful speaker, sir," he added, turning to his nephew. "I wonder you don't go into Parliament[3]."

"Don't be angry, uncle. Come! Dine with us to-morrow."

Scrooge said that he would see him—yes, indeed he did. He went the whole length of the expression, and said that he would see him in that extremity first[4].

"But why?" cried Scrooge's nephew. "Why?"

"Why did you get married?" said Scrooge.

"Because I fell in love."

"Because you fell in love!" growled Scrooge, as if that were the only one thing in the world more ridiculous than a merry Christmas. "Good afternoon!"

---

fellowship or misanthropy will dictate who you spend time with in the afterlife: the mournful, segregated damned or the convivial spirits of Christmas. It needs to be noted that Dickens does not portray a heaven in his text, though it is implied by the existence of Marley's hell, but chooses instead to underscore Heaven-on-Earth: the reward of a good life *is* a good life – its own reward – not an escapist fantasy of heaven. This idea is reflected in the lyrics to Marley's song "Make the Most of This Life" in the musical *Scrooge*: "Make the most of this life / The next life's a curse / The man who kicks the present aside / In a quest for things life doesn't provide / Had better know now his theory is perverse / Make the most of this life / For the next life is far, far worse / Let's talk about heaven a minute / Men dream of it from birth / Heaven, you idiot / You're in it on earth"

[1] A direct argument against the capitalistic values of the Industrial Revolution and in particular against the theories of Thomas Malthus, and English economist who famously argued that famine and disease would weed out the poor and curb population gluts ("to decrease the surplus population," ahem...). He was critical of the Poor Laws – a system of poverty relief analogous to welfare – and supported the Corn Laws which heavily taxed grains and left the poor in a miserable state. Malthus, unsurprisingly, has been viewed by many academics as a possible inspiration for Scrooge

[2] Certainly symbolic: fire, as I have pointed out, is emblematic of hope, fellowship, and truth. Cratchit – in a tradeoff for his job – squelches his last spark of hope for better treatment as penance for his indiscretion (namely, having an opinion)

[3] Presumably as a Whig – the party that (until its 1868 transformation into the Liberal Party) traditionally stood for radical reformation, the correction of social problems, championship of the poor, and improvement of working conditions. Scrooge, unquestionably, is an ardent Tory

[4] *"I'll see you in hell first."* Dickens would occasionally say the expression during live readings, and the euphemism itself was censored in several American editions

"Nay, uncle, but you never came to see me before that happened. Why give it as a reason for not coming now?"

"Good afternoon," said Scrooge.

"I want nothing from you; I ask nothing of you; why cannot we be friends?"

"Good afternoon," said Scrooge.

"I am sorry, with all my heart, to find you so resolute. We have never had any quarrel, to which I have been a party. But I have made the trial in homage to Christmas, and I'll keep my Christmas humour[1] to the last. So A Merry Christmas, uncle!"

"Good afternoon!" said Scrooge.

"And A Happy New Year!"

"Good afternoon!" said Scrooge.

His nephew left the room without an angry word, notwithstanding. He stopped at the outer door to bestow the greetings of the season on the clerk, who, cold as he was, was warmer than Scrooge; for he returned them cordially[2].

"There's another fellow," muttered Scrooge; who overheard him: "my clerk, with fifteen shillings a week[3], and a wife and family, talking about a merry Christmas. I'll retire to Bedlam[4]."

---

[1] Meaning attitude, or state of emotions (which, in a literal sense would include a good sense of humor as well)

[2] Fred and Cratchit represent the communion between the middle and lower-middle classes (despite his cultural depiction as a poor, poor man, Cratchit is still above the working class station – analogous to a temp or a part-time secretary versus a factory worker or janitor). Per Fred's philosophy that we are all fellow passengers en route to the grave, the two men make a connection of fellowship and warmth that spans their social gap (although we never learn Fred's profession, the fact that he keeps a housemaid and the nature of his Christmas party suggest that he is firmly in the middle class and possibly a lawyer (per Scrooge's political suggestion) or a man of letters (per the charge of Dickens' contemporaries that Fred was an dead ringer for his creator))

[3] The wage is actually not a horribly sparse one for a single man (basic laborers were paid eight shillings a week) but the cost of providing for a family would make it a very difficult one to endure. A shilling is worth one-twentieth of a pound, or twelve pence, roughly analogous to an American dime. This is roughly $93 USD a week (2014)

[4] London's infamous insane asylum (Bedlam being a loosening of the pronunciation for Bethlem Royal Hospital). Scrooge implies that if a man like Cratchit, with a wage and a family like Cratchit, are not obsessed with making more money, then perhaps it would be safer in the madhouse than in the streets of the city where such loonies roam free

This lunatic, in letting Scrooge's nephew out, had let two other people in. They were portly gentlemen, pleasant to behold[1], and now stood, with their hats off, in Scrooge's office. They had books and papers in their hands, and bowed to him.

"Scrooge and Marley's, I believe," said one of the gentlemen, referring to his list. "Have I the pleasure of addressing Mr. Scrooge, or Mr. Marley?"

"Mr. Marley has been dead these seven years," Scrooge replied. "He died seven years ago, this very night."

"We have no doubt his liberality is well represented by his surviving partner," said the gentleman, presenting his credentials.

It certainly was; for they had been two kindred spirits. At the ominous word "liberality," Scrooge frowned, and shook his head, and handed the credentials back.

"At this festive season of the year, Mr. Scrooge," said the gentleman, taking up a pen, "it is more than usually desirable that we should make some slight provision for the Poor[2] and destitute, who suffer greatly at the present time. Many thousands are in want of common necessaries; hundreds of thousands are in want of common comforts, sir."

"Are there no prisons[3]?" asked Scrooge.

"Plenty of prisons," said the gentleman, laying down the pen again.

"And the Union workhouses[4]?" demanded Scrooge. "Are they still in operation?"

"They are. Still," returned the gentleman, "I wish I could say they were not."

---

[1] Like his literary master, Washington Irving, Dickens associates girth with congeniality, warmness, and a broad spirit. Fat implies a nature ripe with contentment, pleasure, and mirth, and while today fat characters are often bombastic or corrupt (we associate weight with overindulgence and decadence), to Dickens, a portly gentleman was the sort that carries an aura of good humor and good nature

[2] Dickens' capitalization here is more than just an antiquated, Victorian habit. He is intentionally representing the impoverished masses of England as a people worthy of recognition and respect, like the Scots, the French, or the Russians, whose names are solemnized with a capital letter, and their identities thus owned and acknowledged

[3] Specifically debtors' prisons, like the one that housed Dickens' father during his childhood

[4] With the passing of the New Poor Law in 1834, parishes were consolidated into parish unions, and each union sent funds to support a workhouse. These were essentially prisons where the families of poor men were held and fed while they worked outside. Able bodied children and adults were made to work vicious hours in order to purchase their freedom. In spite of relatively benign intentions – the conditions in the workhouses were miserable, and many saw the practice as little more than a Medieval injustice

"The Treadmill[1] and the Poor Law[2] are in full vigour, then?" said Scrooge.

"Both very busy, sir."

"Oh! I was afraid, from what you said at first, that something had occurred to stop them in their useful course," said Scrooge. "I'm very glad to hear it."

"Under the impression that they scarcely furnish Christian cheer of mind or body to the multitude[3]," returned the gentleman, "a few of us are endeavouring to raise a fund to buy the Poor some meat and drink, and means of warmth. We choose this time, because it is a time, of all others, when Want is keenly felt, and Abundance rejoices. What shall I put you down for?"

"Nothing!" Scrooge replied.

"You wish to be anonymous?"

"I wish to be left alone," said Scrooge. "Since you ask me what I wish, gentlemen, that is my answer. I don't make merry myself at Christmas and I can't afford to make idle[4] people merry. I help to support the establishments I have mentioned[5]—they cost enough; and those who are badly off must go there."

"Many can't go there; and many would rather die[6]."

---

[1] If it were not true it would sound like a cartoon or a farce, but the treadmill was literally a mill whose machinery was turned by prisoners walking on what amounts to the outside surface of a giant hamster wheel. Begun as a form of hard labor early in the century, it was a grisly fate for many who fell in arears – one with the distinct possibility of being crushed to death if one were unfortunate enough to fall from exhaustion

[2] A general reference to a series of so-named legislations that made the workhouses, treadmill, and other social policies possible

[3] A reference that suggests the crowds that Jesus fed with fish and bread and by its nature implies the Christian duty of the well-off to likewise feed and nourish their poorer neighbors

[4] Scrooge imagines that all poverty is caused by a lack of hard work, supposing that if everyone worked as hard as he did, there would be no unemployment. A consummate capitalist, Scrooge is nonetheless a naïve economist

[5] Through his taxes. Scrooge certainly is not making any donations out of pocket

[6] Indeed, for a respectable family to surrender itself to a poorhouse was a humiliation that led to many suicides. Once split apart it was often difficult for a family to pull themselves out of debt, and being sent to a workhouse was tantamount to legalized slavery

"If they would rather die," said Scrooge, "they had better do it, and decrease the surplus population[1]. Besides—excuse me—I don't know that[2]."

"But you might know it," observed the gentleman.

"It's not my business," Scrooge returned. "It's enough for a man to understand his own business, and not to interfere with other people's[3]. Mine occupies me constantly. Good afternoon, gentlemen!"

Seeing clearly that it would be useless to pursue their point, the gentlemen withdrew. Scrooge resumed his labours with an improved opinion of himself, and in a more facetious temper than was usual with him.

Meanwhile the fog and darkness thickened so[4], that people ran about with flaring links[5], proffering their services to go before horses in carriages, and conduct them on their way[6]. The ancient tower of a church, whose gruff old bell was always

---

[1] Thomas Malthus, whom Dickens abhorred, was referenced in an earlier note, and his lasses-faire approach to social welfare once more rears its head here. The minister, sociologist, and economist believed that population control was essential to a nation's success, and that nature or God would trim back the excess if a society didn't do this by its own gumption. As such, plagues, famines, wars, and disasters that eviscerated the poor were viewed as necessary acts of natural selection that prevented the masses from consuming too many resources. For him, a population did not consist of people so much as mouths, and the fewer mouths the better. Malthusian economics is largely concerned with the consumption of resources, and still persists today. Scrooge was clearly an advocate of this approach, viewing the poor as a surplus to be consumed by death rather than living souls to be cared for and nourished

[2] This quote gives me chills every time. It is the manifestation of Ignorance, the bestial child whom Scrooge will meet in the third chapter. Knowing rejection of the truth, knowing condemnation of the suffering poor, knowing negligence of his human capacity to pity and sympathize. Even more so than his injunction to decrease the surplus population, this icy quip is Scrooge's least human, most hellish moment

[3] Dickens thunders the hammer of social responsibility here, calling attention to the callous yet common sentiment that the state of the poor is their concern alone – that a man should keep to his own business and avoid those of others. Dickens, of course, held that the good man saw the persons in his community as fellow passengers to the grave to be comforted and assisted as much as one could

[4] Again, read: the ignorance and denial had thickened so. Immediately after Scrooge's statement of social alienation, the fog rolls in thick as if to illustrate his clouded perception with a metaphor

[5] Staves of firewood the ends of which have been swathed in oil rags or dipped in pitch, and thence set alight. These convenient torches were cheap and easily acquired, and burned with a bright, clear light

[6] A metaphorical counterpoint to Scrooge's fog: these lovers of mankind offer their services to conduct their fellow man through the darkness of societal negligence, literally shining through the murk and offering a reference point of place and

peeping slily down[1] at Scrooge out of a Gothic window in the wall, became invisible[2], and struck the hours and quarters in the clouds, with tremulous vibrations afterwards as if its teeth were chattering in its frozen[3] head up there. The cold became intense. In the main street, at the corner of the court, some labourers were repairing the gas-pipes, and had lighted a great fire in a brazier, round which a party of ragged men and boys were gathered: warming their hands and winking their eyes before the blaze in rapture. The water-plug being left in solitude, its overflowings sullenly congealed, and turned to misanthropic ice. The brightness of the shops where holly sprigs and berries crackled in the lamp heat of the windows, made pale faces ruddy as they passed. Poulterers' and grocers' trades became a splendid joke: a glorious pageant, with which it was next to impossible to believe that such dull principles as bargain and sale had anything to do. The Lord Mayor, in the stronghold of the mighty Mansion House, gave orders to his fifty cooks and butlers to keep Christmas as a Lord Mayor's household should; and even the little tailor, whom he had fined five shillings on the previous Monday for being drunk and bloodthirsty in the streets, stirred up to-morrow's pudding in his garret, while his lean wife and the baby sallied out to buy the beef.

Foggier yet, and colder. Piercing, searching, biting cold. If the good Saint Dunstan had but nipped the Evil Spirit's nose with a touch of such weather as that, instead of using his familiar weapons, then indeed he would have roared to lusty purpose. The owner of one scant young nose, gnawed and mumbled by the hungry cold as bones are gnawed by dogs, stooped down at Scrooge's keyhole to regale him with a Christmas carol: but at the first sound of

"God bless you, merry gentleman!
May nothing you dismay[4]!"

---

individuality that cuts through the selfish fog which blots out the personality of the places it obscures. These ministers to man can be viewed as symbolically fighting back the forces of urban alienation by offering a means of human companionship and guidance to break through the anonymity

[1] A symbol of divine watchfulness. The church bell symbolizes the voice and eye of God, monitoring everything under its vantage, and speaking truth overhead to those who will hear. The sly manner in which it observes Scrooge suggests that it has something planned for him. Indeed it does

[2] Christian morality – specifically the social gospel of brotherhood and fellowship – has been obscured by Scrooge's brewing ignorance

[3] Ice and frost being symbolic of human negligence and alienation, this suggests that the principles of the New Testament – love thy neighbor as thyself – are struggling to be heard amidst the selfish environment of individualism

[4] One of the oldest Christmas carols in existence, certainly one of the oldest still in popular use, "God Rest Ye Merry, Gentlemen" is at least five hundred years old, possibly older, being popularized in the eighteenth century by publications in 1760 and 1775. Dickens makes the common mistake of misunderstanding the verb "rest" – a Tudor-era

Scrooge seized the ruler with such energy of action, that the singer fled in terror, leaving the keyhole to the fog and even more congenial frost[1].

At length the hour of shutting up the counting-house arrived. With an ill-will Scrooge dismounted from his stool, and tacitly admitted the fact to the expectant clerk in the Tank, who instantly snuffed his candle out, and put on his hat.

"You'll want all day to-morrow, I suppose?" said Scrooge.

"If quite convenient, sir."

"It's not convenient," said Scrooge, "and it's not fair. If I was to stop half-a-crown[2] for it, you'd think yourself ill-used, I'll be bound?"

The clerk smiled faintly.

"And yet," said Scrooge, "you don't think me ill-used, when I pay a day's wages for no work."

The clerk observed that it was only once a year.

"A poor excuse for picking a man's pocket every twenty-fifth of December!" said Scrooge, buttoning his great-coat[3] to the chin. "But I suppose you must have the whole day. Be here all the earlier next morning[4]."

The clerk promised that he would; and Scrooge walked out with a growl. The office was closed in a twinkling, and the clerk, with the long ends of his white comforter dangling below his waist (for he boasted no great-coat[5]), went down a slide on Cornhill[6], at the end of a lane of boys, twenty times, in honour of its being Christmas Eve, and then ran home to Camden Town[7] as hard as he could pelt, to play at blindman's-buff.

---

term meaning "keep, maintain, or sustain." The meaning – still widely misinterpreted today – is not "May God give you rest, merry sir," but "May God keep you merry, sir," and the comma is thus required between Merry and Gentlemen

[1] Again: fog and frost = ignorance and want, which filled the vacuum of the space vacated by the genial caroler

[2] A coin worth two shillings and sixpence (30 pence total), or 1/8 of a pound. This is Bob's daily wage – 1/6 of his weekly wage, which tells us that he works Saturdays

[3] A heavy wool outer coat or overcoat made to go over a man's dress coat

[4] It truly must be noted that this is an example of generosity that marbles Scrooge's characterization: if he were a real king-tyrant he would have withheld Christmas as well. One wonders if there are other holidays that Cratchit has off

[5] Being too poor: the garment was a costly one that spoke of status measuring at least with the sturdy middle class. Lower class persons might have a wool sweater or pea jacket, but a greatcoat was more than most could afford

[6] A ward (and a street) in the City of London – today part of the financial district and renowned for its opticians and lens technicians

[7] Entirely swallowed by London today, Camden Town was once a middle to lower-middle classed suburb made largely of rentals located northeast of the city proper

Scrooge took his melancholy dinner in his usual melancholy tavern[1]; and having read all the newspapers, and beguiled the rest of the evening with his banker's-book, went home to bed. He lived in chambers which had once belonged to his deceased partner. They were a gloomy suite of rooms, in a lowering pile of building up a yard, where it had so little business to be, that one could scarcely help fancying it must have run there when it was a young house, playing at hide-and-seek with other houses, and forgotten the way out again[2]. It was old enough now, and dreary enough, for nobody lived in it but Scrooge, the other rooms being all let out as offices[3]. The yard was so dark that even Scrooge, who knew its every stone, was fain to grope with his hands. The fog and frost so hung about the black old gateway of the house, that it seemed as if the Genius of the Weather sat in mournful meditation on the threshold[4].

Now, it is a fact, that there was nothing at all particular about the knocker[5] on the door, except that it was very large. It is also a fact, that Scrooge had seen it,

---

[1] Tantamount to a diner or a dive joint, the fact that Scrooge daily dines at a tavern suggests both his cheapness (rather than a restaurant better suited to his class) and his lack of a cook, a ludicrous thing for a man of his station, since most upper middle class families would employ (at least) a maid and a cook, and often a valet, gardener, or footman depending on the size of the house. Maids and cooks were sometimes rolled into one, and it is surprising that – although he keeps a charwoman – Scrooge has no servant to make his fires, cook his food, clean his rooms, and keep him in a state of respectability. Although this is lost on our republican values today in the West, it is not a sign of republicanism, but one of stingy miserliness

[2] Suggestive of Scrooge himself: a playful little boy who became lost and was never again recovered

[3] Fittingly Scrooge lives amongst businesses rather than living people. It would be like renting an apartment in a depressing, out of date office building. Businesses would lock up at night and you would come home, surrounded by empty rooms, sometimes with a clerk or two working late. Certainly a creepy and alienating situation

[4] "Genius" here refers to the spirit or anthropomorphic manifestation in the same way that Uncle Sam, John Bull, the Grim Reaper, Father Time, and Santa Claus are respectively geniuses of the United States, United Kingdom, death, time, and Christmas. Scrooge's apartment appears to be the source of the fog, which boils heavily from the vicinity in such an intense way that even he is staggered by it. If we continue to nurse the symbolism of fog as ignorance, then the source of the murk is highly suggestive

[5] The knocker consisted of a handle and a plate. The handle could be rapped against the lower end of the plate, or – if this failed – a cane could be gaveled smartly against the polished steel. During the nineteenth century it became fashionable for the plates to be cast images (lions, dogs, eagles). Dickens tellingly commented on the trend in 1839: "Whenever we meet a man for the first time, we contemplate the features of his knocker with the greatest curiosity, for we well know, that between the man and the knocker, there will inevitably be a greater or less degree of resemblance and sympathy."

night and morning, during his whole residence in that place; also that Scrooge had as little of what is called fancy about him as any man in the city of London, even including—which is a bold word—the corporation, aldermen, and livery[1]. Let it also be borne in mind that Scrooge had not bestowed one thought on Marley, since his last mention of his seven years' dead partner that afternoon. And then let any man explain to me, if he can, how it happened that Scrooge, having his key in the lock of the door, saw in the knocker, without its undergoing any intermediate process of change—not a knocker, but Marley's face[2].

Marley's face. It was not in impenetrable shadow as the other objects in the yard were, but had a dismal light about it, like a bad lobster in a dark cellar[3]. It was not angry or ferocious, but looked at Scrooge as Marley used to look: with ghostly spectacles turned up on its ghostly forehead. The hair was curiously stirred, as if by

---

This is telling, as it suggests that Scrooge's vision of Marley is similar to looking into his own personality – into a mirror or a crystal ball as it were, and yet, instead of himself he sees the ghostly face of a denizen of hell

[1] Essentially: the city council, the local politicians, and the guild-belonging tradesmen. The corporation includes the mayor and councilmen, the aldermen each represent a ward, and they are elected by the businessmen who are called the livery because of their legal right to wear the city livery, or colors

[2] E.T.A. Hoffmann – the original master of the weird and horrific, before Poe or Lovecraft or Machen – inspired this episode with his 1814 story "The Golden Pot." In the story, an enchanted student who is being haunted by a crone whom he offended by knocking over her street wares watches with horror as a knocker transforms into a face: "He was looking at the large, fine bronze knocker; but now when, as the last stroke tingled through the air with a loud clang from the steeple-clock … he lifted his hand to grasp this same knocker, the metal visage twisted itself, with horrid rolling of its blue-gleaming eyes into a grinning smile." A very specific knocker also helped inspire the author, too. Belonging to 8 Craven Street, the knocker which features the eyeless, hairless, eerie face resembles a death mask. The feature was removed in the 1890s because it had become an obnoxious sight-seeing attraction to the owners. The knocker in question can be seen online if you Google "8 Craven Street Door Knocker"

[3] Indeed, rotting seafood (seafood in particular, but rodents, meat, and even corpses as well) have been known to emit a blue-green phosphorescence. The color of phosphorescent bacteria – in case you have never encountered it – is a bright, neon blue that peppers the stinking meat in question in pockets, streaks, and veins. This is no cute, clichéd ghostly glow: by comparing it to a rotten lobster in a creepy cellar, Dickens is directly suggesting a corpse in the beginning stages of decay, when its rotting flesh is swarming with radiating putrescence – a real occurrence that happens to many bodies after burial called postmortem luminescence. In the age of embalming we never see this in human corpses, but bodies have been discovered by their dull glow, and neglected battlefields have been known to sparkle with blue light if the bodies were left unburied for more than a few weeks, as postmortem luminescence flickers over the blackening faces

breath or hot air[1]; and, though the eyes were wide open, they were perfectly motionless. That, and its livid colour[2], made it horrible; but its horror seemed to be in spite of the face and beyond its control, rather than a part of its own expression.

As Scrooge looked fixedly at this phenomenon, it was a knocker again.

To say that he was not startled, or that his blood was not conscious of a terrible sensation to which it had been a stranger from infancy, would be untrue. But he put his hand upon the key he had relinquished, turned it sturdily, walked in, and lighted his candle.

He did pause, with a moment's irresolution, before he shut the door; and he did look cautiously behind it first, as if he half expected to be terrified with the sight of Marley's pigtail[3] sticking out into the hall. But there was nothing on the back of the door, except the screws and nuts that held the knocker on, so he said "Pooh, pooh!" and closed it with a bang.

The sound resounded through the house like thunder. Every room above, and every cask in the wine-merchant's cellars below, appeared to have a separate peal of echoes of its own. Scrooge was not a man to be frightened by echoes. He fastened the door, and walked across the hall, and up the stairs; slowly too: trimming his candle as he went.

You may talk vaguely about driving a coach-and-six up a good old flight of stairs, or through a bad young Act of Parliament[4]; but I mean to say you might have got a hearse up that staircase, and taken it broadwise, with the splinter-bar towards the wall and the door towards the balustrades[5]: and done it easy. There was plenty of width for that, and room to spare; which is perhaps the reason why

---

[1] As if in the hot air of hell

[2] Dark blue-black or blue-grey. Make no mistake about it – Marley's face is mottled with decomposition, and the dark color of his skin suggests the grueling stage of putrefaction – no pretty sight

[3] If we imagine this to be set in roughly 1840-1843, and suppose Scrooge to be roughly 60-70, and suppose again that Marley was relatively the same age give or take five years, then Marley would have been born around 1760 – 1770, and would have been a young man when pigtails were going out of vogue. The fact that he retained one thirty years after they went out of fashion (supposing he died circa 1833 – 1836), it testifies to his disregard for society, progress, fashion, and time. To him nothing has changed since his youth, and he is insensible to the tastes of others

[4] A wry political joke: a coach drawn by six horses – three pairs, two abreast – would be able to drive up a very wide staircase, or conceived to ride through a mangled piece of legislation filled with mistakes, poor planning, and unsound logic

[5] The splinter bar is a crossbar attached to the front of the carriage, holding the leather straps that harness the horses

Scrooge thought he saw a locomotive hearse[1] going on before him in the gloom. Half-a-dozen gas-lamps out of the street wouldn't have lighted the entry too well, so you may suppose that it was pretty dark with Scrooge's dip[2].

Up Scrooge went, not caring a button for that. Darkness is cheap, and Scrooge liked it. But before he shut his heavy door, he walked through his rooms to see that all was right. He had just enough recollection of the face to desire to do that.

Sitting-room, bedroom, lumber-room[3]. All as they should be. Nobody under the table, nobody under the sofa; a small fire in the grate; spoon and basin ready; and the little saucepan of gruel[4] (Scrooge had a cold in his head[5]) upon the hob[6]. Nobody under the bed; nobody in the closet; nobody in his dressing-gown, which was hanging up in a suspicious attitude against the wall. Lumber-room as usual. Old fire-guard, old shoes, two fish-baskets, washing-stand on three legs, and a poker.

Quite satisfied, he closed his door, and locked himself in; double-locked himself in, which was not his custom. Thus secured against surprise, he took off

---

[1] A scene depicted in several films with excellent effect. The 1984 version is quite chilling, although the horse driven hearse appears outside, not up the stairs. The 1970 and 1971 versions also succeed in sending shivers up the spine with their phantom hearses

[2] A cheap candle – literally made by dipping a wick in melted tallow

[3] Although the name accurately suggests its use as a pantry used to store fuel, the room was also used to house unused furniture. It suggests that Scrooge probably has stowed away the in-house furniture, living a sparse life in a featureless apartment with minimal furnishings

[4] Oatmeal boiled in water with a soupy consistency. The blandness of the meal was thought to aid several ailments such as head colds and indigestion

[5] The cold (read: social want) has affected Scrooge's head (read: sense of logic and understanding). This handy metaphor seems to suggest that Scrooge's ability to see truth has been clouded by his voluntary ignorance and that he is suffering a psychosomatic cold as a result of his cognitive dissonance. Others have ominously viewed this as the first symptom of the illness that would – had he been unchanged – have killed him on December 24 the following year

[6] A brick shelf in front of the fire that allows containers to be warmed without boiling the contents

his cravat[1]; put on his dressing-gown[2] and slippers, and his nightcap; and sat down before the fire to take his gruel.

It was a very low fire indeed; nothing on such a bitter night. He was obliged to sit close to it, and brood over it, before he could extract the least sensation of warmth from such a handful of fuel. The fireplace was an old one, built by some Dutch merchant long ago[3], and paved all round with quaint Dutch tiles[4], designed to illustrate the Scriptures. There were Cains and Abels, Pharaoh's daughters; Queens of Sheba, Angelic messengers descending through the air on clouds like feather-beds, Abrahams, Belshazzars, Apostles putting off to sea in butter-boats[5],

---

[1] A neckcloth wrapped around the throat and tied in front – the predecessor of the bowtie and necktie. This, by the way, and his shoes are all that Scrooge removes. He is not in a nightshirt in the rest of the tale despite what most films (and the original illustrator) have depicted. Scrooge's attire (trousers, waistcoat, and shirt comfortably warmed by a linen dressing gown) is best depicted in the 1984 film

[2] A comfortable robe often made of silk, muslin, brocade, or linen. These were worn when a person was in a state of some undress, though not usually in the manner of a bathrobe to cover nakedness. Shirtsleeves were rude to display expect by laborers, so a gentleman wearing his shirt and trousers before he was ready to go out to his place of business might wear a dressing gown over his "small clothes" while walking around his room in the morning or in the evening – before dressing or after undressing. A smoking jacket was used similarly as a means of being presentable to company, family, or servants, while wearing a comfortable light robe less restrictive than a coat

[3] William III of Orange ascended to the British throne with his wife and heiress to the British monarchy, Mary II of England during the Glorious Revolution of 1688. William was a Dutch royal, and with his arrival in London, relations between the Netherlands and Great Britain immediately improved. Amsterdam merchants set up offices in British cities and Hollander fashion, art, and design became vogue. The Dutch were stereotyped as being cheap swindlers obsessed with money, brilliant at banking, and renowned for their frugality and wealth – a fitting background for Scrooge's dark, under furnished home

[4] Delftware. Delft pottery was tin-glazed porcelain famous for its white pottery with blue designs and illustrations. The Dutch had a long standing reputation for baking high quality pottery, and when the trade with China introduced them to Chinese pottery with its trademark white-and-blue characteristics, they rapidly reproduced the look, to European acclaim. Tiles were used to decorate many things, although the tile-lined fireplace is perhaps the most iconic. Tiles often featured geometric patterns or scenes from life, literature, or mythology. One very popular theme in Calvinist Holland was illustrating stories from the Old and New Testaments

[5] Cain – oldest son of Adam and Eve – killed his brother Abel in a jealous rage in the book of Genesis. Pharaoh's unnamed daughter rescued the infant Moses from the Nile, raising him as her own in Exodus. The Queen of Sheba visited King Solomon to view his empire in a brief episode recorded in 1 Kings. Angels are seen giving advice in a variety of passages in both Testaments. Abraham is the founder of the Hebrew race, second

hundreds of figures to attract his thoughts; and yet that face of Marley, seven years dead, came like the ancient Prophet's rod[1], and swallowed up the whole. If each smooth tile had been a blank at first, with power to shape some picture on its surface from the disjointed fragments of his thoughts, there would have been a copy of old Marley's head on every one.

"Humbug!" said Scrooge; and walked across the room.

After several turns, he sat down again. As he threw his head back in the chair, his glance happened to rest upon a bell[2], a disused bell, that hung in the room, and communicated for some purpose now forgotten with a chamber in the highest story of the building. It was with great astonishment, and with a strange, inexplicable dread, that as he looked, he saw this bell begin to swing. It swung so softly in the outset that it scarcely made a sound; but soon it rang out loudly, and so did every bell in the house[3].

This might have lasted half a minute, or a minute, but it seemed an hour. The bells ceased as they had begun, together. They were succeeded by a clanking noise, deep down below; as if some person were dragging a heavy chain over the casks in the wine-merchant's cellar. Scrooge then remembered to have heard that ghosts in haunted houses were described as dragging chains[4].

---

only to Moses in Jewish renown. Belshazzar was the ill-fated king of Babylon in the book of Daniel, who literally saw the proverbial "writing on the wall." The Twelve Apostles who followed Christ – of whom several were fishermen – are featured in boats on the Sea of Galilee in several stories. Nearly all of these incidents were favorite subjects of the Dutch master painters, Rembrandt in particular

[1] Moses was challenged by the Pharaoh's magicians, who changed their staffs into snakes. Moses' brother Aaron responded by throwing his staff on the ground, which transformed into a great serpent and swallowed the magician's snakes whole

[2] While it is unclear what Scrooge's room was originally, it certainly was used by servants, who were alerted to a need upstairs by its ringing

[3] Most rooms would have bells in them – the kitchen, cellar, scullery, servant's quarters, lumber room, store rooms, and others – each communicating to a different room. Looking under the bell, where either a name or a number would relate its origin, they could quickly respond. Depending on how many bells are in each room (there could be as many as ten or twelve in a large building), this sound could be maddening

[4] The tradition comes from Antiquity, being most famously associated with Pliny the Younger's famous description of a ghost in a letter to Sula: "*It happened that Athenodorus the philosopher came to Athens at this tìme, and reading the bill [for a house] ascertained the price. The extraordinary cheapness raised his suspicion; nevertheless, when he heard tbe whole story, he was so far from being discouraged, that he was more strongly inclined to hire it, and, in short, actually did so. When it grew towards evening, he ordered a couch to be prepared for him in the fore-part of the house, and after calling for a light, together with his pen and tablets, he directed all his people to retire within. But that his mind might not, for want of employment, be open to the vain terrors of imaginary noises and apparitions, he applied himself to writing with*

The cellar-door flew open with a booming sound, and then he heard the noise much louder, on the floors below; then coming up the stairs; then coming straight towards his door.

"It's humbug still!" said Scrooge. "I won't believe it."

His colour changed though, when, without a pause, it came on through the heavy door, and passed into the room before his eyes. Upon its coming in, the dying flame leaped up, as though it cried, "I know him; Marley's Ghost!" and fell again[1].

The same face: the very same. Marley in his pigtail, usual waistcoat, tights and boots; the tassels on the latter bristling, like his pigtail, and his coat-skirts, and the hair upon his head[2]. The chain he drew was clasped about his middle. It was long, and wound about him like a tail; and it was made (for Scrooge observed it closely) of cash-boxes, keys, padlocks, ledgers, deeds, and heavy purses wrought in steel. His body was transparent; so that Scrooge, observing him, and looking through his waistcoat, could see the two buttons on his coat behind.

---

all his faculties. The first part of the night passed with usual silence, then began the clanking of iron fetters; however, he neither lifted up his eyes, nor laid down his pen, but closed his ears by concentrating his attention. The noise increased and advanced nearer, till it seemed at the door, and at last in the chamber. He looked round and saw the apparition exactly as it had been described to him: it stood before him, beckoning with the finger. Athenodorus made a sign with his hand that it should wait a little, and bent again to his writing, but the ghost rattling its chains over his head as he wrote, he looked round and saw it beckoning as before. Upon this he immediately took up his lamp and followed it. The ghost slowly stalked along, as if encumbered with its chains; and having turned into the courtyard of the house, suddenly vanished. Athenodorus being thus deserted, marked the spot with a handful of grass and leaves. The next day he went to the magistrates, and advised them to order that spot to be dug up. There they found bones commingled and intertwined with chains; for the body had mouldered away by long lying in the ground, leaving them bare, and corroded by the fetters. The bones were collected, and buried at the public expense; and after the ghost was thus duly laid the house was haunted no more." It has been noted that chains do not feature in many English ghost stories and are seen as a primarily European fashion

[1] Depicted literally in John Leech's original illustration, wherein an anthropomorphic candle flame – blue in the fashion of folklore – is drawn with a shocked if whimsical face

[2] Marley is robed in the fashion of the early Regency: the early 1810s – the era of Jane Austen, the Battle of Waterloo, *Pride and Prejudice*, Keats, Shelley, and Lord Byron. His boots have tassels on the crest of the shin, indicating Hessian boots which were popular at the time, and his pigtail is from a still earlier generation since it went out of fashion before the French Revolution when men began cutting their hair short in an emulation of the Greeks and Romans

Scrooge had often heard it said that Marley had no bowels[1], but he had never believed it until now.

No, nor did he believe it even now. Though he looked the phantom through and through, and saw it standing before him; though he felt the chilling influence of its death-cold eyes; and marked the very texture of the folded kerchief bound about its head and chin[2], which wrapper he had not observed before; he was still incredulous, and fought against his senses.

"How now!" said Scrooge, caustic and cold as ever. "What do you want with me?"

"Much!"—Marley's voice, no doubt about it.

"Who are you?"

"Ask me who I was."

"Who were you then?" said Scrooge, raising his voice. "You're particular, for a shade[3]." He was going to say "to a shade," but substituted this, as more appropriate.

"In life I was your partner, Jacob Marley."

"Can you—can you sit down?" asked Scrooge, looking doubtfully at him.

"I can."

"Do it, then."

Scrooge asked the question, because he didn't know whether a ghost so transparent might find himself in a condition to take a chair; and felt that in the event of its being impossible, it might involve the necessity of an embarrassing explanation. But the ghost sat down on the opposite side of the fireplace, as if he were quite used to it[4].

"You don't believe in me," observed the Ghost.

"I don't," said Scrooge.

"What evidence would you have of my reality beyond that of your senses[5]?"

"I don't know," said Scrooge.

---

[1] An antiquated expression today analogous to "he had no heart." As odd as it is to our culture, where bowels might be associated with courage if anything, guts were formerly seen to be the zone of feeling and emotion

[2] A cloth winder was bound tightly under the chin of a corpse and over the head to keep the jaw clenched. This was done as a point of dignity to keep the lips from opening as gasses force their way out of the orifices, the tongue from swelling out of their mouth, and their mouth from twisting into a chilling rictus smile. Note that he speaks while his jaw is tied shut, and thus must be speaking (and screaming later) without moving his lips

[3] A pun wrought with classic, Dickensian dark humor: shade was a common term for a ghost

[4] Marley's later testimony suggests that this is because he does just that – sitting next to Scrooge in phantom form on a regular basis

[5] This is destined to become a chilling commentary on Scrooge's social ignorance: he sees the misery of the poor, yet denies his senses

"Why do you doubt your senses?"

"Because," said Scrooge, "a little thing affects them. A slight disorder of the stomach makes them cheats. You may be an undigested bit of beef, a blot of mustard, a crumb of cheese, a fragment of an underdone potato[1]. There's more of gravy than of grave about you, whatever you are!"

Scrooge was not much in the habit of cracking jokes, nor did he feel, in his heart, by any means waggish then. The truth is, that he tried to be smart, as a means of distracting his own attention, and keeping down his terror; for the spectre's voice disturbed the very marrow in his bones.

To sit, staring at those fixed glazed eyes[2], in silence for a moment, would play, Scrooge felt, the very deuce with him. There was something very awful, too, in the spectre's being provided with an infernal atmosphere of its own. Scrooge could not feel it himself, but this was clearly the case; for though the Ghost sat perfectly motionless, its hair, and skirts, and tassels, were still agitated as by the hot vapour from an oven[3].

"You see this toothpick?" said Scrooge, returning quickly to the charge, for the reason just assigned; and wishing, though it were only for a second, to divert the vision's stony gaze from himself.

"I do," replied the Ghost.

"You are not looking at it," said Scrooge.

"But I see it[4]," said the Ghost, "notwithstanding."

"Well!" returned Scrooge, "I have but to swallow this, and be for the rest of my days persecuted by a legion of goblins, all of my own creation. Humbug, I tell you! humbug!"

---

[1] Scrooge is referring to the largely discredited concept of the "cheese dream," which posits that different foods eaten before bed will cause the diner to have dreams particular to their meals, cheese and lobster most infamously being associated with weird visions and surreal nightmares. Scrooge's comments in Stave Two suggest that he believes that he is currently asleep and dreaming

[2] Fixed in a corpse stare, a disturbing condition of death that was one of the first things addressed after a death: the pulling down of the eyelids, sometimes overlaid with pennies. This measure is traditionally seen as a gesture done to preserve the corpse's dignity – the stare leaving a shocked, bug-eyed expression – was actually just as much done to ease the living who could be deeply distraught by seeing their loved ones stricken with such a pained, ghoulish expression. Marley's eyes may also have clouded over if he is indeed in the state of putrefaction which causes postmortem luminescence, and their soulless, white irises would be deeply repulsive to look on

[3] As if he is still in hell. In fact, it could be said that Marley does in fact remain physically in hell, that his appearance is a mere projection from that steamy region

[4] Like his disembodied voice, the Ghost's eyes see without looking. His physical appearance is just a shade or projection with no bearing or restrictions on his senses: his eyes are mere symbols of eyes rather than effective organs of vision

At this the spirit raised a frightful cry, and shook its chain with such a dismal and appalling noise, that Scrooge held on tight to his chair, to save himself from falling in a swoon. But how much greater was his horror, when the phantom taking off the bandage round its head, as if it were too warm to wear indoors, its lower jaw dropped down upon its breast[1]!

Scrooge fell upon his knees, and clasped his hands before his face.

"Mercy!" he said. "Dreadful apparition, why do you trouble me?"

"Man of the worldly mind!" replied the Ghost, "do you believe in me or not?"

"I do," said Scrooge. "I must. But why do spirits walk the earth[2], and why do they come to me?"

"It is required of every man," the Ghost returned, "that the spirit within him should walk abroad among his fellowmen, and travel far and wide; and if that spirit goes not forth in life, it is condemned to do so after death. It is doomed to wander through the world—oh, woe is me!—and witness what it cannot share, but might have shared on earth, and turned to happiness!"

Again the spectre raised a cry, and shook its chain and wrung its shadowy hands.

"You are fettered[3]," said Scrooge, trembling. "Tell me why?"

"I wear the chain I forged in life," replied the Ghost. "I made it link by link, and yard by yard; I girded it on of my own free will, and of my own free will I wore it. Is its pattern strange to you?"

Scrooge trembled more and more.

"Or would you know," pursued the Ghost, "the weight and length of the strong coil you bear yourself? It was full as heavy and as long as this, seven Christmas Eves ago. You have laboured on it, since. It is a ponderous chain!"

---

[1] Certainly suggestive of putrefaction. Marley's dislocated jaw does not merely fall open, but on his breast, as if the tendons and flesh that hold it to the skull have rotted away or grown soft and mushy. If you try it yourself as I did, I could only get my chin within two inches of my collarbone. Marley's flesh must be in a very sad, very elastic state, which few screen adaptations or illustrations are willing to depict

[2] Scrooge wonders why it is that the dead do not stay in their coffins, as he assumed. This is fitting, since he views life as individualistic and segregated, and a man who sees life divided into non-communicating compartments would naturally be disturbed to learn that the dead are not relegated to the land of death. Indeed, Marley roaming the streets of London is analogous to Scrooge learning that the poor – far from being a separate species with no relationship to him – are his brothers and sisters on earth

[3] Pliny's ghost was a slave who had died in his fetters. Marley has died in his fetters as well, although they are invisible and self-imposed. Dickens uses them to symbolize the restrictions that a closed-off life leads to. Rather than having a free, robust spirit in life, Marley was restrained, cloistered, and asocial – much like a prisoner who has been shut out from society. Marley's physical restraints – borne after death – are the manifestation of psychological restraints fostered in life

Scrooge glanced about him on the floor, in the expectation of finding himself surrounded by some fifty or sixty fathoms[1] of iron cable: but he could see nothing.

"Jacob," he said, imploringly. "Old Jacob Marley, tell me more. Speak comfort to me, Jacob!"

"I have none to give," the Ghost replied. "It comes from other regions, Ebenezer Scrooge, and is conveyed by other ministers, to other kinds of men[2]. Nor can I tell you what I would[3]. A very little more is all permitted to me. I cannot rest, I cannot stay, I cannot linger anywhere. My spirit never walked beyond our counting-house—mark me!—in life my spirit never roved beyond the narrow limits of our money-changing hole; and weary journeys lie before me[4]!"

It was a habit with Scrooge, whenever he became thoughtful, to put his hands in his breeches pockets. Pondering on what the Ghost had said, he did so now, but without lifting up his eyes, or getting off his knees.

"You must have been very slow about it, Jacob," Scrooge observed, in a business-like manner, though with humility and deference.

"Slow!" the Ghost repeated.

"Seven years dead," mused Scrooge. "And travelling all the time!"

"The whole time," said the Ghost. "No rest, no peace. Incessant torture of remorse."

"You travel fast?" said Scrooge.

"On the wings of the wind," replied the Ghost.

"You might have got over a great quantity of ground in seven years," said Scrooge.

The Ghost, on hearing this, set up another cry, and clanked its chain so hideously in the dead silence of the night, that the Ward[5] would have been justified in indicting it for a nuisance.

---

[1] 300 and 360 feet in length respectively

[2] Suggestive that there are other ghosts whose jobs are to encourage living men. Marley, however, is a walking warning, a pilloried example to frighten wicked men into goodness, the supernatural version of a "scare them straight" motivational speaker (a la a felon who is brought in to address problem students on the horrors of prison life), and Scrooge is about to go to Christmas Spirit Boot Camp

[3] A fascinating implication: what information is Marley privy to that he is holding back?

[4] This calls to mind the myth of the Wandering Jew: a man who spat on Christ as he was marched to the cross and was condemned to immortality, wandering ceaselessly, unable to find a home until Judgment Day. This also brings to mind the Ancient Mariner who Coleridge describes as travelling without rest, telling his story to all that he feels compelled to accost as a form of penance

[5] The night watchman, one of whom was assigned to each district, or ward

"Oh! captive, bound, and double-ironed[1]," cried the phantom, "not to know, that ages of incessant labour by immortal creatures, for this earth must pass into eternity before the good of which it is susceptible is all developed. Not to know that any Christian spirit working kindly in its little sphere, whatever it may be, will find its mortal life too short for its vast means of usefulness. Not to know that no space of regret can make amends for one life's opportunity misused! Yet such was I! Oh! such was I!"

"But you were always a good man of business, Jacob," faltered Scrooge, who now began to apply this to himself.

"Business!" cried the Ghost, wringing its hands again. "Mankind was my business. The common welfare was my business; charity, mercy, forbearance, and benevolence, were, all, my business. The dealings of my trade were but a drop of water in the comprehensive ocean of my business!"[2]

It held up its chain at arm's length, as if that were the cause of all its unavailing grief, and flung it heavily upon the ground again[3].

"At this time of the rolling year," the spectre said, "I suffer most. Why did I walk through crowds of fellow-beings with my eyes turned down, and never raise them to that blessed Star which led the Wise Men to a poor abode[4]! Were there no poor homes to which its light[5] would have conducted me!"

---

[1] To be double-ironed is to be shackled both hand and foot. While Marley is apparently only burdened by a chain which is girded about his waist, the phrase is used to describe his complete, thorough, and redundant captivity

[2] This lovely speech was never more beautifully rendered with more tragic pathos and heartbreaking feeling than by Frank Finlay in the tale's 1984 version. The Ghost's delivery is tempered by anger, intensity, and sorrow in a way that is almost always glossed over by actors. Finlay's performance of this passage as much as anything has cemented his reputation as the definitive Jacob Marley. Finlay, incidentally, also performed what some consider to be one of the best renditions of Dr Van Helsing in the 1977 version of *Dracula*, an adaptation which itself is seen by many critics as the essential version of the Stoker's novel

[3] Indeed, the chain – presumably – being manufactured, link by link, through a long series of acts of human dereliction, each twist of iron representing a moment of vice, and each item, each purse, lock, and box, being forged from great acts of wickedness. Marley holds out his chain as a prisoner might woefully look at a copy of the crimes and charges which had placed them in custody

[4] Marley is reminded that Christ's parents were quite poor, being homeless on the night of his birth, and transient renters by the time the Magi arrived in Bethlehem

[5] The Star of Bethlehem has often been used as a metaphor for the guiding light of salvation: a reference point which draws the sinful and dejected in the direction of peace and forgiveness, something of a manifestation of the Holy Spirit. Marley implies that though the light of godly guidance was ever around him, he never lost sight of his own selfish interests long enough to notice it, and as a result has been damned

Scrooge was very much dismayed to hear the spectre going on at this rate, and began to quake exceedingly.

"Hear me!" cried the Ghost. "My time is nearly gone."

"I will," said Scrooge. "But don't be hard upon me! Don't be flowery[1], Jacob! Pray!"

"How it is that I appear before you in a shape that you can see, I may not tell. I have sat invisible beside you many and many a day[2]."

It was not an agreeable idea. Scrooge shivered, and wiped the perspiration from his brow.

"That is no light part of my penance[3]," pursued the Ghost. "I am here to-night to warn you, that you have yet a chance and hope of escaping my fate. A chance and hope of my procuring[4], Ebenezer."

"You were always a good friend to me," said Scrooge. "Thank'ee!"

"You will be haunted," resumed the Ghost, "by Three Spirits."

Scrooge's countenance fell almost as low as the Ghost's had done.

"Is that the chance and hope you mentioned, Jacob?" he demanded, in a faltering voice.

"It is."

"I—I think I'd rather not," said Scrooge.

"Without their visits," said the Ghost, "you cannot hope to shun the path I tread. Expect the first to-morrow, when the bell tolls One."

"Couldn't I take 'em all at once, and have it over, Jacob?" hinted Scrooge.

"Expect the second on the next night at the same hour. The third upon the next night when the last stroke of Twelve has ceased to vibrate. Look to see me no more; and look that, for your own sake, you remember what has passed between us!"

When it had said these words, the spectre took its wrapper from the table, and bound it round its head, as before. Scrooge knew this, by the smart sound its teeth

---

[1] "Stop your whining and get on with it" is essentially what Scrooge means. "Don't be hard upon me" doesn't mean "don't be cross or stern," but rather "don't bother me with your troubles" or, put in our parlance "You're getting pretty heavy on me; stop harshing my mellow"

[2] Explaining his seeming familiarity with Scrooge's armchair

[3] Marley, like Dante's Virgil, to whom he has been compared, seems to be a denizen of Purgatory, and his appeal to Scrooge seems to be a part of his sentence – not unlike cleaning up a dirty highway after being arrested for littering

[4] This is a very humane and touching moment which many adaptations and critical readings seem to skim over: Marley has appealed to his supernatural masters on Scrooge's behalf, requesting a few minutes of time – and the aid of three other spirits – in order that Scrooge may have a chance at salvation. Whether this compassion for his partner is the result of their earthly friendship or a development of his rehabilitated personality is unclear

made[1], when the jaws were brought together by the bandage. He ventured to raise his eyes again, and found his supernatural visitor confronting him in an erect attitude, with its chain wound over and about its arm.

The apparition walked backward from him; and at every step it took, the window raised itself a little, so that when the spectre reached it, it was wide open.

It beckoned Scrooge to approach, which he did. When they were within two paces of each other, Marley's Ghost held up its hand, warning him to come no nearer. Scrooge stopped.

Not so much in obedience, as in surprise and fear: for on the raising of the hand, he became sensible of confused noises in the air; incoherent sounds of lamentation and regret; wailings inexpressibly sorrowful and self-accusatory. The spectre, after listening for a moment, joined in the mournful dirge[2]; and floated out upon the bleak, dark night.

Scrooge followed to the window: desperate in his curiosity. He looked out.

The air was filled with phantoms, wandering hither and thither in restless haste, and moaning as they went. Every one of them wore chains like Marley's Ghost; some few (they might be guilty governments) were linked together; none were free. Many had been personally known to Scrooge in their lives. He had been quite familiar with one old ghost, in a white waistcoat, with a monstrous iron safe attached to its ankle, who cried piteously at being unable to assist a wretched woman with an infant, whom it saw below, upon a door-step. The misery with them all was, clearly, that they sought to interfere, for good, in human matters, and had lost the power for ever.

Whether these creatures faded into mist, or mist enshrouded them, he could not tell. But they and their spirit voices faded together; and the night became as it had been when he walked home.

Scrooge closed the window, and examined the door by which the Ghost had entered. It was double-locked, as he had locked it with his own hands, and the bolts were undisturbed. He tried to say "Humbug!" but stopped at the first syllable. And being, from the emotion he had undergone, or the fatigues of the day, or his glimpse of the Invisible World, or the dull[3] conversation of the Ghost, or the lateness of the hour, much in need of repose; went straight to bed, without

---

[1] A revolting detail. The hollow clamp of teeth being smote together, along with the pop of the dislocated jaw would surely be enough to turn one's stomach. It should be noted that – like his eyes which see but do not look – the organ of voice is disembodied, that while his jaw is shut, Marley is able to speak. In fact, he talks much before the wrapper is removed, and after it is taken off, there is no suggestion that the jaw returns to its place to move normally. Therefore, what we have is a picture of Marley speaking, wailing, and screaming without moving his lips or mouth. A truly ghastly thing to picture
[2] Again, he wails expressively with his jaw clenched shut
[3] Meaning serious, grim, severe, or heavy, not boring as we exclusively use the word today

undressing, and fell asleep upon the instant.

SCROOGE'S whole universe is haunted. The streets of London are invaded and obscured by the genius of Ignorance – the thick-boiling brown smog – and pinched bitterly by the genius of Want – the icy brine of frost that nips everything within sight. Dickens warns us well in advance that the supernatural and natural worlds are due to clash, both with his memorable opening line and with his personified elements ruling the city streets like a monopoly: the ignorant smog which hides light, creates anonymity, and prevents perspective, and the avaricious frost which squelches life, proliferates misery, and is felt universally regardless of class. Marley's appearance is the culmination of a haunting that has been occurring since the book's first pages: London is haunted by Scrooge and Scrooges. We know of course that three spirits do follow – the Ghost of the Past who re-familiarizes Scrooge with his origins and innocence, the Ghost of the Present who acquaints Scrooge with the joys and tenderness of the common man, and the Ghost of the Future who haunts Scrooge with a promise of a miserable death and an infamous legacy – but we often forget that there are two more spirits. At the conclusion of his visitation, the Ghost of Christmas Present pulls back his robe to reveal two animallike children – Scrooge's – the taloned geniuses of Ignorance, upon whose forehead is written "doom," and Want. Scrooge in that moment understands that he has been the cause of far more haunting than he has experienced in the past three hours, and he understands to a degree, the shame and misery suffered by the damned Marley, whose heart is broken by his inability to intercede in the events of mankind, and who is ironically more of a man after becoming a ghost, having been more of a ghost than a man when alive (truly a crossbreeding of "Goblins" and "Lawyer and the Ghost"). A Christmas Carol, like most of its predecessors, was made to generate understanding and conversation around the dreadful conditions of the industrial and urban poor, and to plead for humanitarianism and universal goodwill. In the many decades since A Christmas Carol's release, it has suffered horribly from over-familiarization and infantilization. While there are several movie versions which do justice to Dickens' desperate cause, I recommend to your attention the 1984 version starring George C. Scott as a robust, self-important capitalist (unlike the feminized, doddering, night-cap-bedecked fussbudgets popularized by most productions) and Frank Finlay as the single most effective Marley ever to appear on screen (Edward Woodward offers up the single most effective Ghost of Present: a leering, disgusted observer rather than the jolly simpleton). Simply attired in leaden makeup and glazed contact lenses, this creature of hell is a figure of pathos and wretched sympathy rather than a fun opportunity to implement CGI gore and trick photography. The film is startling, uncomfortable, and convicting, and none – with the single exception of Alastair Sim's iconic Scrooge – come nearly as close to rendering Dickens' urgent vision.

OFTEN underrated and under-anthologized, the following story – or more accurately, two stories couched within a frame narrative (we will comment on both, individually) – is perhaps one of Dickens' most complex and thematically dark tales. Often misunderstood and typically criticized for its plot, "To be Read at Dusk" is an intricate study in dualism, repression, fate, and psychological influences on personal identity. Dickens uses the frame narrative – which is disarming in spite of its truly unsettling nature – to commence a conversation on the nature of reality, the source of identity, and the pull of the unconscious – those shadowy things which we avoid or try to deny – on the conscious – the (ostensible) basis of human identity. In the three stories which he twines and threads, Dickens will attempt to cause you to question the power of nurture over nature, of will over fate, and of self over psychology. And then he will turn the tables again.

To Be Read at Dusk
{1852}

ONE, two, three, four, five.[1]. There were five of them[2].

Five couriers[3], sitting on a bench outside the convent on the summit of the Great St. Bernard[4] in Switzerland, looking at the remote heights, stained by the setting sun as if a mighty quantity of red wine had been broached upon the mountain top, and had not yet had time to sink into the snow[5].

---

[1] Fading in like a shadowy procession flitting through the fog, the central group of this tale already retain the qualities of ghosts – shiftless, airy, and immaterial

[2] "Them" – the subject of this narrative may elucidate the objectivity of these five "thems"

[3] Diplomatic messengers. Switzerland, being the geographical hub of Europe, is an understandable place for the representatives of European nations to mingle in between trips. Meeting at the crossroads of Europe, the couriers themselves are go-betweens, strongly suggesting a borderland or a neutral convergence of otherwise opposite entities – in this case, the dead and the living, the natural and the supernatural

[4] The Great St. Bernard Pass (home to the famous Great St. Bernard Pass Hostel), is the third highest road pass in Switzerland, located on the southeastern border, near France and Italy

[5] Kimberly Jackson argues that we are absolutely meant to jump from the simile "red like wine" to "wine like blood" – Dickens' narrator disowns the simile in the next line, allowing the reader to question its appropriateness and to fill in the gap left by "wine" – the mountain, a deadly symbol of mortality and fate, is soaked in the blood of its victims, and Dickens plays with the reader, allowing them to arrive at the conclusion that it is sinister without being heavy handed

This is not my simile[1]. It was made for the occasion by the stoutest courier, who was a German. None of the others took any more notice of it than they took of me[2], sitting on another bench on the other side of the convent door, smoking my cigar, like them[3], and — also like them — looking at the reddened snow, and at the lonely shed hard by, where the bodies of belated travellers, dug out of it, slowly wither away, knowing no corruption in that cold region[4].

The wine upon the mountain top soaked in as we looked[5]; the mountain became white; the sky, a very dark blue; the wind rose; and the air turned piercing cold. The five couriers buttoned their rough coats. There being no safer man to imitate in all such proceedings than a courier[6], I buttoned mine.

The mountain in the sunset had stopped the five couriers in a conversation. It is a sublime[7] sight, likely to stop conversation. The mountain being now out of the sunset, they resumed[8]. Not that I had heard any part of their previous discourse; for

---

[1] Figure of speak used to draw comparisons, employing "like" or "as." Similes play a critical role in Dickens' literary structure – several critics have suggested that this is a ghost story about "likeness" – about similarity, relationship, inversion, and categorical sameness

[2] Initially the narrator is unnoticed – almost ghostlike. That will change

[3] Similes and comparisons are already cropping up – why might Dickens be encouraging juxtaposition between the narrator and the "thems"? This story probes how those things which we insist on (and hope to) disassociating ourselves from – evil, death, corruption... ghosts – are not nearly so neatly compartmentalized. Who are the ghosts and who the men?

[4] Firstly, if Dickens was too deft in using his wine simile, then the "reddened snow" mentioned in this context will undoubtedly conjure something ravenous and sinister. Secondly, Dickens gruesomely explains that beneath that sheet of crimson down are the frozen bodies of unfortunate travelers who have been overtaken by storms. Their bodies, once dug out, are stacked in a shed like cord wood, where they remain preserved by the extreme cold – the dead encroach on the world of the living in this borderland, failing to decay properly ("knowing no corruption" – one would not immediately be able to identify them as "dead"), and in their grisly proximity to the living, stored in a shed "hard by," within eyesight

[5] Dickens suggests that like the mountain, whose snows hide the dead, and whose scarlet tones imply their nature, the story hides dark secrets about the nature of its characters and literary themes. Like the mountain, which sinks into inoffensive blue, the story, too, will momentarily disarm us, allowing us to ignore what it encloses for the time being

[6] A courier, someone prone to long, exposed travel conditions, would certainly know how to stay warm, and be worth emulating on a chilly Swiss peak

[7] A vision of natural power inspiring awe, fear, dread, admiration, and beauty, such as a violent storm, a vast ocean, an endless desert, or an enormous woodland

[8] Once the uncomfortable nature of the mountain has been disassociated from its visible features – once the blood-red light has faded – the couriers are no longer prevented

indeed, I had not then broken away from the American gentleman, in the travellers' parlour of the convent, who, sitting with his face to the fire[1], had undertaken to realise to me the whole progress of events which had led to the accumulation by the Honourable Ananias Dodger[2] of one of the largest acquisitions of dollars ever made in our country.

'My God!' said the Swiss courier, speaking in French, which I do not hold (as some authors appear to do) to be such an all-sufficient excuse for a naughty word, that I have only to write it in that language to make it innocent[3]; 'if you talk of ghosts — '

'But I DON'T talk of ghosts,' said the German.

'Of what then?' asked the Swiss.

'If I knew of what then,' said the German, 'I should probably know a great deal more[4].'

It was a good answer, I thought, and it made me curious. So, I moved my position to that corner of my bench which was nearest to them, and leaning my back against the convent wall, heard perfectly, without appearing to attend.

'Thunder and lightning[5]!' said the German, warming, 'when a certain man is coming to see you, unexpectedly; and, without his own knowledge, sends some invisible messenger, to put the idea of him into your head all day, what do you call that? When you walk along a crowded street — at Frankfort, Milan, London, Paris — and think that a passing stranger is like your friend Heinrich, and then that another passing stranger is like your friend Heinrich, and so begin to have a strange foreknowledge that presently you'll meet your friend Heinrich — which you do, though you believed

---

from continuing their discourse on the relationships of ghosts to men – a topic the reality of which is made abundantly clear by the mountain's gory spectre, rendering such a conversation unnecessary until the vision fades once more, allowing speculation to once more reign

[1] Important: this materialistic capitalist has removed himself as far as possible from the looming phantom of human mortality and moral ambiguity, as represented by the mountain. Instead, he thrusts his face into the fire – symbolic of human industry and contrivance

[2] A likely reference to *Oliver Twist's* Artful Dodger – lampooning the morals and virtue of American opportunists – hypocritical shysters who manipulate and scheme in order to accumulate power and wealth

[3] Once more, Dickens conjures the spirit of hypocrisy – "If it's a curse in English, writing it in French does nothing to dilute its genuine import"

[4] They speak not of categorical "ghosts" but of the murky middle country between the living and the dead

[5] *"Donder und Blitzen!"* A traditional German oath (it extends to all German speaking nations, Scandinavians, and the Dutch) used in English literature, most famously employed to name two of the reindeer in "A Visit from St. Nicholas" (so used because of Sinter Klaas' Germano-Dutch etymology)

him at Trieste[1] — what do you call THAT?'

'It's not uncommon, either,' murmured the Swiss and the other three.

'Uncommon!' said the German. 'It's as common as cherries in the Black Forest. It's as common as maccaroni at Naples. And Naples reminds me! When the old Marchesa Senzanima shrieks at a card- party on the Chiaja[2] — as I heard and saw her, for it happened in a Bavarian family of mine, and I was overlooking the service that evening — I say, when the old Marchesa starts up at the card-table, white through her rouge, and cries, "My sister in Spain is dead! I felt her cold touch on my back!" — and when that sister IS dead at the moment — what do you call that?'

'Or when the blood of San Gennaro liquefies[3] at the request of the clergy — as all the world knows that it does regularly once a-year, in my native city,' said the Neapolitan courier after a pause, with a comical look, 'what do you call that?'

'THAT!' cried the German. 'Well, I think I know a name for that[4].'

'Miracle?' said the Neapolitan, with the same sly face.

The German merely smoked and laughed; and they all smoked and laughed.

'Bah!' said the German, presently. 'I speak of things that really do happen. When I want to see the conjurer, I pay to see a professed one, and have my money's worth. Very strange things do happen without ghosts[5]. Ghosts! Giovanni Baptista, tell your story of the English bride. There's no ghost in that, but something full as strange[6]. Will any man tell me what?'

As there was a silence among them, I glanced around. He whom I took to be Baptista was lighting a fresh cigar. He presently went on to speak. He was a Genoese, as I judged.

'The story of the English bride?' said he. 'Basta[7]! one ought not to call so slight a

---

[1] A seaport in N.E. Italy – a crossroads (and melting pot) of Slavic, Latin, and German culture

[2] Chiaia : a neighborhood in Naples

[3] Januarius (272 C.E. – 305 C.E.) was an Italian saint. The so-called "Blood Miracle" occurs when a vile of his dried blood reportedly returns to liquid form. This manner of miracle is not uncommon amongst Catholic relics – weeping statues, bleeding paintings, etc. – although hoaxes and natural phenomena explain nearly all of them

[4] Likely a Lutheran, the German – like most Anglican Englishmen – would be almost condescendingly anti-Catholic, viewing relics and related miracles as dangerous superstitions

[5] The ways of ghosts and the ways of men are not, Dickens continues to suggest, mutually exclusive – the line between the natural and supernatural is thin and shaded, for humanity is haunted by its own complex psychological and spiritual nature

[6] Rumblings of weird fiction. E. T. A. Hoffmann, Edgar Allan Poe, Goethe, the Brothers Grimm, and several other folklorists, literati, and dramatists had spread tales of the bizarre and uncanny which occur outside of strict literary archetypes such as "ghost" or "vampire," but Dickens extends beyond Victorian conventions by searching out the truly uncanny, nonetheless, and should be applauded for it

[7] Italian: *Stop*! *Enough*!

thing a story. Well, it's all one. But it's true. Observe me well, gentlemen, it's true. That which glitters is not always gold; but what I am going to tell, is true.'

He repeated this more than once.

THIS tale is a classic example of the Demon Lover genre – the story of a fated supernatural abduction; it was employed earlier by J. W. von Goethe in "The Erlking" and by Fitz-James O'Brien in "The Demon of the Gibbet." Le Fanu would use the theme in "Schalken the Painter" and "Ultor de Lacy," and this very story would later serve to inspire the classic supernatural works of Rhoda Broughton ("The Man with the Nose") and E. F. Benson ("The Face"). This story is one of split identity – light and darkness, transparency and shadow, Super-Ego and Id – the impossibility of maintaining their separation, and the potentially violent coup that one can have when repressed by the other.

Ten years ago, I took my credentials to an English gentleman at Long's Hotel, in Bond Street, London, who was about to travel — it might be for one year, it might be for two. He approved of them; likewise of me. He was pleased to make inquiry. The testimony that he received was favourable. He engaged me by the six months, and my entertainment was generous.

He was young, handsome, very happy. He was enamoured of a fair young English lady, with a sufficient fortune, and they were going to be married. It was the wedding-trip[1], in short, that we were going to take. For three months' rest in the hot weather (it was early summer then) he had hired an old place on the Riviera, at an easy distance from my city, Genoa, on the road to Nice.   Did I know that place? Yes; I told him I knew it well. It was an old palace with great gardens. It was a little bare, and it was a little dark and gloomy, being close surrounded by trees; but it was spacious, ancient, grand, and on the seashore. He said it had been so described to him exactly, and he was well pleased that I knew it. For its being a little bare of furniture, all such places were. For its being a little gloomy, he had hired it principally for the gardens, and he and my mistress would pass the summer weather in their shade.

'So all goes well, Baptista?' said he.

'Indubitably[2], signore; very well.'

We had a travelling chariot for our journey, newly built for us, and in all respects complete. All we had was complete; we wanted for nothing. The marriage took place. They were happy. I was happy, seeing all so bright, being so well situated, going to my own city, teaching my language in the rumble to the maid, la bella[3] Carolina, whose heart was gay with laughter: who was young and rosy.

---

[1] A honeymoon
[2] Doubtlessly, without a doubt
[3] The adorable, the lovely

The time flew. But I observed — listen to this, I pray[1]! (and here the courier dropped his voice) — I observed my mistress[2] sometimes brooding in a manner very strange; in a frightened manner; in an unhappy manner; with a cloudy, uncertain alarm upon her. I think that I began to notice this when I was walking up hills by the carriage side, and master had gone on in front. At any rate, I remember that it impressed itself upon my mind one evening in the South of France, when she called to me to call master back; and when he came back, and walked for a long way, talking encouragingly and affectionately to her, with his hand upon the open window, and hers in it. Now and then, he laughed in a merry way, as if he were bantering[3] her out of something. By-and-by, she laughed, and then all went well again.

It was curious. I asked la bella Carolina, the pretty little one, *Was mistress unwell?* — No. — *Out of spirits?* — No. — *Fearful of bad roads, or brigands[4]?* — No. And what made it more mysterious was, the pretty little one would not look at me in giving answer, but WOULD look at the view.

But, one day she told me the secret.

'If you must know,' said Carolina, 'I find, from what I have overheard, that mistress is haunted.'

'How haunted?'

'By a dream.'

'What dream?'

'By a dream of a face. For three nights before her marriage, she saw a face in a dream — always the same face, and only One.'

'A terrible face?'

'No. The face of a dark, remarkable-looking man, in black, with black hair and a grey moustache — a handsome man except for a reserved and secret air. Not a face she ever saw, or at all like a face she ever saw. Doing nothing in the dream but looking at her fixedly, out of darkness[5].'

'Does the dream come back?'

'Never. The recollection of it is all her trouble.'

'And why does it trouble her?'

Carolina shook her head.

'That's master's question,' said la bella. 'She don't know. She wonders why, herself. But I heard her tell him, only last night, that if she was to find a picture of that face in our Italian house (which she is afraid she will) she did not know how she could ever bear it.'

---

[1] I beg you

[2] Female employer – not a lover

[3] Using quick, chatty language

[4] Italy was famous for its bandits, highwaymen, and bands of robbers that waylaid rural travel routes, especially those used by foreign tourists and diplomats

[5] The figure is tailored in and surrounded by funereal black – both sinister in its morbid cultural symbolism, and emblematic of Nothingness – cosmic emptiness and spiritual desolation

Upon my word I was fearful after this (said the Genoese courier) of our coming to the old palazzo[1], lest some such ill-starred[2] picture should happen to be there. I knew there were many there; and, as we got nearer and nearer to the place, I wished the whole gallery in the crater of Vesuvius[3]. To mend the matter, it was a stormy dismal evening when we, at last, approached that part of the Riviera. It thundered; and the thunder of my city and its environs, rolling among the high hills, is very loud. The lizards ran in and out of the chinks in the broken stone wall of the garden, as if they were frightened; the frogs bubbled and croaked their loudest; the sea-wind moaned, and the wet trees dripped; and the lightning — body of San Lorenzo, how it lightened!

We all know what an old palace in or near Genoa is — how time and the sea air have blotted it — how the drapery painted on the outer walls has peeled off in great flakes of plaster — how the lower windows are darkened with rusty bars of iron — how the courtyard is overgrown with grass — how the outer buildings are dilapidated — how the whole pile seems devoted to ruin. Our palazzo was one of the true kind. It had been shut up close for months. Months? — years! — it had an earthy smell, like a tomb. The scent of the orange trees on the broad back terrace, and of the lemons ripening on the wall, and of some shrubs that grew around a broken fountain, had got into the house somehow, and had never been able to get out again. There was, in every room, an aged smell, grown faint with confinement[4]. It pined in all the cupboards and drawers. In the little rooms of communication between great rooms, it was stifling. If you turned a picture — to come back to the pictures — there it still was, clinging to the wall behind the frame, like a sort of bat[5].

The lattice-blinds were close shut, all over the house. There were two ugly, grey old women in the house, to take care of it; one of them with a spindle, who stood winding and mumbling in the doorway, and who would as soon have let in the devil as the air[6]. Master, mistress, la bella Carolina, and I, went all through the palazzo. I went first, though I have named myself last, opening the windows and the lattice-blinds, and

[1] Palace, mansion

[2] Cursed, ill-fated

[3] A giant Italian volcano

[4] Confinement – the word evokes repression, sublimation, and the pent up impulses of the unconscious mind. This episode certainly mulls the anxieties of unconscious urges and thoughts

[5] Although *Dracula* is yet to appear in culture, the bat still possessed a leering, lurking cultural currency which saw it as a symbol of devilish perversion – the diabolical, nocturnal foil to the spiritual and melodious bird. Like a bat, repressed terrors hang silently in this house during the daylight of consciousness, only to descend and strike in the blind nocturne of dreams

[6] Symbolic of spiritual purification, truth, speech (confession, testimony), and communication

shaking down on myself splashes of rain, and scraps of mortar[1], and now and then a dozing mosquito, or a monstrous, fat, blotchy, Genoese spider[2].

When I had let the evening light into a room, master, mistress, and la bella Carolina, entered. Then, we looked round at all the pictures, and I went forward again into another room. Mistress secretly had great fear of meeting with the likeness of that face — we all had; but there was no such thing. The Madonna and Bambino, San Francisco, San Sebastiano, Venus, Santa Caterina, Angels, Brigands, Friars, Temples at Sunset, Battles, White Horses, Forests, Apostles, Doges, all my old acquaintances many times repeated[3]? — yes. Dark, handsome man in black, reserved and secret, with black hair and grey moustache, looking fixedly at mistress out of darkness? — no[4].

At last we got through all the rooms and all the pictures, and came out into the gardens. They were pretty well kept, being rented by a gardener, and were large and shady. In one place there was a rustic theatre, open to the sky; the stage a green slope; the coulisses[5], three entrances upon a side, sweet-smelling leafy screens. Mistress moved her bright eyes, even there, as if she looked to see the face come in upon the scene; but all was well.

'Now, Clara[6],' master said, in a low voice, 'you see that it is nothing? You are happy.'

Mistress was much encouraged. She soon accustomed herself to that grim palazzo, and would sing, and play the harp, and copy the old pictures, and stroll with master under the green trees and vines all day. She was beautiful. He was happy. He would laugh and say to me, mounting his horse for his morning ride before the heat:

'All goes well, Baptista!'

'Yes, signore, thank God, very well.'

We kept no company. I took la bella to the Duomo and Annunciata, to the Cafe, to the Opera, to the village Festa, to the Public Garden, to the Day Theatre, to the Marionetti[7]. The pretty little one was charmed with all she saw. She learnt Italian — heavens! miraculously! Was mistress quite forgetful of that dream? I asked Carolina

---

[1] The mineral cement used to hold building materials together – symbolically, the restraints and regulators of the unconscious mind are crumbling away

[2] Symbolic of dark, venomous, unsightly elements of the unconscious

[3] These are archetypes which represent the romantic, holy, familiar, noble, historic, patriotic, chivalric, manly, maternal, and sacred things that inhabit the middling areas of the Freudian model of consciousness – the Super-Ego: the symbols, ideas, and feelings which inspire good behavior and idealism. The Super-Ego has been widely represented, yes, but the Id – the dark impulses and selfish lusts that we deny or restrict – has failed to appear

[4] As previously mentioned: the Id – the dark impulses and selfish lusts that we deny or restrict – has failed to appear

[5] Backstage area, or a screen between the stage wings

[6] Importantly, we learn that her name is Clara – from the Latin for *clear, bright, radiant*

[7] Petty amusements: a cathedral; coffee shops; operas; a festival day; a beer garden; stageplays; marionette puppet shows, etc.

sometimes. Nearly, said la bella — almost. It was wearing out.

One day master received a letter, and called me.

'Baptista!'

'Signore!'

'A gentleman who is presented to me will dine here to-day. He is called the Signor Dellombra[1]. Let me dine like a prince.'

It was an odd name. I did not know that name. But, there had been many noblemen and gentlemen pursued by Austria on political suspicions, lately, and some names had changed. Perhaps this was one. Altro[2]! Dellombra was as good a name to me as another.

When the Signor Dellombra came to dinner (said the Genoese courier in the low voice, into which he had subsided once before), I showed him into the reception-room, the great sala[3] of the old palazzo. Master received him with cordiality, and presented him to mistress. As she rose, her face changed, she gave a cry, and fell upon the marble floor.

Then, I turned my head to the Signor Dellombra, and saw that he was dressed in black, and had a reserved and secret air, and was a dark, remarkable-looking man, with black hair and a grey moustache.

Master raised mistress in his arms, and carried her to her own room, where I sent la bella Carolina straight. La bella told me afterwards that mistress was nearly terrified to death, and that she wandered in her mind about her dream, all night.

Master was vexed and anxious — almost angry, and yet full of solicitude. The Signor Dellombra was a courtly[4] gentleman, and spoke with great respect and sympathy of mistress's being so ill. The African wind[5] had been blowing for some days (they had told him at his hotel of the Maltese Cross), and he knew that it was often hurtful. He hoped the beautiful lady would recover soon. He begged permission to retire, and to renew his visit when he should have the happiness of hearing that she was better.

---

[1] A very, *very* sinister omen – his name is Italian for "Of Shadow," "Of Darkness," literally, title included, "Lord Shadow" or "Lord of Shadows." His identity is fused with the concept of hidden things – things invisible but nonetheless extant. Shadows are the opposite of brightness ("Clara"), and Lord Shadow represents Clara's unapparent, repressed inversed, libidinal nature

[2] Italian: Other

[3] Italian: Room

[4] Refined and aristocratic, with the telltale breeding that identifies him as a high-born noble. Like Dracula, his aristocratic background allows a discussion of the hypocritical perils of privileging wealth, power, class, breeding, gender, and title. Alternatively, it serves to illustrate the elegant persuasion of impulse and passion, which are sometimes played down as crude and thuggish: to the contrary – it can be authoritative, commanding, and alluring

[5] The simoon – a dry, sandy, hurricanical that shuttles through North Africa, across to Southern Europe (especially Italy). Clouded with romance, it is suggestive of passion and lust

Master would not allow of this, and they dined alone.

He withdrew early. Next day he called at the gate, on horse-back, to inquire for mistress. He did so two or three times in that week.

What I observed myself, and what la bella Carolina told me, united to explain to me that master had now set his mind on curing mistress of her fanciful terror. He was all kindness, but he was sensible and firm. He reasoned with her, that to encourage such fancies was to invite melancholy, if not madness. That it rested with herself to be herself. That if she once resisted her strange weakness, so successfully as to receive the Signor Dellombra as an English lady would receive any other guest, it was for ever conquered. To make an end, the signore came again, and mistress received him without marked distress (though with constraint and apprehension still), and the evening passed serenely. Master was so delighted with this change, and so anxious to confirm it, that the Signor Dellombra became a constant guest. He was accomplished in pictures, books, and music; and his society, in any grim palazzo, would have been welcome.

I used to notice, many times, that mistress was not quite recovered. She would cast down her eyes and droop her head, before the Signor Dellombra, or would look at him with a terrified and fascinated glance, as if his presence had some evil influence or power upon her. Turning from her to him, I used to see him in the shaded gardens, or the large half-lighted sala, looking, as I might say, 'fixedly upon her out of darkness[1].' But, truly, I had not forgotten la bella Carolina's words describing the face in the dream.

After his second visit I heard master say:

'Now, see, my dear Clara, it's over! Dellombra has come and gone, and your apprehension is broken like glass.'

'Will he — will he ever come again?' asked mistress.

'Again? Why, surely, over and over again! Are you cold?' (she shivered).

'No, dear — but — he terrifies me: are you sure that he need come again?'

'The surer for the question, Clara!' replied master, cheerfully.

But, he was very hopeful of her complete recovery now, and grew more and more so every day. She was beautiful. He was happy.

'All goes well, Baptista?' he would say to me again.

'Yes, signore, thank God; very well.'

We were all (said the Genoese courier, constraining himself to speak a little louder), we were all at Rome for the Carnival. I had been out, all day, with a Sicilian, a friend of mine, and a courier, who was there with an English family. As I returned at night to our hotel, I met the little Carolina, who never stirred from home alone, running distractedly along the Corso[2].

'Carolina! What's the matter?'

'O Baptista! O, for the Lord's sake! where is my mistress?'

'Mistress, Carolina?'

---

[1] The very image of the lady's vision

[2] Italian: Course

'Gone since morning — told me, when master went out on his day's journey, not to call her, for she was tired with not resting in the night (having been in pain), and would lie in bed until the evening; then get up refreshed. She is gone! — she is gone! Master has come back, broken down the door, and she is gone! My beautiful, my good, my innocent[1] mistress!'

The pretty little one so cried, and raved, and tore herself that I could not have held her, but for her swooning on my arm as if she had been shot. Master came up — in manner, face, or voice, no more the master that I knew, than I was he. He took me (I laid the little one upon her bed in the hotel, and left her with the chamber-women), in a carriage, furiously through the darkness[2], across the desolate Campagna[3]. When it was day, and we stopped at a miserable post-house[4], all the horses had been hired twelve hours ago, and sent away in different directions. Mark me! by the Signor Dellombra, who had passed there in a carriage, with a frightened English lady crouching in one corner[5].

I never heard (said the Genoese courier, drawing a long breath) that she was ever traced beyond that spot. All I know is, that she vanished into infamous oblivion[6], with the dreaded face beside her that she had seen in her dream.

TALES of twins are common throughout literature, and are well-represented in horror, especially by the Doppelgänger, an apparition that – whether physical or psychical – represents the split nature of humanity. Algernon Blackwood ("The Terror of the Twins"), Poe ("William Wilson," "...House of Usher"), and Robert Louis Stevenson ("...Dr Jekyll and Mr Hyde") are just a few of the writers who have employed this

---

[1] These positive qualities demonstrate moral homogeneity, good behavior, social respectability, and polite conformity – qualities at odd with the selfish, lustful urges of the Id. It is naturally important that this is her servant's first reaction, to defend her mistress's virtuous reputation, rather than to assume it will be understood. Lord Shadow's influence in the household has clearly alerted at least *her* to her mistress's complex psychological makeup

[2] He begins to acknowledge his wife's turbulent unconscious by acquainting himself with and entering the darkness that he has so long disregarded. It is too late

[3] Italian: countryside, wilderness – implications of vastness

[4] Way station for rest, refreshment, and changing horses

[5] Out of fear or shame? Sometimes I read it one way, others another. Is she an abductee or an accomplice? Certainly Dickens leaves it vague with great intentionality . In either case, Shadow has now become united with Brightness, and the two natures – once forced apart – are now hurdled towards one another in a violent and desperate reunification

[6] Infamous implies a level of lost reputation. Oblivion – like the darkness that houses Lord Shadow – not only hides, but devours. Whatever motives or truths may have been involved in this mystery are now consigned to the same dark void that masks our minds from each other

motif. The story that follows, while not nearly as elegant as the previous, is perhaps more structurally complicated; it concerns the nature of identity – is it material or is it spiritual? – and the messy, unclear borderlands between Self and Other, between Haunter and Haunted.

'What do you call THAT[1]?' said the German courier, triumphantly. 'Ghosts! There are no ghosts THERE! What do you call this, that I am going to tell you? Ghosts! There are no ghosts HERE!'

I took an engagement once (pursued the German courier) with an English gentleman[2], elderly and a bachelor, to travel through my country, my Fatherland. He was a merchant who traded with my country and knew the language, but who had never been there since he was a boy — as I judge, some sixty years before.

His name was James, and he had a twin-brother[3] John[4], also a bachelor. Between these brothers there was a great affection. They were in business together, at Goodman's Fields, but they did not live together. Mr. James dwelt in Poland Street, turning out of Oxford Street, London; Mr. John resided by Epping Forest[5].

Mr. James and I were to start for Germany in about a week. The exact day depended on business. Mr. John came to Poland Street (where I was staying in the house), to pass that week with Mr. James. But, he said to his brother on the second day, 'I don't feel very well, James. There's not much the matter with me; but I think I am a little gouty[6]. I'll go home and put myself under the care of my old housekeeper, who understands my ways. If I get quite better, I'll come back and see you before you go. If I don't feel well enough to resume my visit where I leave it off, why YOU will come and see me before you go[7].' Mr. James, of course, said he would, and they shook hands

---

[1] German and Italian tales of the fantastic are often seen as competing schools, even within English literature, Gothic tales featuring Italian settings were rivaled by those featuring German backdrops. German Gothic is often typified as grotesque – violent, monstrous, brooding, with hate as its common element – and the Italian Gothic as arabesque – romantic, magical, mysterious, with lust as its common element

[2] Once more, an Englishman is the subject of the tale. Dickens is almost certainly using this international gab fest as an opportunity to critique English culture and hypocrisy

[3] Likeness once more appears in the plot – the two brothers are identical, meaning that while different persons, they nonetheless hold common elements of the same identity

[4] Infamously, James and John, apostles to Jesus, battled over which would have the honor to sit at his right side in the Kingdom of Heaven. Christ chastised their greed and rivalry

[5] Some 27 miles between the two areas

[6] Gout is an inflammation of the feet caused by a welling of uric acid in the lower extremities

[7] A fateful exclamation. While this story lacks the elegance of its predecessor, it deals with a dualism that is perhaps more complicated; John tells James that if he recovers his brother shall see him again, and that if he does not, he shall see his brother. Both men

— both hands, as they always did — and Mr. John ordered out his old-fashioned chariot and rumbled home.

It was on the second night after that — that is to say, the fourth in the week — when I was awoke out of my sound sleep by Mr. James coming into my bedroom in his flannel-gown, with a lighted candle. He sat upon the side of my bed, and looking at me, said:

'Wilhelm, I have reason to think I have got some strange illness upon me.'

I then perceived that there was a very unusual expression in his face.

'Wilhelm,' said he, 'I am not afraid or ashamed to tell you what I might be afraid or ashamed to tell another man. You come from a sensible country[1], where mysterious things are inquired into and are not settled to have been weighed and measured — or to have been unweighable and unmeasurable — or in either case to have been completely disposed of, for all time — ever so many years ago. I have just now seen the phantom of my brother[2].'

I confess (said the German courier) that it gave me a little tingling of the blood to hear it.

'I have just now seen,' Mr. James repeated, looking full at me, that I might see how collected he was, 'the phantom of my brother John. I was sitting up in bed, unable to sleep, when it came into my room, in a white dress, and regarding me earnestly, passed up to the end of the room, glanced at some papers on my writing-desk, turned, and, still looking earnestly at me as it passed the bed, went out at the door. Now, I am not in the least mad, and am not in the least disposed to invest that phantom with any external existence out of myself. I think it is a warning to me that I am ill[3]; and I

---

share a facial identity, and to see one is to see the self; they are both distinct individualities and shared partners of a common nature. Dickens once more alludes to the indivisibility of huamnity's complex soup of psychologies, spiritualities, identities, and wills

[1] Germany was infamous for its involvement in the Gothic movement. Stories like those of Goethe, Hoffmann, the Grimms, and Gotthelf were gruesome and weird enough to match Poe, Stoker, and Le Fanu. Being one of the few Protestant regions that did not have a thoroughly successful Enlightenment, avoided humanist influences, and eschewed the republicanization that swept France, Britain, Holland, the United States, and Italy, Germany continued to have a general population that was educated by folklore and superstition rather than Plutarch and Locke, and tales of ghosts, wizards, witchcraft, monsters, vampires, and visions abounded fruitfully in German peasants' cottages and in German intellectuals' libraries alike

[2] Or perhaps the phantom of his own self? They are identical, why so sure as to who he saw?

[3] In a sense, he is: John is the one who is ill, but considering their joint identity, when one suffers so does the other. Like Clara and Dellombra who represented the disparate elements of the unconscious – the socially proper and the shunned libido – James and John represent the divided human identity: the physical and the psychical, the tangible

think I had better be bled[1].'

I got out of bed directly (said the German courier) and began to get on my clothes, begging him not to be alarmed, and telling him that I would go myself to the doctor. I was just ready, when we heard a loud knocking and ringing at the street door. My room being an attic at the back, and Mr. James's being the second-floor room in the front, we went down to his room, and put up the window, to see what was the matter.

'Is that Mr. James?' said a man below, falling back to the opposite side of the way to look up.

'It is,' said Mr. James, 'and you are my brother's man, Robert.'

'Yes, Sir. I am sorry to say, Sir, that Mr. John is ill. He is very bad, Sir. It is even feared that he may be lying at the point of death. He wants to see you, Sir. I have a chaise here. Pray come to him. Pray lose no time.'

Mr. James and I looked at one another. 'Wilhelm,' said he, 'this is strange. I wish you to come with me!' I helped him to dress, partly there and partly in the chaise; and no grass grew under the horses' iron shoes between Poland Street and the Forest[2].

Now, mind! (said the German courier) I went with Mr. James into his brother's room, and I saw and heard myself what follows.

His brother lay upon his bed, at the upper end of a long bed-chamber. His old housekeeper was there, and others were there: I think three others were there, if not four, and they had been with him since early in the afternoon. He was in white, like the figure — necessarily so, because he had his night-dress on. He looked like the figure — necessarily so, because he looked earnestly at his brother when he saw him come into the room.

But, when his brother reached the bed-side, he slowly raised himself in bed, and looking full upon him, said these words:

'JAMES, YOU HAVE SEEN ME BEFORE, TO-NIGHT— AND YOU KNOW IT![3]'
And so died!

---

and the spiritual. James and John's spiritual identities are unique (or so they think) – one can visit the other supernaturally – but their physical identities are common

[1] The infamous practice of opening a vein and allowing it to momentarily empty was a gambit on the part of pre-Darwinian physicians to balance out the bodily fluids – too much blood was considered the cause of most fevers, diseases, and hysterias

[2] That is to say, they flew like the wind – to use a simile

[3] James incorrectly mistook the omen to represent a turn in his own health, but death had invaded his brother's physical nature instead. They share a physical identity, but when the body failed to bring about a reunion, the psychical individuation extended itself to his brother. The accusation that John appears to make is that his brother misinterpreted the meaning of his spectral appearance, taking it to foretell disaster to his own body, while the doom was intended for his brothers'. The mistake is due to their shared physicality – an identity thought to split evenly between the material and the spiritual is in fact divided coarsely by a jagged, smeared border that occasions James' failure to respond to his brother's psychic message

I waited, when the German courier ceased, to hear something said of this strange story. The silence was unbroken. I looked round, and the five couriers were gone: so noiselessly that the ghostly mountain[1] might have absorbed them[2] into its eternal snows[3]. By this time, I was by no means in a mood to sit alone in that awful[4] scene, with the chill air coming solemnly upon me — or, if I may tell the truth, to sit alone anywhere. So I went back into the convent- parlour, and, finding the American gentleman still disposed to relate the biography of the Honourable Ananias Dodger, heard it all out.

---

[1] Symbolic of mortality and man's ineffectuality in the face of a bizarre, untamable cosmos, the mountain re-dominates the landscape in the conclusion just as it did in the introduction. You will recall that the couriers were speechless while the sunset poured over its face like spilled wine (sun like wine, wine like blood) because the mountain's encrimsoned face was testimony to the warped chaos of the natural/supernatural worlds, and that once it faded into the blue twilight, their conversation – a debate on the nature of the relationship between the natural and supernatural – was revived, capable of being had while the mountain didn't so obviously attest to the grotesque reality. Now that the conversation has abruptly ceased, the mountain is left looming ominously in the dusk – a closing *"Finis"* that underscores their grim conclusion

[2] Not unlike the bodies of the frozen travelers buried on the mountainside – bodies which, incidentally, might include those of five unfortunate couriers

[3] Just as the narrator began the story as a spectral eavesdropping, unnoticed by his storytellers, he is left alone without a word. The departure is abrupt, jarring, and alienating. Once the object, the narrator becomes the subject – once in control of the narrative, he is now almost helpless to continue it, deciding to return to the greedy American's tales. The couriers may simply have left abruptly, they may have been ghosts themselves, or they may have been visions sent to communicate a message. But one way or another, they are absorbed into the monolithic mountain representing the vast mystery and horror of the unprobed natural world. The universe is indifferent, immense, and prone to deception. Just so is the human mind, Dickens suggests, juxtaposing the vast vista with the labyrinthine psychology of his characters

[4] Both "full of awe" because of the mountain's grand and terrifying sublimity, and "repugnant" because of the corpses that have, throughout time, been absorbed by those eternal snows

FATE and identity, Dickens suggests, are under the sway of the unconscious, and regardless of our breeding, our higher aspirations, or our conscious desires, reality cannot be altered to fit the needs of the conscience or society. A woman of noble virtue cannot banish the dark impulses of a schizophrenic moral identity; a man whose physical self is shared nebulously with his twin brother cannot rationally expect his psychical self to be neatly split between them; a mountain which is, in reality, bathed in the blood of its victims, cannot be compared to spilled wine without suggesting its true nature; and a party of story tellers bent on arriving at a satisfactory understanding of what is things – ghosts and yet not ghosts – which inhabit the spaces between the natural and the supernatural may not be able to avoid calling attention to their own ambiguous supernaturality. As in "The Signalman" and "The Trial by Murder," Dickens uses the ghost story as a vehicle for illuminating the shadowy territories between unconscious knowledge and conscious denial.

THIS tale is among the best of Dickens' straightforward ghost stories, standing ably alongside the psychological horrors of "A Madman's Manuscript" and "The Mother's Eyes," in something of a triumvirate of chilling murder tales. "The Hanged Man's Bride" begins on a humorous note – a ghost appears to two lazy rogues who fail to pick up on his obviously supernatural condition – but it rapidly deepens into a tale of emotional abuse, brutal homicide, and surging Poe-esque guilt. In fact, while Dickens has a undeniable claim on influencing Poe's major murder stories, it appears that by this point, after Poe's death, the worm had turned: "The Hanged Man's Bride" bears several striking similarities to "Metzengerstein," "The Tell-Tale Heart," and most especially "The Black Cat." Also influenced by Gothic masterpieces "The Rime of the Ancient Mariner" and "Schalken the Painter," this disturbing tale went on to inspire many of the ghost stories of J. Sheridan Le Fanu, Wilkie Collins, Algernon Blackwood, E. F. Benson, and M. R. James among others.

The Hanged Man's Bride
Or, The Ghost in the Bridal Chamber
EXCERPTED *from* THE LAZY TOUR OF TWO IDLE APPRENTICES, CHP. *Four*
{1857}

NIGHT had come again, and they had been writing for two or three hours: writing, in short, a portion of the lazy notes from which these lazy sheets are taken. They had left off writing, and glasses were on the table between them. The house was closed and quiet. Around the head of Thomas Idle, as he lay upon his sofa, hovered light wreaths of fragrant smoke. The temples of Francis Goodchild, as he leaned back in his chair, with his two hands clasped behind his head, and his legs crossed, were similarly decorated.

They had been discussing several idle subjects of speculation, not omitting the strange old men, and were still so occupied, when Mr. Goodchild abruptly changed his attitude to wind up his watch. They were just becoming drowsy enough to be stopped in their talk by any such slight check. Thomas Idle, who was speaking at the moment, paused and said, 'How goes it?'

'One,' said Goodchild.

As if he had ordered One old man, and the order were promptly executed (truly, all orders were so, in that excellent hotel), the door opened, and One old man stood there.

He did not come in, but stood with the door in his hand.

'One of the six, Tom, at last!' said Mr. Goodchild, in a surprised whisper.—'Sir, your pleasure?'

'Sir, your pleasure?' said the One old man.

'I didn't ring.'

'The bell did,' said the One old man.

He said BELL, in a deep, strong way, that would have expressed the church Bell.

'I had the pleasure, I believe, of seeing you, yesterday?' said Goodchild.

'I cannot undertake to say for certain,' was the grim reply of the One old man.

'I think you saw me? Did you not?'

'Saw you?' said the old man. 'O yes, I saw you. But, I see many who never see me.'

A chilled, slow, earthy, fixed old man. A cadaverous old man of measured speech. An old man who seemed as unable to wink, as if his eyelids had been nailed to his forehead. An old man whose eyes—two spots of fire—had no more motion than if they had been connected with the back of his skull by screws driven through it, and rivetted and bolted outside, among his grey hair.

The night had turned so cold, to Mr. Goodchild's sensations, that he shivered. He remarked lightly, and half apologetically, 'I think somebody is walking over my grave.'

'No,' said the weird old man, 'there is no one there.'

Mr. Goodchild looked at Idle, but Idle lay with his head enwreathed in smoke.

'No one there?' said Goodchild.

'There is no one at your grave, I assure you,' said the old man.

He had come in and shut the door, and he now sat down. He did not bend himself to sit, as other people do, but seemed to sink bolt upright, as if in water, until the chair stopped him.

'My friend, Mr. Idle,' said Goodchild, extremely anxious to introduce a third person into the conversation.

'I am,' said the old man, without looking at him, 'at Mr. Idle's service.'

'If you are an old inhabitant of this place,' Francis Goodchild resumed.

'Yes.'

'Perhaps you can decide a point my friend and I were in doubt upon, this morning. They hang condemned criminals at the Castle, I believe?'

'I believe so,' said the old man.

'Are their faces turned towards that noble prospect?'

'Your face is turned,' replied the old man, 'to the Castle wall. When you are tied up, you see its stones expanding and contracting violently, and a similar expansion and contraction seem to take place in your own head and breast. Then, there is a rush of fire and an earthquake, and the Castle springs into the air, and you tumble down a precipice.'

His cravat appeared to trouble him. He put his hand to his throat, and moved his neck from side to side. He was an old man of a swollen character of face, and his nose was immoveably hitched up on one side, as if by a little hook inserted in that nostril. Mr. Goodchild felt exceedingly uncomfortable, and began to think the night was hot, and not cold.

'A strong description, sir,' he observed.

'A strong sensation,' the old man rejoined.

Again, Mr. Goodchild looked to Mr. Thomas Idle; but Thomas lay on his back with his face attentively turned towards the One old man, and made no sign. At this time Mr. Goodchild believed that he saw threads of fire stretch from the old man's eyes to his own, and there attach themselves. (Mr. Goodchild writes the present account of his experience, and, with the utmost solemnity, protests that he

had the strongest sensation upon him of being forced to look at the old man along those two fiery films, from that moment.)

'I must tell it to you,' said the old man, with a ghastly and a stony stare.

'What?' asked Francis Goodchild.

'You know where it took place. Yonder!'

Whether he pointed to the room above, or to the room below, or to any room in that old house, or to a room in some other old house in that old town, Mr. Goodchild was not, nor is, nor ever can be, sure. He was confused by the circumstance that the right forefinger of the One old man seemed to dip itself in one of the threads of fire, light itself, and make a fiery start in the air, as it pointed somewhere. Having pointed somewhere, it went out.

'You know she was a Bride,' said the old man.

'I know they still send up Bride-cake,' Mr. Goodchild faltered. 'This is a very oppressive air.'

'She was a Bride,' said the old man. 'She was a fair, flaxen-haired, large-eyed girl, who had no character, no purpose. A weak, credulous, incapable, helpless nothing. Not like her mother. No, no. It was her father whose character she reflected.

'Her mother had taken care to secure everything to herself, for her own life, when the father of this girl (a child at that time) died—of sheer helplessness; no other disorder—and then He renewed the acquaintance that had once subsisted between the mother and Him. He had been put aside for the flaxen-haired, large-eyed man (or nonentity) with Money. He could overlook that for Money. He wanted compensation in Money.

'So, he returned to the side of that woman the mother, made love to her again, danced attendance on her, and submitted himself to her whims. She wreaked upon him every whim she had, or could invent. He bore it. And the more he bore, the more he wanted compensation in Money, and the more he was resolved to have it.

'But, lo! Before he got it, she cheated him. In one of her imperious states, she froze, and never thawed again. She put her hands to her head one night, uttered a cry, stiffened, lay in that attitude certain hours, and died. And he had got no compensation from her in Money, yet. Blight and Murrain on her! Not a penny.

'He had hated her throughout that second pursuit, and had longed for retaliation on her. He now counterfeited her signature to an instrument, leaving all she had to leave, to her daughter—ten years old then—to whom the property passed absolutely, and appointing himself the daughter's Guardian. When He slid it under the pillow of the bed on which she lay, He bent down in the deaf ear of Death, and whispered: "Mistress Pride, I have determined a long time that, dead or alive, you must make me compensation in Money.'

'So, now there were only two left. Which two were, He, and the fair flaxen-haired, large-eyed foolish daughter, who afterwards became the Bride.

'He put her to school. In a secret, dark, oppressive, ancient house, he put her to school with a watchful and unscrupulous woman. "My worthy lady," he said, "here is a mind to be formed; will you help me to form it?" She accepted the trust. For which she, too, wanted compensation in Money, and had it.

'The girl was formed in the fear of him, and in the conviction, that there was no escape from him. She was taught, from the first, to regard him as her future husband—the man who must marry her—the destiny that overshadowed her—the appointed certainty that could never be evaded. The poor fool was soft white wax in their hands, and took the impression that they put upon her. It hardened with time. It became a part of herself. Inseparable from herself, and only to be torn away from her, by tearing life away from her.

'Eleven years she had lived in the dark house and its gloomy garden. He was jealous of the very light and air getting to her, and they kept her close. He stopped the wide chimneys, shaded the little windows, left the strong-stemmed ivy to wander where it would over the house-front, the moss to accumulate on the untrimmed fruit-trees in the red-walled garden, the weeds to over-run its green and yellow walks. He surrounded her with images of sorrow and desolation. He caused her to be filled with fears of the place and of the stories that were told of it, and then on pretext of correcting them, to be left in it in solitude, or made to shrink about it in the dark. When her mind was most depressed and fullest of terrors, then, he would come out of one of the hiding-places from which he overlooked her, and present himself as her sole resource.

'Thus, by being from her childhood the one embodiment her life presented to her of power to coerce and power to relieve, power to bind and power to loose, the ascendency over her weakness was secured. She was twenty-one years and twenty-one days old, when he brought her home to the gloomy house, his half-witted, frightened, and submissive Bride of three weeks.

'He had dismissed the governess by that time—what he had left to do, he could best do alone—and they came back, upon a rain night, to the scene of her long preparation. She turned to him upon the threshold, as the rain was dripping from the porch, and said:

'"O sir, it is the Death-watch ticking for me!"

'"Well!" he answered. "And if it were?"

'"O sir!" she returned to him, "look kindly on me, and be merciful to me! I beg your pardon. I will do anything you wish, if you will only forgive me!"

'That had become the poor fool's constant song: "I beg your pardon," and "Forgive me!"

'She was not worth hating; he felt nothing but contempt for her. But, she had long been in the way, and he had long been weary, and the work was near its end, and had to be worked out.

'"You fool," he said. "Go up the stairs!"

'She obeyed very quickly, murmuring, "I will do anything you wish!" When he came into the Bride's Chamber, having been a little retarded by the heavy fastenings of the great door (for they were alone in the house, and he had arranged that the people who attended on them should come and go in the day), he found her withdrawn to the furthest corner, and there standing pressed against the paneling as if she would have shrunk through it: her flaxen hair all wild about her face, and her large eyes staring at him in vague terror.

"'What are you afraid of? Come and sit down by me."

"'I will do anything you wish. I beg your pardon, sir. Forgive me!" Her monotonous tune as usual.

"'Ellen, here is a writing that you must write out to-morrow, in your own hand. You may as well be seen by others, busily engaged upon it. When you have written it all fairly, and corrected all mistakes, call in any two people there may be about the house, and sign your name to it before them. Then, put it in your bosom to keep it safe, and when I sit here again to-morrow night, give it to me."

"'I will do it all, with the greatest care. I will do anything you wish."

"'Don't shake and tremble, then."

"'I will try my utmost not to do it—if you will only forgive me!"

'Next day, she sat down at her desk, and did as she had been told. He often passed in and out of the room, to observe her, and always saw her slowly and laboriously writing: repeating to herself the words she copied, in appearance quite mechanically, and without caring or endeavouring to comprehend them, so that she did her task. He saw her follow the directions she had received, in all particulars; and at night, when they were alone again in the same Bride's Chamber, and he drew his chair to the hearth, she timidly approached him from her distant seat, took the paper from her bosom, and gave it into his hand.

'It secured all her possessions to him, in the event of her death. He put her before him, face to face, that he might look at her steadily; and he asked her, in so many plain words, neither fewer nor more, did she know that?

'There were spots of ink upon the bosom of her white dress, and they made her face look whiter and her eyes look larger as she nodded her head. There were spots of ink upon the hand with which she stood before him, nervously plaiting and folding her white skirts.

'He took her by the arm, and looked her, yet more closely and steadily, in the face. "Now, die! I have done with you."

'She shrunk, and uttered a low, suppressed cry.

"'I am not going to kill you. I will not endanger my life for yours. Die!"

'He sat before her in the gloomy Bride's Chamber, day after day, night after night, looking the word at her when he did not utter it. As often as her large unmeaning eyes were raised from the hands in which she rocked her head, to the stern figure, sitting with crossed arms and knitted forehead, in the chair, they read in it, "Die!" When she dropped asleep in exhaustion, she was called back to shuddering consciousness, by the whisper, "Die!" When she fell upon her old entreaty to be pardoned, she was answered "Die!" When she had out-watched and out-suffered the long night, and the rising sun flamed into the sombre room, she heard it hailed with, "Another day and not dead?—Die!"

'Shut up in the deserted mansion, aloof from all mankind, and engaged alone in such a struggle without any respite, it came to this—that either he must die, or she. He knew it very well, and concentrated his strength against her feebleness. Hours upon hours he held her by the arm when her arm was black where he held it, and bade her Die!

'It was done, upon a windy morning, before sunrise. He computed the time to be half-past four; but, his forgotten watch had run down, and he could not be sure. She had broken away from him in the night, with loud and sudden cries— the first of that kind to which she had given vent—and he had had to put his hands over her mouth. Since then, she had been quiet in the corner of the paneling where she had sunk down; and he had left her, and had gone back with his folded arms and his knitted forehead to his chair.

'Paler in the pale light, more colourless than ever in the leaden dawn, he saw her coming, trailing herself along the floor towards him—a white wreck of hair, and dress, and wild eyes, pushing itself on by an irresolute and bending hand.

"'O, forgive me! I will do anything. O, sir, pray tell me I may live!"

"'Die!"

"'Are you so resolved? Is there no hope for me?"

"'Die!"

'Her large eyes strained themselves with wonder and fear; wonder and fear changed to reproach; reproach to blank nothing. It was done. He was not at first so sure it was done, but that the morning sun was hanging jewels in her hair—he saw the diamond, emerald, and ruby, glittering among it in little points, as he stood looking down at her—when he lifted her and laid her on her bed.

'She was soon laid in the ground. And now they were all gone, and he had compensated himself well.

'He had a mind to travel. Not that he meant to waste his Money, for he was a pinching man and liked his Money dearly (liked nothing else, indeed), but, that he had grown tired of the desolate house and wished to turn his back upon it and have done with it. But, the house was worth Money, and Money must not be thrown away. He determined to sell it before he went. That it might look the less wretched and bring a better price, he hired some labourers to work in the overgrown garden; to cut out the dead wood, trim the ivy that drooped in heavy masses over the windows and gables, and clear the walks in which the weeds were growing mid-leg high.

'He worked, himself, along with them. He worked later than they did, and, one evening at dusk, was left working alone, with his bill-hook in his hand. One autumn evening, when the Bride was five weeks dead.

"'It grows too dark to work longer," he said to himself, "I must give over for the night."

'He detested the house, and was loath to enter it. He looked at the dark porch waiting for him like a tomb, and felt that it was an accursed house. Near to the porch, and near to where he stood, was a tree whose branches waved before the old bay-window of the Bride's Chamber, where it had been done. The tree swung suddenly, and made him start. It swung again, although the night was still. Looking up into it, he saw a figure among the branches.

'It was the figure of a young man. The face looked down, as his looked up; the branches cracked and swayed; the figure rapidly descended, and slid upon its feet before him. A slender youth of about her age, with long light brown hair.

'"What thief are you?" he said, seizing the youth by the collar.

'The young man, in shaking himself free, swung him a blow with his arm across the face and throat. They closed, but the young man got from him and stepped back, crying, with great eagerness and horror, "Don't touch me! I would as like be touched by the Devil!"

'He stood still, with his bill-hook in his hand, looking at the young man. For, the young man's look was the counterpart of her last look, and he had not expected ever to see that again.

'"I am no thief. Even if I were, I would not have a coin of your wealth, if it would buy me the Indies. You murderer!"

'"What!"

'"I climbed it," said the young man, pointing up into the tree, "for the first time, nigh four years ago. I climbed it, to look at her. I saw her. I spoke to her. I have climbed it, many a time, to watch and listen for her. I was a boy, hidden among its leaves, when from that bay-window she gave me this!"

'He showed a tress of flaxen hair, tied with a mourning ribbon.

'"Her life," said the young man, "was a life of mourning. She gave me this, as a token of it, and a sign that she was dead to every one but you. If I had been older, if I had seen her sooner, I might have saved her from you. But, she was fast in the web when I first climbed the tree, and what could I do then to break it!"

'In saying those words, he burst into a fit of sobbing and crying: weakly at first, then passionately.

'"Murderer! I climbed the tree on the night when you brought her back. I heard her, from the tree, speak of the Death-watch at the door. I was three times in the tree while you were shut up with her, slowly killing her. I saw her, from the tree, lie dead upon her bed. I have watched you, from the tree, for proofs and traces of your guilt. The manner of it, is a mystery to me yet, but I will pursue you until you have rendered up your life to the hangman. You shall never, until then, be rid of me. I loved her! I can know no relenting towards you. Murderer, I loved her!"

'The youth was bare-headed, his hat having fluttered away in his descent from the tree. He moved towards the gate. He had to pass—Him—to get to it. There was breadth for two old-fashioned carriages abreast; and the youth's abhorrence, openly expressed in every feature of his face and limb of his body, and very hard to bear, had verge enough to keep itself at a distance in. He (by which I mean the other) had not stirred hand or foot, since he had stood still to look at the boy. He faced round, now, to follow him with his eyes. As the back of the bare light-brown head was turned to him, he saw a red curve stretch from his hand to it. He knew, before he threw the bill-hook, where it had alighted—I say, had alighted, and not, would alight; for, to his clear perception the thing was done before he did it. It cleft the head, and it remained there, and the boy lay on his face.

'He buried the body in the night, at the foot of the tree. As soon as it was light in the morning, he worked at turning up all the ground near the tree, and hacking and hewing at the neighbouring bushes and undergrowth. When the labourers came, there was nothing suspicious, and nothing suspected.

'But, he had, in a moment, defeated all his precautions, and destroyed the triumph of the scheme he had so long concerted, and so successfully worked out. He had got rid of the Bride, and had acquired her fortune without endangering his life; but now, for a death by which he had gained nothing, he had evermore to live with a rope around his neck.

'Beyond this, he was chained to the house of gloom and horror, which he could not endure. Being afraid to sell it or to quit it, lest discovery should be made, he was forced to live in it. He hired two old people, man and wife, for his servants; and dwelt in it, and dreaded it. His great difficulty, for a long time, was the garden. Whether he should keep it trim, whether he should suffer it to fall into its former state of neglect, what would be the least likely way of attracting attention to it?

'He took the middle course of gardening, himself, in his evening leisure, and of then calling the old serving-man to help him; but, of never letting him work there alone. And he made himself an arbour over against the tree, where he could sit and see that it was safe.

'As the seasons changed, and the tree changed, his mind perceived dangers that were always changing. In the leafy time, he perceived that the upper boughs were growing into the form of the young man—that they made the shape of him exactly, sitting in a forked branch swinging in the wind. In the time of the falling leaves, he perceived that they came down from the tree, forming tell-tale letters on the path, or that they had a tendency to heap themselves into a churchyard mound above the grave. In the winter, when the tree was bare, he perceived that the boughs swung at him the ghost of the blow the young man had given, and that they threatened him openly. In the spring, when the sap was mounting in the trunk, he asked himself, were the dried-up particles of blood mounting with it: to make out more obviously this year than last, the leaf-screened figure of the young man, swinging in the wind?

'However, he turned his Money over and over, and still over. He was in the dark trade, the gold-dust trade, and most secret trades that yielded great returns. In ten years, he had turned his Money over, so many times, that the traders and shippers who had dealings with him, absolutely did not lie—for once—when they declared that he had increased his fortune, Twelve Hundred Per Cent.

'He possessed his riches one hundred years ago, when people could be lost easily. He had heard who the youth was, from hearing of the search that was made after him; but, it died away, and the youth was forgotten.

'The annual round of changes in the tree had been repeated ten times since the night of the burial at its foot, when there was a great thunder-storm over this place. It broke at midnight, and roared until morning. The first intelligence he heard from his old serving-man that morning, was, that the tree had been struck by Lightning.

'It had been riven down the stem, in a very surprising manner, and the stem lay in two blighted shafts: one resting against the house, and one against a portion of the old red garden-wall in which its fall had made a gap. The fissure went down the tree to a little above the earth, and there stopped. There was great curiosity to see the tree, and, with most of his former fears revived, he sat in his arbour— grown quite an old man—watching the people who came to see it.

'They quickly began to come, in such dangerous numbers, that he closed his garden-gate and refused to admit any more. But, there were certain men of science who travelled from a distance to examine the tree, and, in an evil hour, he let them in!—Blight and Murrain on them, let them in!

'They wanted to dig up the ruin by the roots, and closely examine it, and the earth about it. Never, while he lived! They offered money for it. They! Men of science, whom he could have bought by the gross, with a scratch of his pen! He showed them the garden-gate again, and locked and barred it.

'But they were bent on doing what they wanted to do, and they bribed the old serving-man—a thankless wretch who regularly complained when he received his wages, of being underpaid—and they stole into the garden by night with their lanterns, picks, and shovels, and fell to at the tree. He was lying in a turret-room on the other side of the house (the Bride's Chamber had been unoccupied ever since), but he soon dreamed of picks and shovels, and got up.

'He came to an upper window on that side, whence he could see their lanterns, and them, and the loose earth in a heap which he had himself disturbed and put back, when it was last turned to the air. It was found! They had that minute lighted on it. They were all bending over it. One of them said, "The skull is fractured;" and another, "See here the bones;" and another, "See here the clothes;" and then the first struck in again, and said, "A rusty bill-hook!"

'He became sensible, next day, that he was already put under a strict watch, and that he could go nowhere without being followed. Before a week was out, he was taken and laid in hold. The circumstances were gradually pieced together against him, with a desperate malignity, and an appalling ingenuity. But, see the justice of men, and how it was extended to him! He was further accused of having poisoned that girl in the Bride's Chamber. He, who had carefully and expressly avoided imperilling a hair of his head for her, and who had seen her die of her own incapacity!

'There was doubt for which of the two murders he should be first tried; but, the real one was chosen, and he was found Guilty, and cast for death. Bloodthirsty wretches! They would have made him Guilty of anything, so set they were upon having his life.

'His money could do nothing to save him, and he was hanged. I am He, and I was hanged at Lancaster Castle with my face to the wall, a hundred years ago!'

At this terrific announcement, Mr. Goodchild tried to rise and cry out. But, the two fiery lines extending from the old man's eyes to his own, kept him down, and he could not utter a sound. His sense of hearing, however, was acute, and he could hear the clock strike Two. No sooner had he heard the clock strike Two, than he saw before him Two old men!

"THERE was a ship!" This is how the eponymous Ancient Mariner of Coleridge's Gothic poem begins his ritualistic narration. Condemned to wander the earth and relate the tale of his crimes, the old man with gleaming eyes arrests the attention of his listeners before disappearing. "She was a bride!" exclaims Dickens' ancient murderer. This grotesque phantom is likewise damned to transmit the story of his deeds on a regular basis (one o'clock each night) as a part of his penance. The story would have an obvious influence on E. F. Benson, Algernon Blackwood, Wilkie Collins, M.R. James – particularly "Martin's Close," "The Story of a Disappearance and an Appearance," "Lost Hearts," "The Ash Tree," and "The Stalls of Barchester" – and on Britain's master ghost story writer, J. Sheridan Le Fanu. Indeed, the tale reads very much like a Le Fanu tale, closely resembling elements of "Schalken the Painter" (which, in this case, being written in the 1830s, was possibly an influence on this episode), "Mr Justice Harbottle," "The Haunted Baronet," "Madam Crowl's Ghost," and "Squire Toby's Will." Like Le Fanu's grisly oeuvre, Dickens uses this story to examine the blurred lines between good and evil, health and illness, innocence and guilt (the killer is innocent of the first death... or is he? It is nebulous), the natural and the supernatural, past and present, falsehood and truth. It is a dark, chiaroscuro landscape of human sin, shame, and corruption, spotted with gleams of virtue, but overwhelmingly cloaked in featureless shadow.

As with "Christmas Ghosts," the following excerpt is a set of nursery tales (quite literally; the piece is sometimes titled "Nurse's Stories") which ostensibly have haunted the author throughout childhood and his adult life. It is not entirely clear whether these are Dickens' invention or those of his childhood nursemaid, Mary Weller, but many literary historians seem to take Dickens' word that they are not his invention, and with good reason. The narratives he selected to represent follow the model of folkloric horror stories (he notes the relation of the first to the Blue-Beard myth) being gruesome, fantastical, and disturbing. Either could have easily been penned by the Brothers Grimm, Hans Christian Andersen, or Charles Perrault, whose grisly fairy tales are astonishing gory and horrific. The two stories follow the general theme that has been developing in Dickens supernatural fiction – first with a flourish from "Madman's," then regularly after "Baron Koeldwethout" – a building sense of moral bankruptcy, cosmic alienation, the consistent victory of evil over good (even when good wins out, it is a pyrrhic triumph), and the lonesome situation of the virtuous person who must rely upon their own energies to defeat evil – often with either mixed or entirely disheartening results.

Captain Murder & the Devil's Bargain
Or, Nurse's Stories
EXCERPTED *from* THE UNCOMMERCIAL TRAVELLER, CHAPTER *Fifteen*
{1857}

WHEN I was in Dullborough one day, revisiting the associations of my childhood as recorded in previous pages of these notes, my experience in this wise was made quite inconsiderable and of no account, by the quantity of places and people-- utterly impossible places and people, but none the less alarmingly real--that I found I had been introduced to by my nurse before I was six years old, and used to be forced to go back to at night without at all wanting to go. If we all knew our own minds (in a more enlarged sense than the popular acceptation of that phrase), I suspect we should find our nurses responsible for most of the dark corners we are forced to go back to, against our wills.

The first diabolical character who intruded himself on my peaceful youth (as I called to mind that day at Dullborough), was a certain Captain Murderer. This wretch must have been an off-shoot of the Blue Beard family, but I had no suspicion of the consanguinity in those times. His warning name would seem to have awakened no general prejudice against him, for he was admitted into the best society and possessed immense wealth. Captain Murderer's mission was matrimony, and the gratification of a cannibal appetite with tender brides. On his marriage morning, he always caused both sides of the way to church to be planted with curious flowers; and when his bride said, 'Dear Captain Murderer, I ever saw flowers like these before: what are they called?' he answered, 'They are called Garnish for house-lamb,' and laughed at his ferocious practical joke in a horrid manner, disquieting the minds of the noble bridal company, with a very sharp show of teeth, then displayed for the first time. He made love in a coach and six, and married in a coach and twelve, and all his horses were milk-white horses with one red spot on the back which he caused to be hidden by the harness. For, the spot WOULD come there, though every horse was milk-white when Captain Murderer bought him. And the spot was young bride's blood. (To this terrific point I am indebted for my first personal experience of a shudder and cold beads on the forehead.) When Captain Murderer had made an end of feasting and revelry, and had dismissed the noble guests, and was alone with his wife on the day month after their marriage, it was his whimsical custom to produce a golden rolling-pin and a silver pie-board. Now, there was this special feature in the Captain's courtships, that he always asked if the young lady could make pie-crust; and if she couldn't by nature or education, she was taught. Well. When the bride saw Captain Murderer produce the golden rolling-pin and silver pie-board, she remembered this, and turned up her laced-silk sleeves to make a pie. The Captain brought out a silver pie-dish of immense capacity, and the Captain brought out flour and butter and eggs and all things needful, except the inside of the pie; of materials for the staple of the pie itself, the Captain brought out none. Then said the lovely bride, 'Dear Captain Murderer, what pie is this to be?' He replied, 'A meat pie.' Then said the lovely bride, 'Dear Captain Murderer, I see no meat.' The Captain humorously retorted, 'Look in the glass.' She looked in the glass, but still she saw no meat, and then the Captain roared with laughter, and suddenly frowning and drawing his sword, bade her roll out the crust. So she rolled out the crust, dropping large tears upon it all the time because he was so cross, and when she had lined the dish with crust and had cut the crust all ready to fit the top, the Captain called out, 'I see the meat in the glass!' And the bride looked up at the glass, just in time to see the Captain cutting her head off; and he chopped her in pieces, and peppered her, and salted her, and put her in the pie, and sent it to the baker's, and ate it all, and picked the bones.

Captain Murderer went on in this way, prospering exceedingly, until he came to choose a bride from two twin sisters, and at first didn't know which to choose. For, though one was fair and the other dark, they were both equally beautiful. But the fair twin loved him, and the dark twin hated him, so he chose the fair one. The dark twin would have prevented the marriage if she could, but she couldn't; however, on the night before it, much suspecting Captain Murderer, she stole out and climbed his garden wall, and looked in at his window through a chink in the shutter, and saw him having his teeth filed sharp. Next day she listened all day, and heard him make his joke about the house-lamb. And that day month, he had the paste rolled out, and cut the fair twin's head off, and chopped her in pieces, and peppered her, and salted her, and put her in the pie, and sent it to the baker's, and ate it all, and picked the bones.

Now, the dark twin had had her suspicions much increased by the filing of the Captain's teeth, and again by the house-lamb joke. Putting all things together when he gave out that her sister was dead, she divined the truth, and determined to be revenged. So, she went up to Captain Murderer's house, and knocked at the knocker and pulled at the bell, and when the Captain came to the door, said: 'Dear Captain Murderer, marry me next, for I always loved you and was jealous of my sister.' The Captain took it as a compliment, and made a polite answer, and the marriage was quickly arranged. On the night before it, the bride again climbed to his window, and again saw him having his teeth filed sharp. At this sight she laughed such a terrible laugh at the chink in the shutter, that the Captain's blood curdled, and he said: 'I hope nothing has disagreed with me!' At that, she laughed again, a still more terrible laugh, and the shutter was opened and search made, but she was nimbly gone, and there was no one. Next day they went to church in a coach and twelve, and were married. And that day month, she rolled the pie-crust out, and Captain Murderer cut her head off, and chopped her in pieces, and peppered her, and salted her, and put her in the pie, and sent it to the baker's, and ate it all, and picked the bones.

But before she began to roll out the paste she had taken a deadly poison of a most awful character, distilled from toads' eyes and spiders' knees; and Captain Murderer had hardly picked her last bone, when he began to swell, and to turn blue, and to be all over spots, and to scream. And he went on swelling and turning bluer, and being more all over spots and screaming, until he reached from floor to ceiling and from wall to wall; and then, at one o'clock in the morning, he blew up with a loud explosion. At the sound of it, all the milk-white horses in the stables broke their halters and went mad, and then they galloped over everybody in Captain Murderer's house (beginning with the family blacksmith who had filed his teeth) until the whole were dead, and then they galloped away.

Hundreds of times did I hear this legend of Captain Murderer, in my early youth, and added hundreds of times was there a mental compulsion upon me in bed, to peep in at his window as the dark twin peeped, and to revisit his horrible house, and look at him in his blue and spotty and screaming stage, as he reached from floor to ceiling and from wall to wall. The young woman who brought me acquainted with Captain Murderer had a fiendish enjoyment of my terrors, and used to begin, I remember--as a sort of introductory overture--by clawing the air with both hands, and uttering a long low hollow groan. So acutely did I suffer from this ceremony in combination with this infernal Captain, that I sometimes used to plead I thought I was hardly strong enough and old enough to hear the story again just yet. But, she never spared me one word of it, and indeed commanded the awful chalice to my lips as the only preservative known to science against 'The Black Cat'--a weird and glaring-eyed supernatural Tom, who was reputed to prowl about the world by night, sucking the breath of infancy, and who was endowed with a special thirst (as I was given to understand) for mine.

This female bard--may she have been repaid my debt of obligation to her in the matter of nightmares and perspirations!--reappears in my memory as the daughter of a shipwright. Her name was Mercy, though she had none on me. There was something of a shipbuilding flavour in the following story. As it always recurs to me in a vague association with calomel pills, I believe it to have been reserved for dull nights when I was low with medicine.

There was once a shipwright, and he wrought in a Government Yard, and his name was Chips. And his father's name before him was Chips, and HIS father's name before HIM was Chips, and they were all Chipses. And Chips the father had sold himself to the Devil for an iron pot and a bushel of tenpenny nails and half a ton of copper and a rat that could speak; and Chips the grandfather had sold himself to the Devil for an iron pot and a bushel of tenpenny nails and half a ton of copper and a rat that could speak; and Chips the great-grandfather had disposed of himself in the same direction on the same terms; and the bargain had run in the family for a long, long time. So, one day, when young Chips was at work in the Dock Slip all alone, down in the dark hold of an old Seventy-four that was haled up for repairs, the Devil presented himself, and remarked:

'A Lemon has pips, And a Yard has ships, And *I'll* have Chips!'

(I don't know why, but this fact of the Devil's expressing himself in rhyme was peculiarly trying to me.) Chips looked up when he heard the words, and there he saw the Devil with saucer eyes that squinted on a terrible great scale, and that struck out sparks of blue fire continually. And whenever he winked his eyes, showers of blue sparks came out, and his eyelashes made a clattering like flints and steels striking lights. And hanging over one of his arms by the handle was an iron pot, and under that arm was a bushel of tenpenny nails, and under his other arm was half a ton of copper, and sitting on one of his shoulders was a rat that could speak. So, the Devil said again:

'A Lemon has pips, And a Yard has ships, And *I'll* have Chips!'

(The invariable effect of this alarming tautology on the part of the Evil Spirit was to deprive me of my senses for some moments.) So, Chips answered never a word, but went on with his work. 'What are you doing, Chips?' said the rat that could speak. 'I am putting in new planks where you and your gang have eaten old away,' said Chips. 'But we'll eat them too,' said the rat that could speak; 'and we'll let in the water and drown the crew, and we'll eat them too.' Chips, being only a shipwright, and not a Man-of- war's man, said, 'You are welcome to it.' But he couldn't keep his eyes off the half a ton of copper or the bushel of tenpenny nails; for nails and copper are a shipwright's sweethearts, and shipwrights will run away with them whenever they can. So, the Devil said, 'I see what you are looking at, Chips. You had better strike the bargain. You know the terms. Your father before you was well acquainted with them, and so were your grandfather and great-grandfather before him.' Says Chips, 'I like the copper, and I like the nails, and I don't mind the pot, but I don't like the rat.' Says the Devil, fiercely, 'You can't have the metal without him--and HE'S a curiosity. I'm going.' Chips, afraid of losing the half a ton of copper and the bushel of nails, then said, 'Give us hold!' So, he got the copper and the nails and the pot and the rat that could speak, and the Devil vanished. Chips sold the copper, and he sold the nails, and he would have sold the pot; but whenever he offered it for sale, the rat was in it, and the dealers dropped it, and would have nothing to say to the bargain. So, Chips resolved to kill the rat, and, being at work in the Yard one day with a great kettle of hot pitch on one side of him and the iron pot with the rat in it on the other, he turned the scalding pitch into the pot, and filled it full. Then, he kept his eye upon it till it cooled and hardened, and then he let it stand for twenty days, and then he heated the pitch again and turned it back into the kettle, and then he sank the pot in water for twenty days more, and then he got the smelters to put it in the furnace for twenty

days more, and then they gave it him out, red hot, and looking like red-hot glass instead of iron-yet there was the rat in it, just the same as ever! And the moment it caught his eye, it said with a jeer:

'A Lemon has pips, And a Yard has ships, And *I'll* have Chips!'

(For this Refrain I had waited since its last appearance, with inexpressible horror, which now culminated.) Chips now felt certain in his own mind that the rat would stick to him; the rat, answering his thought, said, 'I will--like pitch!'

Now, as the rat leaped out of the pot when it had spoken, and made off, Chips began to hope that it wouldn't keep its word. But, a terrible thing happened next day. For, when dinner-time came, and the Dock-bell rang to strike work, he put his rule into the long pocket at the side of his trousers, and there he found a rat--not that rat, but another rat. And in his hat, he found another; and in his pocket-handkerchief, another; and in the sleeves of his coat, when he pulled it on to go to dinner, two more. And from that time he found himself so frightfully intimate with all the rats in the Yard, that they climbed up his legs when he was at work, and sat on his tools while he used them. And they could all speak to one another, and he understood what they said. And they got into his lodging, and into his bed, and into his teapot, and into his beer, and into his boots. And he was going to be married to a corn-chandler's daughter; and when he gave her a workbox he had himself made for her, a rat jumped out of it; and when he put his arm round her waist, a rat clung about her; so the marriage was broken off, though the banns were already twice put up--which the parish clerk well remembers, for, as he handed the book to the clergyman for the second time of asking, a large fat rat ran over the leaf. (By this time a special cascade of rats was rolling down my back, and the whole of my small listening person was overrun with them. At intervals ever since, I have been morbidly afraid of my own pocket, lest my exploring hand should find a specimen or two of those vermin in it.)

You may believe that all this was very terrible to Chips; but even all this was not the worst. He knew besides, what the rats were doing, wherever they were. So, sometimes he would cry aloud, when he was at his club at night, 'Oh! Keep the rats out of the convicts' burying-ground! Don't let them do that!' Or, 'There's one of them at the cheese down-stairs!' Or, 'There's two of them smelling at the baby in the garret!' Or, other things of that sort. At last, he was voted mad, and lost his work in the Yard, and could get no other work. But, King George wanted men, so before very long he got pressed for a sailor. And so he was taken off in a boat one evening to his ship, lying at Spithead, ready to sail. And so the first thing he made out in her as he got near her, was the figure-head of the old Seventy-four, where he had seen the Devil. She was called the Argonaut, and they rowed right under the bowsprit where the figure-head of the Argonaut, with a sheepskin in his hand and a blue gown on, was looking out to sea; and sitting staring on his forehead was the rat who could speak, and his exact words were these: 'Chips ahoy! Old boy! We've pretty well eat them too, and we'll drown the crew, and will eat them too!' (Here I always became exceedingly faint, and would have asked for water, but that I was speechless.)

The ship was bound for the Indies; and if you don't know where that is, you ought to it, and angels will never love you. (Here I felt myself an outcast from a future state.) The ship set sail that very night, and she sailed, and sailed, and sailed. Chips's feelings were dreadful. Nothing ever equalled his terrors. No wonder. At last, one day he asked leave to speak to the Admiral. The Admiral giv' leave. Chips went down on his knees in the Great State Cabin. 'Your Honour, unless your Honour, without a moment's loss of time, makes sail for the nearest shore, this is a doomed ship, and her name is the Coffin!' 'Young man, your words are a madman's words.' 'Your Honour no; they are nibbling us away.' 'They?' 'Your Honour, them dreadful rats. Dust and hollowness where solid oak ought to be! Rats nibbling a grave for every man on board! Oh! Does your Honour love your Lady and your pretty children?' 'Yes, my man, to be sure.' 'Then, for God's sake, make for the nearest shore, for at this present moment the rats are all stopping in their work, and are all looking straight towards you with bare teeth, and are all saying to one another that you shall never, never, never, never, see your Lady and your children more.' 'My poor fellow, you are a case for the doctor. Sentry, take care of this man!'

So, he was bled and he was blistered, and he was this and that, for six whole days and nights. So, then he again asked leave to speak to the Admiral. The Admiral giv' leave. He went down on his knees in the Great State Cabin. 'Now, Admiral, you must die! You took no warning; you must die! The rats are never wrong in their calculations, and they make out that they'll be through, at twelve to-night. So, you must die!--With me and all the rest!' And so at twelve o'clock there was a great leak reported in the ship, and a torrent of water rushed in and nothing could stop it, and they all went down, every living soul. And what the rats--being water-rats- -left of Chips, at last floated to shore, and sitting on him was an immense overgrown rat, laughing, that dived when the corpse touched the beach and never came up. And there was a deal of seaweed on the remains. And if you get thirteen bits of seaweed, and dry them and burn them in the fire, they will go off like in these thirteen words as plain as plain can be:

'A Lemon has pips, And a Yard has ships, And I've got Chips!'

The same female bard--descended, possibly, from those terrible old Scalds who seem to have existed for the express purpose of addling the brains of mankind when they begin to investigate languages-- made a standing pretence which greatly assisted in forcing me back to a number of hideous places that I would by all means have avoided. This pretence was, that all her ghost stories had occurred to her own relations. Politeness towards a meritorious family, therefore, forbade my doubting them, and they acquired an air of authentication that impaired my digestive powers for life. There was a narrative concerning an unearthly animal foreboding death, which appeared in the open street to a parlour-maid who 'went to fetch the beer' for supper: first (as I now recall it) assuming the likeness of a black dog, and gradually rising on its hind-legs and swelling into the semblance of some quadruped greatly surpassing a hippopotamus: which apparition--not because I deemed it in the least improbable, but because I felt it to be really too large to bear--I feebly endeavoured to explain away. But, on Mercy's retorting with wounded dignity that the parlour-maid was her own sister-in-law, I perceived there was no hope, and resigned myself to this zoological phenomenon as one of my many pursuers. There was another narrative describing the apparition of a young woman who came out of a glass-case and haunted another young woman until the other young woman questioned it and elicited that its bones (Lord! To think of its being so particular about its bones!) were buried under the glass-case, whereas she required them to be interred, with every Undertaking solemnity up to twenty-four pound ten, in another particular place. This narrative I considered--I had a personal interest in disproving, because we had glass-cases at home, and how, otherwise, was I to be guaranteed from the intrusion of young women requiring ME TO bury them up to twenty- four pound ten, when I had only twopence a week? But my remorseless nurse cut the ground from under my tender feet, by informing me that She was the other young woman; and I couldn't say 'I don't believe you;' it was not possible.

Such are a few of the uncommercial journeys that I was forced to make, against my will, when I was very young and unreasoning. And really, as to the latter part of them, it is not so very long ago-- now I come to think of it--that I was asked to undertake them once again, with a steady countenance.

SIMILARLY to "To Be Read at Dusk," we are handed two stories couched in a framing narrative, both of which are drearily mysterious, neither of which offer the redemption of their protagonists. Instead, we meet a vicious woman (a twin whose sibling has died, like those in "Dusk") who becomes a suicide murderer, basting her flesh with poison before she is cannibalized by the man who consumed her far more sane and innocent sister. This is a portrait of hate and revenge and bitter spite, one which spurns the help of society or law in favor of rash and reckless vigilantism. Secondly we meet Chips (who, incidentally is nearly perfectly modelled on the eponymous Scroogian miser from Irving's "The Devil and Tom Walker") whose valiant attempts to resist his hereditary destiny (compare to "Madman's") are ineffectual, and his sin proves contagious, destroying the complement of an entire battleship. Free will and agency are slaves to human nature and destiny. A lemon encases its seeds, and a shipyard is home to immobilized vessels, and in the same way, the devil intimates that Chips has just as much chance of escaping his ownership. The failure of external systems – of religion, law, community, family – and the miserable vanity of human agency is the focus of this double feature. Perhaps the most unsettling fact of all is that these cynical tales of frailty, hopelessness, and moral ineptitude were forced down the gullets of entire generations of small children. And yet we might be forced to ask ourselves which is the more dangerous: a nursery story that jolts youngsters out of their egocentric worldview with the shocking realization that good does not always triumph, and mommy will not always make everything better, or our sanitized, censored, and sanctified children's tales that build up a fruitless expectation of invincibility, moral clarity, and reliable rescue?

MOST famous of Dickens' ghost stories (somewhat undeservingly when compared to the original, weird, and mystifying mainstays "Signal-Man," "Dusk," and "Bride"), the following tale is arguably the grand dame of English spook tales. Based loosely on the real-life murder of Lord William Russell, "The Trial for Murder" was once considered the exemplar of a respectable ghost story (largely because of its author) and was included with "The Turn of the Screw," "The Body-Snatchers," and "The Legend of Sleepy Hollow" in early-to-mid twentieth century anthologies of ghost stories. In our current century, "Trial" loses a great deal of momentum due to its perspective, narration, and delivery, all of which diminish the intrusion of the supernatural, making it eerie and chilly but never really frightening or weird. Until the end. While early anthologists were correct in choosing this tale as a relatively tame and reputable example of the decent ghost story (good lord, what would they have done with Onions, Hodgson, Machen, Blackwood, Wakefield, or God forbid, Lovecraft, Aickman, or De la Mare?), they missed the utterly thrilling implications of its conclusion – that we are all ghosts of something, that our society is crippled and inept, and that justice is not to be expected without the goodly puppeteering of a supernatural overlord, one which – as the secondary title suggests – Dickens sadly writes off.

The Trial for Murder
Or, To Be Taken With a Grain of Salt
{1865}

I have always noticed a prevalent want of courage, even among persons of superior intelligence and culture, as to imparting their own psychological experiences when those have been of a strange sort. Almost all men are afraid that what they could relate in such wise would find no parallel or response in a listener's internal life, and might be suspected or laughed at[1]. A truthful traveller, who should have seen some extraordinary creature in the likeness of a sea-serpent, would have no fear of mentioning it; but the same traveller, having had some singular presentiment, impulse, vagary of thought, vision (so-called), dream, or other remarkable mental impression, would hesitate considerably before he would own to it[2]. To this

---

[1] Dickens introduces us to a theme which will run throughout his tale: the stupidity and lack of understanding of others. Almost as if to illustrate how difficult it is to reason with people, Dickens begins a tale that is self-reflective: it is the sort of story which others would deride, and it is one which involves human laziness and lack of vision as a main concept

[2] Dickens asserts that it is far easier to confess to an aberration originating outside of the mind (claiming to see a flying saucer or fairy for instance), than to admit to any aberration of the mind (having a dream or vision or feeling a premonition). For whatever reason, he grumbles, it is easier to relate the former than the later, even though there

reticence I attribute much of the obscurity in which such subjects are involved. We do not habitually communicate our experiences of these subjective things as we do our experiences of objective creation. The consequence is, that the general stock of experience in this regard appears exceptional, and really is so, in respect of being miserably imperfect.

In what I am going to relate, I have no intention of setting up, opposing, or supporting, any theory whatever[1]. I know the history of the Bookseller of Berlin[2], I have studied the case of the wife of a late Astronomer Royal as related by Sir David Brewster[3], and I have followed the minutest details of a much more remarkable case of Spectral Illusion occurring within my private circle of friends. It may be necessary to state as to this last, that the sufferer (a lady) was in no degree, however distant, related to me. A mistaken assumption on that head might suggest an explanation of a part of my own case[4] — but only a part — which would be wholly without foundation. It cannot be referred to my inheritance of any

---

may be more validity in the intuitive psychology than in the cryptozoological observations. The reason he provides is that the lenses of the five senses are keenly understood to us while the lens of the mind and the spirit still lurk in a shadowy environment hidden from view. It is therefore less anxiety-producing to admit to *seeing* a ghost than – for instance – to admit to having a *mental vision* of a dead man. This is the crux of Dickens' story: mankind's hesitation to listen to reason and their lazy propensity to avoid the evidence of their senses (as Jacob Marley would say) in a bid to preserve their simplistic worldviews. This does, of course, transfer into social matters: just as a man might find it easier to hear a friend's story about a flying saucer than to trust his wife's intuition about a foreseen disaster – writing it off as hokum while entertaining the less sensitive, spiritual tale – it is easier for men to swallow the myths of the world around them than to admit to the harsh realities of life. For example, it might be easier for a fellow to claim that big business should be unopposed due to popular capitalist narratives about the heroism of the free market than to accept the misery of oppressed workers and their families as credible reasons to oppose those libertarian measures

[1] This objective approach would be adopted by the Society for Psychical Research in their explorations of supernatural phenomena – the scientific method, necessary for ensuring objectivity

[2] Christoph Frederich Nicolai, the said bookseller, was an eighteenth century German intellectual who began to see phantoms after missing a doctor appointment. At first terrified of losing his sanity, he decided to hold off calling the doctor, and instead kept a journal describing his interactions with the dozens of ghosts that visited his house. His pragmatic and measured approach to what was likely a bout of psychosis is copied here in Dickens' narrator's cool narrative

[3] The Scottish inventor of the kaleidoscope and the stereoscope developed a daguerreotype only to discover a spectral blur. This was the first recorded description of a ghost caught on film

[4] Namely that they might both suffer from hereditary insanity

developed peculiarity, nor had I ever before any at all similar experience, nor have I ever had any at all similar experience since.

It does not signify how many years ago, or how few, a certain murder was committed in England, which attracted great attention. We hear more than enough of murderers as they rise in succession to their atrocious eminence, and I would bury the memory of this particular brute, if I could, as his body was buried, in Newgate Jail[1]. I purposely abstain from giving any direct clue to the criminal's individuality[2].

When the murder was first discovered, no suspicion fell — or I ought rather to say, for I cannot be too precise in my facts, it was nowhere publicly hinted that any suspicion fell — on the man who was afterwards brought to trial[3]. As no reference was at that time made to him in the newspapers, it is obviously impossible that any description of him can at that time have been given in the newspapers. It is essential that this fact be remembered.

Unfolding at breakfast my morning paper, containing the account of that first discovery, I found it to be deeply interesting, and I read it with close attention. I read it twice, if not three times. The discovery had been made in a bedroom, and, when I laid down the paper, I was aware of a flash — rush — flow — I do not know

---

[1] The London prison where defendants were jailed and executed after being tried in the Old Bailey

[2] And yet, I shall try to unveil the murder in question. This is almost undoubtedly based on the sensational murder of Lord William Russell by his valet Francois Benjamin Courvoisier on May 6 1840. Lord William was a Member of Parliament and a member of a renowned family of aristocrats. On the morning after his slaying, his maid came into his bedchamber to find the room in great disarray, seemingly to have been burgled. Frightened, she sent his valets (including Courvoisier) to check on the master. He was found in bed with his throat cut open, his pillows saturated in blood. At first the murderer seemed stupefied, and the police merely questioned him as a witness, but when they searched the house, they found a variety of Lord William's personal valuables hidden throughout the valet's room, and then a gold locket was discovered on his person. He was arrested for the murder and tried at the Old Bailey where he pled not guilty. Even as evidence piled up against him, and even after confessing to his lawyers, Courvoisier refused to change his plea. He only confessed after being found guilty. In his confession he claimed to have slain his master after angering him to the point that Lord William hinted at firing him in the morning. Terrified of losing his position, reputation, and character, he cut his throat in the night: "I went near the bed by the side of the window, and then I murdered him. He just moved his arm a little; he never spoke a word." Courvoisier was executed on July 6 at Newgate in front of a crowd of 40,000. Among the throng were many aristocrats, nobles, and members of Parliament, as well as opponents of the death penalty. One such activist was William Makepeace Thackeray, who was accompanied by his like-minded friend, a 28 year old Charles Dickens

[3] As in the Lord William Russell case

what to call it — no word I can find is satisfactorily descriptive — in which I seemed to see that bedroom passing through my room, like a picture impossibly painted on a running river[1]. Though almost instantaneous in its passing, it was perfectly clear; so clear that I distinctly, and with a sense of relief, observed the absence of the dead body from the bed[2].

It was in no romantic place[3] that I had this curious sensation, but in chambers in Piccadilly, very near to the corner of St. James's Street[4]. It was entirely new to me. I was in my easy-chair at the moment, and the sensation was accompanied with a peculiar shiver which started the chair from its position. (But it is to be noted that the chair ran easily on castors.) I went to one of the windows (there are two in the room, and the room is on the second floor) to refresh my eyes with the moving objects down in Piccadilly. It was a bright autumn morning, and the street was sparkling and cheerful. The wind was high. As I looked out, it brought down from the Park[5] a quantity of fallen leaves, which a gust took, and whirled into a spiral pillar. As the pillar fell and the leaves dispersed, I saw two men on the opposite side of the way[6], going from West to East. They were one behind the other. The foremost man often looked back over his shoulder. The second man followed him, at a distance of some thirty paces[7], with his right hand menacingly raised. First, the singularity and steadiness of this threatening gesture in so public a thoroughfare attracted my attention; and next, the more remarkable circumstance that nobody heeded it. Both men threaded their way among the other passengers with a smoothness hardly consistent even with the action of walking on a pavement; and no single creature, that I could see, gave them place, touched them, or looked after them. In passing before my windows, they both stared up at me[8]. I saw their two faces very distinctly, and I knew that I could

---

[1] This calls to mind the ghostly hearse that Scrooge witnesses trundling up the stairs ahead of him

[2] He must count himself lucky if this murder is in all respects similar to its model. Samuel Warren describes the scene thusly: "His face was covered over with a towel; on removing which, and pulling down the [bedclothes], a ghastly spectacle presented itself. He lay weltering in his blood, and his head was nearly severed from his body by the stroke of some weapon"

[3] Meaning wild, sublime, or fanciful – like a churchyard, moorland, mountain range, or tarn

[4] A major intersection in one of the poshest parts of Westminster's business district, known for having some of the highest rents in the world

[5] St. James's Park

[6] The sidewalk opposite his chambers

[7] It must be noted that this is a fairly far distance to connect two people in a crowd, since we are talking about approximately thirty meters

[8] We note, therefore, that he is not watching a ghost pursuing a living man, but the ghost of a dead man tormenting and chasing the spirit of a living man. Dickens has a

recognise them anywhere. Not that I had consciously noticed anything very remarkable in either face, except that the man who went first had an unusually lowering[1] appearance, and that the face of the man who followed him was of the colour of impure wax[2].

I am a bachelor, and my valet and his wife constitute my whole establishment. My occupation is in a certain Branch Bank, and I wish that my duties as head of a Department were as light as they are popularly supposed to be. They kept me in town[3] that autumn, when I stood in need of change. I was not ill, but I was not well. My reader is to make the most that can be reasonably made of my feeling jaded, having a depressing sense upon me of a monotonous life, and being "slightly dyspeptic[4]." I am assured by my renowned doctor that my real state of health at that time justifies no stronger description, and I quote his own from his written answer to my request for it[5].

As the circumstances of the murder, gradually unravelling, took stronger and stronger possession of the public mind, I kept them away from mine by knowing as little about them as was possible in the midst of the universal excitement. But I knew that a verdict of Wilful Murder had been found against the suspected murderer, and that he had been committed to Newgate for trial. I also knew that his trial had been postponed over one Sessions of the Central Criminal Court[6], on the ground of general prejudice and want of time for the preparation of the defence[7]. I may further have known, but I believe I did not, when, or about when, the Sessions to which his trial stood postponed would come on.

My sitting-room, bedroom, and dressing-room[8], are all on one floor. With the last there is no communication but through the bedroom. True, there is a door in it, once communicating with the staircase; but a part of the fitting of my bath has

---

notoriously liberal definition of ghosts, and in Dickens a man need not be dead to appear in spirit to his fellow

[1] Sullen, droopy, depressed

[2] Impure wax which has not been refined, or tallow, is a sickly, grey-ish yellow hue, similar to butter or lard – to color of a man's face after he has bled to death and been dead for seven hours or so

[3] "Town" is a British euphemism for London

[4] Cranky, crotchety, depressed

[5] The narrator wants to assure his reader that other than a subtle bout of nervous moodiness, there was nothing ailing him in such a way as to cause hallucinations or psychosis

[6] Also known as the Crown Court of England and Wales, this is the highest trial court in the nation, with 92 trial locations across Britain. The "Central" Court is the Old Bailey

[7] Though the murder has been committed elsewhere, the trial is being moved to London to avoid a local jury. This same plot point is used by M. R. James in his "Martin's Close," which is a Jamesian version of Dickens' original story

[8] We would call a sitting room a den, parlor, or living room, and a dressing room – in the days before closets – was essentially a walk-in closet with wardrobes and chests

been — and had then been for some years — fixed across it. At the same period, and as a part of the same arrangement — the door had been nailed up and canvased over.

I was standing in my bedroom late one night, giving some directions to my servant before he went to bed. My face was towards the only available door of communication with the dressing-room, and it was closed. My servant's back was towards that door. While I was speaking to him, I saw it open, and a man look in, who very earnestly and mysteriously beckoned to me. That man was the man who had gone second of the two along Piccadilly, and whose face was of the colour of impure wax.

The figure, having beckoned, drew back, and closed the door. With no longer pause than was made by my crossing the bedroom, I opened the dressing-room door, and looked in. I had a lighted candle already in my hand. I felt no inward expectation of seeing the figure in the dressing-room, and I did not see it there.

Conscious that my servant stood amazed[1], I turned round to him, and said: "Derrick, could you believe that in my cool senses I fancied I saw a —" As I there laid my hand upon his breast, with a sudden start he trembled violently, and said, "O Lord, yes, sir! A dead man beckoning!"

Now I do not believe that this John Derrick, my trusty and attached servant for more than twenty years, had any impression whatever of having seen any such figure, until I touched him. The change in him was so startling, when I touched him, that I fully believe he derived his impression in some occult manner from me at that instant.

I bade John Derrick bring some brandy, and I gave him a dram, and was glad to take one myself. Of what had preceded that night's phenomenon, I told him not a single word. Reflecting on it, I was absolutely certain that I had never seen that face before, except on the one occasion in Piccadilly. Comparing its expression when beckoning at the door with its expression when it had stared up at me as I stood at my window, I came to the conclusion that on the first occasion it had sought to fasten itself upon my memory, and that on the second occasion it had made sure of being immediately remembered[2].

I was not very comfortable that night, though I felt a certainty, difficult to explain, that the figure would not return. At daylight I fell into a heavy sleep, from

---

[1] Important to note that while the master is calm, the servant is excited. This lends validity to the idea that the ghost is not imagined because the servant was horrified by its appearance – not by his master screaming and falling to the ground, or by his master asking him if he had also "seen a dead man beckoning"

[2] Now the spirit begins his intervention into human affairs. Not trusting the distracted, unprofessional, and lazy general public to see to his justice, the ghost makes sure that his face is remembered in connection with the defendant, and proceeds to supernaturally push his pupils aggressively along – witnesses, jurors, lawyers, and all – until the conviction of his murderer is secured

which I was awakened by John Derrick's coming to my bedside with a paper in his hand.

This paper, it appeared, had been the subject of an altercation at the door between its bearer and my servant. It was a summons to me to serve upon a Jury at the forthcoming Sessions of the Central Criminal Court at the Old Bailey[1]. I had never before been summoned on such a Jury, as John Derrick well knew. He believed — I am not certain at this hour whether with reason or otherwise — that that class of Jurors were customarily chosen on a lower qualification than mine[2], and he had at first refused to accept the summons. The man who served it had taken the matter very coolly. He had said that my attendance or non-attendance was nothing to him; there the summons was; and I should deal with it at my own peril, and not at his.

For a day or two I was undecided whether to respond to this call, or take no notice of it. I was not conscious of the slightest mysterious bias, influence, or attraction, one way or other. Of that I am as strictly sure as of every other statement that I make here. Ultimately I decided, as a break in the monotony of my life, that I would go.

The appointed morning was a raw morning in the month of November. There was a dense brown fog in Piccadilly, and it became positively black and in the last degree oppressive[3] East of Temple Bar[4]. I found the passages and staircases of the Court-House flaringly lighted with gas, and the Court itself similarly illuminated[5]. I *think* that, until I was conducted by officers into the Old Court and saw its crowded state, I did not know that the Murderer was to be tried that day. I *think* that, until I was so helped into the Old Court with considerable difficulty, I did not know into which of the two Courts sitting my summons would take me. But this

---

[1] First organized in 1585, the current edifice dates from 1774. Part of the present building stands on the site of the medieval Newgate gaol, on a road named Old Bailey which follows the line of the City of London's fortified wall (or bailey), which runs from Ludgate Hill to the junction of Newgate Street and Holborn Viaduct. The Crown Court sitting at the Central Criminal Court deals with major criminal cases from within Greater London and, in exceptional cases, from other parts of England and Wales. Trials at the Old Bailey, as at other courts, are open to the public, albeit subject to stringent security procedures.

[2] Hardly. Indeed, British juries originally consisted wholly of gentlemen, and it was considered a civic duty to serve as a juror

[3] In Dickens' fiction fog is used as a motif for ignorance or willful denial of truth – it obscures, avoids, and conceals

[4] The point where Fleet Street, London, transitions into the Strand, Westminster

[5] So in this cloud of ignorance, evasion, and secrecy, the Old Bailey merely flickers with the dull promise of truth. It is a light, yes, but a dim one, and justice is promised but not garunteed

must not be received as a positive assertion, for I am not completely satisfied in my mind on either point[1].

I took my seat in the place appropriated to Jurors in waiting, and I looked about the Court as well as I could through the cloud of fog and breath that was heavy in it. I noticed the black vapour hanging like a murky curtain outside the great windows, and I noticed the stifled sound of wheels on the straw or tan[2] that was littered in the street; also, the hum of the people gathered there, which a shrill whistle, or a louder song or hail than the rest, occasionally pierced. Soon afterwards the Judges, two in number, entered, and took their seats. The buzz in the Court was awfully hushed. The direction was given to put the Murderer to the bar. He appeared there. And in that same instant I recognised in him the first of the two men who had gone down Piccadilly.

If my name had been called then, I doubt if I could have answered to it audibly. But it was called about sixth or eighth in the panel, and I was by that time able to say, "Here!" Now, observe. As I stepped into the box, the prisoner, who had been looking on attentively, but with no sign of concern, became violently agitated, and beckoned to his attorney. The prisoner's wish to challenge me[3] was so manifest, that it occasioned a pause, during which the attorney, with his hand upon the dock, whispered with his client, and shook his head. I afterwards had it from that gentleman, that the prisoner's first affrighted words to him were, *"At all hazards challenge that man!"* But that, as he would give no reason for it, and admitted that he had not even known my name until he heard it called and I appeared, it was not done.

Both on the ground already explained, that I wish to avoid reviving the unwholesome memory of that Murderer, and also because a detailed account of his long trial is by no means indispensable to my narrative, I shall confine myself closely to such incidents in the ten days and nights during which we, the Jury, were kept together, as directly bear on my own curious personal experience. It is in that, and not in the Murderer, that I seek to interest my reader. It is to that, and not to a page of the Newgate Calendar, that I beg attention.

I was chosen Foreman of the Jury. On the second morning of the trial, after evidence had been taken for two hours (I heard the church clocks strike), happening to cast my eyes over my brother jurymen, I found an inexplicable difficulty in counting them[4]. I counted them several times, yet always with the same difficulty. In short, I made them one too many.

---

[1] There are hints here at more supernatural guidance

[2] Tan are strips of tree bark which are used to produce tannin to convert hide into leather. This and straw were spread over cobblestones to lessen the noise of traffic within the courtroom

[3] As the jurors are vetted, the legal teams have the right to challenge any of them – to question their suitability based on bias

[4] A formal step taken to ensure that all jurors are present

I touched[1] the brother jurymen whose place was next me, and I whispered to him, "Oblige me by counting us." He looked surprised by the request, but turned his head and counted. "Why," says he, suddenly, "we are Thirt-; but no, it's not possible. No. We are twelve[2]."

According to my counting that day, we were always right in detail, but in the gross we were always one too many. There was no appearance — no figure — to account for it; but I had now an inward foreshadowing of the figure that was surely coming.

The Jury were housed at the London Tavern. We all slept in one large room on separate tables, and we were constantly in the charge and under the eye of the officer sworn to hold us in safe-keeping. I see no reason for suppressing the real name of that officer. He was intelligent, highly polite, and obliging, and (I was glad to hear) much respected in the City. He had an agreeable presence, good eyes, enviable black whiskers, and a fine sonorous voice. His name was Mr. Harker.

When we turned into our twelve beds at night, Mr. Harker's bed was drawn across the door[3]. On the night of the second day, not being disposed to lie down, and seeing Mr. Harker sitting on his bed, I went and sat beside him, and offered him a pinch of snuff. As Mr. Harker's hand touched mine in taking it from my box, a peculiar shiver crossed him[4], and he said, "Who is this?"

Following Mr. Harker's eyes, and looking along the room, I saw again the figure I expected — the second of the two men who had gone down Piccadilly. I rose, and advanced a few steps; then stopped, and looked round at Mr. Harker. He was quite unconcerned, laughed, and said in a pleasant way, "I thought for a moment we had a thirteenth juryman, without a bed. But I see it is the moonlight."

Making no revelation to Mr. Harker, but inviting him to take a walk with me to the end of the room, I watched what the figure did. It stood for a few moments by the bedside of each of my eleven brother jurymen, close to the pillow. It always went to the right-hand side of the bed, and always passed out crossing the foot of the next bed. It seemed, from the action of the head, merely to look down pensively at each recumbent figure. It took no notice of me, or of my bed, which was that nearest to Mr. Harker's. It seemed to go out where the moonlight came in, through a high window, as by an aerial flight of stairs.

Next morning at breakfast, it appeared that everybody present had dreamed of the murdered man last night, except myself and Mr. Harker[5].

---

[1] The psychic touch returns

[2] M. R. James adored this subtle enchantment, and in several of his stories included incidents where a person miscounted the number of people in a room or carriage, etc., while the reader suspects that the extra head counted is that of a malicious and predatory ghost

[3] Harker's role is to prevent jury tampering or attacks on the juror's persons

[4] Once more we see the psychic touch in action

[5] The spirit had no need to influence them since it had been seen walking about the room inoculating the jurors against forgetting him. Indeed, this seems to be the

I now felt as convinced that the second man who had gone down Piccadilly was the murdered man (so to speak), as if it had been borne into my comprehension by his immediate testimony. But even this took place, and in a manner for which I was not at all prepared.

On the fifth day of the trial, when the case for the prosecution was drawing to a close, a miniature of the murdered man, missing from his bedroom upon the discovery of the deed, and afterwards found in a hiding-place where the Murderer had been seen digging, was put in evidence. Having been identified by the witness under examination, it was handed up to the Bench, and thence handed down to be inspected by the Jury. As an officer in a black gown was making his way with it across to me, the figure of the second man who had gone down Piccadilly impetuously started from the crowd, caught the miniature from the officer, and gave it to me with his own hands[1], at the same time saying, in a low and hollow tone — before I saw the miniature, which was in a locket[2] — *"I was younger then, and my face was not then drained of blood[3]."* It also came between me and the brother juryman to whom I would have given the miniature, and between him and the brother juryman to whom he would have given it, and so passed it on through the whole of our number, and back into my possession. Not one of them, however, detected this.

---

specter's game: he is concerned that if the humanity of his murder is forgotten, then it will be easy to acquit his murderer. It is crucial that none of the jurors enter the trial distracted by their outside lives, bored, annoyed, or daydreaming. They must focus on the loss of life and the tragic horror of a man's death

[1] What is happening here suddenly becomes clearer: the ghost is literally interceding on his own behalf, subverting the mortal agents of justice out of distrust. He doesn't entrust the officer to adequately convey the message of the miniature – evidence which the prosecution is using to establish guilt, but which the ghost hopes will remind the jury of his humanity, and of the tragedy of his murder. While the officer calmly shows it to the jurors, the ghost all but snatches it from his hand and thrusts it in their faces: "I was alive, and now I am dead; have pity on my lost life," he seems to cry out. By literally maneuvering the officer's hands – or at the very least covering them with his own – the ghost steps into the world of mortal affairs and tries to subvert the miscarriage of justice that he seems to fear if he does not intervene supernaturally

[2] Compare to the gold locket found on Courvoisier's person

[3] This desperate plea is not a logical appeal to the murderer's guilt, nor to the importance of the evidence; instead, it is an emotional appeal – one of pathos rather than logos – to the dead man's former vitality and lost life. He hopes that they will not just focus on carrying out a civic duty, but that they will become humanly embroiled in an outrageous loss of life – that they would not be so focused on avenging his death, but that they would come to understand, feel, and mourn the gravity of his untimely slaughter: "look at me; I was a man like you are – alive and well, not hideous or maimed, and now I am no longer. Have pity on me and remember me..."

At table, and generally when we were shut up together in Mr. Harker's custody, we had from the first naturally discussed the day's proceedings a good deal. On that fifth day, the case for the prosecution being closed, and we having that side of the question in a completed shape before us, our discussion was more animated and serious. Among our number was a vestryman[1] — the densest idiot I have ever seen at large — who met the plainest evidence with the most preposterous objections, and who was sided with by two flabby parochial parasites; all the three impanelled from a district so delivered over to Fever that they ought to have been upon their own trial for five hundred Murders[2]. When these mischievous blockheads were at their loudest, which was towards midnight, while some of us were already preparing for bed, I again saw the murdered man. He stood grimly behind them, beckoning to me. On my going towards them, and striking into the conversation, he immediately retired[3]. This was the beginning of a separate series of appearances, confined to that long room in which we were confined. Whenever a knot of my brother jurymen laid their heads together, I saw the head of the murdered man among
theirs. Whenever their comparison of notes was going against him, he would solemnly and irresistibly beckon to me[4].

It will be borne in mind that down to the production of the miniature, on the fifth day of the trial, I had never seen the Appearance in Court. Three changes occurred now that we entered on the case for the defence. Two of them I will

---

[1] A member his local church's vestry, or governing body. Often the church vestry was just as political as it was ecclesiastical, having influence on local politics, and such a person would in some circumstances be more comparable to a city councilman than to a church deacon

[2] The area of country where these three come from is ravaged by (presumably) Typhoid fever, and the narrator suspects that they are partially to blame. Typhoid could be prevented by washing hands after bowel movements and before touching food, using clean utensils, and sterilizing medical equipment. But no one was safe if sewage was introduced into sources of drinking water. Typhoid was one of a class of diseases that the Victorians termed "filth diseases," called bowel fever by some, and many among the educated middle classes blamed minor functionaries and local government boards for refusing to educate the poor, clean the rivers, instigate sanitation measures, or updating sewage disposal techniques

[3] The ghost is allayed when the narrator takes over for him as an active agent. Dickens seems to be suggesting that the supernatural must intervene when the mortal world is complacent and disinterested in justice, but that once living men inspire themselves with compassion, generosity, and outrage, the need for divine intervention passes, or to quote Burke, "all that is necessary for the triumph of evil is that good men do nothing"

[4] He begins to step back in some cases – letting the narrator actively disturb the complacency and gullibility of his fellow jurors – but the ghost is far from retired, and is still quite worried that the channels of human justice will be clogged and polluted with stupidity and apathy

mention together, first. The figure was now in Court continually, and it never there addressed itself to me, but always to the person who was speaking at the time. For instance: the throat of the murdered man had been cut straight across. In the opening speech for the defence, it was suggested that the deceased might have cut his own throat. At that very moment, the figure, with its throat in the dreadful condition referred to (this it had concealed before), stood at the speaker's elbow, motioning across and across its windpipe, now with the right hand, now with the left, vigorously suggesting to the speaker himself the impossibility of such a wound having been self-inflicted by either hand[1]. For another instance: a witness to character, a woman, deposed to the prisoner's being the most amiable of mankind. The figure at that instant stood on the floor before her, looking her full in the face, and pointing out the prisoner's evil countenance with an extended arm and an outstretched finger[2].

The third change now to be added impressed me strongly as the most marked and striking of all. I do not theorise upon it; I accurately state it, and there leave it. Although the Appearance was not itself perceived by those whom it addressed, its coming close to such persons was invariably attended by some trepidation or disturbance on their part. It seemed to me as if it were prevented, by laws to which I was not amenable, from fully revealing itself to others, and yet as if it could invisibly, dumbly, and darkly overshadow their minds. When the leading counsel for the defence suggested that hypothesis of suicide, and the figure stood at the learned gentleman's elbow, frightfully sawing at its severed throat, it is undeniable that the counsel faltered in his speech, lost for a few seconds the thread of his ingenious discourse, wiped his forehead with his handkerchief, and turned extremely pale[3]. When the witness to character was confronted by the Appearance, her eyes most certainly did follow the direction of its pointed finger, and rest in great hesitation and trouble upon the prisoner's face. Two additional illustrations will suffice. On the eighth day of the trial, after the pause which was every day made early in the afternoon for a few minutes' rest and refreshment, I came back into Court with the rest of the Jury some little time before the return of the Judges. Standing up in the box and looking about me, I thought the figure was not there, until, chancing to raise my eyes to the gallery, I saw it bending forward, and

---

[1] Lord Russell William was so badly mutilated that he was nearly decapitated by the razor strokes. If his injuries are – as I suspect – identical to those of the fictional victim, then suicide would be a ridiculous, ludicrous theory

[2] Previously happy to urge the jurors forward into recognizing the way to equity, the ghost is now forced to deal with perjurers, hacks, and lying character witnesses. In these cases he can only hope to haunt their consciences, confound their logic, and expose their lies through guilt and shame. If the jurors dreamed of the dead man at night, just imagine how awful this woman's nightmares will be when she goes home from court

[3] The ghost may have appeared to him in a vision at this moment, or it may simply have been an act of psychically-induced guilt, but in any case, his physical response to what we must presume to be the ghost's interference is fairly severe

leaning over a very decent woman[1], as if to assure itself whether the Judges had resumed their seats or not. Immediately afterwards that woman screamed, fainted, and was carried out. So with the venerable, sagacious, and patient Judge who conducted the trial. When the case was over, and he settled himself and his papers to sum up, the murdered man, entering by the Judges' door, advanced to his Lordship's desk, and looked eagerly over his shoulder at the pages of his notes which he was turning. A change came over his Lordship's face; his hand stopped; the peculiar shiver, that I knew so well, passed over him; he faltered, "Excuse me, gentlemen, for a few moments. I am somewhat oppressed by the vitiated[2] air;" and did not recover until he had drunk a glass of water.

Through all the monotony of six of those interminable ten days — the same Judges and others on the bench, the same Murderer in the dock, the same lawyers at the table, the same tones of question and answer rising to the roof of the court, the same scratching of the Judge's pen, the same ushers going in and out, the same lights kindled at the same hour when there had been any natural light of day, the same foggy curtain outside the great windows when it was foggy, the same rain pattering and dripping when it was rainy, the same footmarks of turnkeys and prisoner day after day on the same sawdust, the same keys locking and unlocking the same heavy doors[3] — through all the wearisome monotony which made me feel as if I had been Foreman of the Jury for a vast cried of time, and Piccadilly had flourished coevally with Babylon, the murdered man never lost one trace of his distinctness in my eyes, nor was he at any moment less distinct than anybody else[1].

---

[1] Her decency is important: by this Dickens means to say that she exhibited a gentility that assured the narrator of her breeding – whether wealthy or poor, she appears to be a lady of discretion, restraint, and ladylike composure. It would not be uncommon for a sensational court trial to be attended by all kinds and classes of people, and the more sensational, the more likelihood of attracting unsavory sorts of citizens. What Dickens wants to underscore is that the woman was not drunk or mad

[2] Spoiled, rotten. During any season the Old Bailey would be a stinking atmosphere ripe with body odor, steam, and pollution from the chimneys and sewers of London, and since it took place near the winter, it would also reek of oil, smoke, and soot

[3] Dickens drones on and on about the monotonous courtroom for a very good reason: he is underscoring the lack of humanity and passion that sedates modern law, causing apathy to blow into the Old Bailey like sedating smoke into a beehive, and like those bees who fall asleep when smoke trickles into their precious fortresses, the jurors and the judges and the lawyers and the bailiffs are susceptible to a lethargy that renders their venomous stings useless. The ghost is aware of this, and his intrusion into the sleepy courtroom is perhaps the only thing which prevents the barbed stinger of justice from failing to punish his murderer. Amidst all the monotony and all the laziness and all the stupidity and all the corruption and all the perjury and all the deceit, the ghost manages to find a living agent in our narrator, and hand in hand they combat the drowsy influence of an apathetic society

else[1]. I must not omit, as a matter of fact, that I never once saw the Appearance which I call by the name of the murdered man look at the Murderer. Again and again I wondered, "Why does he not?" But he never did[2].

Nor did he look at me, after the production of the miniature, until the last closing minutes of the trial arrived. We retired to consider, at seven minutes before ten at night. The idiotic vestryman and his two parochial parasites gave us so much trouble that we twice returned into Court to beg to have certain extracts from the Judge's notes re-read. Nine of us had not the smallest doubt about those passages, neither, I believe, had any one in the Court; the dunder-headed triumvirate, having no idea but obstruction, disputed them for that very reason. At length we prevailed, and finally the Jury returned into Court at ten minutes past twelve.

The murdered man at that time stood directly opposite the Jury-box, on the other side of the Court. As I took my place, his eyes rested on me with great attention; he seemed satisfied, and slowly shook a great gray veil, which he carried

---

[1] Indeed, his humanity and the horror of his abbreviated life and potential are not lost to the narrator – not abstracted or distanced just because of his being dead and buried. To the narrator, the dead man may in fact be the most vivid and vital of all the court's occupants, because his life was the one most affected by the crime, and it is because of him that they are there at all. The narrator never loses sight of the murdered man, and as a result, never loses sight of his civic mission to prevent his death from becoming just another forgotten and unresolved tragedy

[2] In veridical narratives of ghosts in courtrooms (the genre is vastly stocked) from this time period and the previous two centuries, ghosts are usually depicted as stalking their killers, choking them with ghostly hands, glowering at them from the stalls, or hovering angrily over them. Dickens refuses to have his ghost condescend to these theatrics. Instead of focusing on the killer, he is principally concerned with his own legacy – reminding the jurors and spectators of his life and loss. As a result, the ghost does what the families of victims often do in sensational trials: they bemoan the celebrity of the perpetrator and urge the public to focus on the victims, not their malefactor. Serial killers certainly develop a cult of sensationalism and become household names – Dahmer, Bundy, BTK, Jack the Ripper – while their victims are killed time over time again when their names, faces, and lives are forgotten and their murderers ascend into public immortality. Dickens ghost hopes to avoid this fate, turning the thoughts of the courtroom spectators to his loss, not to his killer

on his arm for the first time, over his head and whole form[1]. As I gave in our verdict, "Guilty," the veil collapsed, all was gone, and his place was empty[2].

The Murderer, being asked by the Judge, according to usage, whether he had anything to say before sentence of Death should be passed upon him[3], indistinctly muttered something which was described in the leading newspapers of the following day as "a few rambling, incoherent, and half-audible words, in which he was understood to complain that he had not had a fair trial, because the Foreman of the Jury was prepossessed against him[4]." The remarkable declaration that he really made was this: "*MY LORD, I KNEW I WAS A DOOMED MAN, WHEN THE FOREMAN OF MY JURY CAME INTO THE BOX. MY LORD, I KNEW HE WOULD NEVER LET ME OFF, BECAUSE,*

---

[1] While it is traditional for ghosts to be sheeted in veils, shrouds, or cloaks, this specter has appeared just as he was in life. Now that his justice is being delivered, he prepares himself to cross over to the supernatural world – "through the veil," as the expression goes. There is also the added symbolism of the judge's black cap: when a judge passes capital sentence upon a prisoner, he places a black cloth atop his head

[2] Appeased by justice, the ghost vanishes into the hereafter: "his place was empty." The narrator's choice of words is interesting, since they seem to dwell on the gap left after his disappearance. Apparently the phantom's appeals to remember him have worked, and his living agent continues to sense an unoccupied place in society where the man's spirit used to dwell. To borrow a similar sentiment of tangible loss from another tale: "I see a vacant seat in the poor chimney-corner, and a crutch without an owner, carefully preserved..."

[3] Traditionally the condemned man was given a chance to appeal to the judge before he passed sentence of death, and it was technically within his power to overrule the jury's recommendation and to commute his sentence based on the prisoner's appeal. The tradition "according to usage," however, was essentially that: a matter of usage done according to tradition, but without any real chance of affecting a change in the inevitable sentencing

[4] Apathetic and disinterested like the majority of humanity (as Dickens depicts it in this tale), the newspapers skim over the prisoner's statement and miss the incredible importance of his claim

---

"To be taken with a grain of salt." The phrase suggests that the morsel about to be swallowed would not be palatable without some cynicism, humor, or other allowance. It also suggests a farce, a fantasy, or a flight of fancy. And this, I believe, is what Dickens' original title implied. Like *"To be Read at Dusk,"* Dickens refers his readership to the optimal condition for understanding the text. In this case, it is to suspend belief, judgment, or critique for a moment, and to enjoy a fantasy. The dream he projects is one in which the universe steps in to correct the mistakes of bumbling clerks, electees, officials, judges, rogues, criminals, idiots, and whole seas of unchecked corruption. It is a cosmos that permits the laws of nature to be suspended – the very definition of supernaturalism – in order that justice and right might be served. The tale is a relative of *"The Lawyer and the Ghost"* in that it uses a preternatural experience to highlight a foible of natural life. Like the ghost who is more socially mobile after death and the poor wretch who envies him, the specter in the courtroom corrects for the stupidity of the jury, the idiocy of the jurists, and the corruption of the witnesses. And eventually our narrator joins the spirit, appearing himself at the criminal's bedside. What Dickens suggests here is that we have the ability to do what the ghost does – to rise above our bumbling, mortal situation and interfere with the status quo. After all, not only did his specter divert the course of events, but the living narrator acted in them, too, presaging the criminal's doom and

---

[1] Ambiguous ghosts are Dickens' favorite. In "To be Read at Dusk" the ghosts include living people, dying people, dead people, and possibly dead people. In "The Signalman," the ghost is not really a ghost so much as a weird vision, faceless and vague. Here we have a man who is thoroughly alive (make no mistake, this isn't a *Sixth Sense* ending: the narrator is not also a ghost – in the conventional sense) making a supernatural appearance without being aware of it. Ghosts to Dickens are not the spirits of the dead; they are the shadows of truth – the projections of reality – which may in some cases be the souls of the departed or other supernatural elementals, but there is no requirement in his fiction that a ghost (or any other such being) be a clear cut dead spirit

[2] Dickens adores parallelism (as we see in "To be Read at Dusk"), and we see here how the ghost found an agent among the living, and the agent among the living himself became a ghost. Just as the murder victim returned from death as a phantom, his living helpmate projected (before his own death) the form of a phantom. Dickens demonstrates how the living can be just as impactful as a ghost, if only they would care enough. We wouldn't need ghosts to influence jurors, intimidate perjurers, or muddle defense lawyers if those people would take the initiative and live earnest, caring lives – we would then be our own ghosts of vengeance, just as the narrator became one himself

making intellectual decisions which lead to that turn of events. Otherwise, the only suspect – and the favorite of the papers – would have escaped without paying so much as a fine. But Dickens warns us – take it with a dash of realism, because far too often a situation like this is without guiding spirits, without moral inference, without mindful justice, and without hope. As a brief aside, this tale was a tremendous influence to M. R. James, who adored Dickens ("Count Magnus," "A Warning to the Curious," "Story of a Disappearance and an Appearance," and "Casting the Runes," include wry nods to the tale, but it is "Martin's Close" that is its unmistakable descendent) and to Le Fanu, whose "Mr Justice Harbottle" contains more than one clear reference to Dickens' story.

ON June 9, 1865 at 3:13 in the afternoon, an elderly Charles Dickens was travelling by train with his mistress and her mother in southeastern England when the Folkestone-to-London train derailed near Staplehurst due to a signalman's negligence. The Staplehurst Rail Crash took the lives of ten and left forty injured – some of whom died in Dickens' arms. The author was traumatized. He lost his voice for two weeks afterward, and avoided trains with phobic anxiety. Dying five years later on June 9, 1870, Dickens, as his son stated, "never fully recovered" from the shock. Written a year after the disaster, this cathartic ghost tale features a responsible signalman haunted in an emotionally exhaustive sense by Dickens' own wasting phantom: the helplessness to save life in spite of one's best efforts. The titular railroadman's angst mirrors Dickens' eerily. He is a man who accepts his unnecessarily menial role in society, not daring to change his station or aspire to better himself. "The Signal-Man" is a grim and chilling study both in man's desperate inability to alter the fates of others, and in his stubborn unwillingness to affect the one life which he may reasonably hope to better, or even save: his own.

The Signal Man[1]
{1866}

"HALLOA! BELOW THERE[2]!"

When he[3] heard a voice thus calling to him, he was standing at the door of his box[4], with a flag in his hand, furled round its short pole. One would have thought, considering the nature of the ground, that he could not have doubted from what quarter the voice came; but instead of looking up to where I stood on the top of the steep cutting[5] nearly over his head, he turned himself about, and looked down the Line. There was something remarkable in his manner of doing so, though I could not have said for my life what. But I know it was remarkable

---

[1] An employee of the railroad transport network who operates the signals from a signal box overlooking the rails in order to control the movement of trains

[2] "Bellow _there_" – Immediately, separation and isolation are thematically introduced

[3] Although the story is told in first person, it begins in third – the signalman is instantly made the tale's focus – a solitary man who is the object rather than the subject of human society

[4] Usually a small brick building with large windows on three sides, elevated high over the tracks to allow the signalman a means of warmth, shelter, and perspective, allowing him to see the rails in both directions. From here he operates mechanical (telegram signals raised by pulleys) and manual (flags and colored lanterns) signals in order to direct engineers or warn of danger. Bells engaged by passing locomotives communicated when a train was approaching, and telegraphs communicated between signal boxes down the line and from conductors' cabooses

[5] A hill or rock formation that has been transfixed (or "cut through") to allow for a narrow road, canal, or railway track to pass through an otherwise impassible landscape

enough to attract my notice, even though his figure was foreshortened and shadowed, down in the deep trench, and mine was high above him, so steeped in the glow of an angry sunset[1], that I had shaded my eyes with my hand before I saw him at all.

"Halloa! Below!"

From looking down the Line, he turned himself about again, and, raising his eyes, saw my figure high above him.

"Is there any path by which I can come down and speak to you?"

He looked up at me without replying, and I looked down at him without pressing him too soon with a repetition of my idle question. Just then there came a vague vibration in the earth and air[2], quickly changing into a violent pulsation, and an oncoming rush that caused me to start back, as though it had force to draw me down. When such vapour as rose to my height from this rapid train had passed me, and was skimming away over the landscape, I looked down again, and saw him refurling the flag he had shown while the train went by.

I repeated my inquiry. After a pause, during which he seemed to regard me with fixed attention, he motioned with his rolled-up flag towards a point on my level, some two or three hundred yards distant. I called down to him, "All right!" and made for that point. There, by dint of looking closely about me, I found a rough zigzag descending path notched out, which I followed.

The cutting was extremely deep, and unusually precipitate[3]. It was made through a clammy stone, that became oozier and wetter as I went down. For these reasons, I found the way long enough to give me time to recall a singular air of reluctance or compulsion[4] with which he had pointed out the path.

When I came down low enough upon the zigzag descent to see him again, I saw that he was standing between the rails on the way by which the train had lately passed, in an attitude as if he were waiting for me to appear. He had his left hand at his chin, and that left elbow rested on his right hand, crossed over his breast. His attitude was one of such expectation and watchfulness that I stopped a moment, wondering at it.

I resumed my downward way, and stepping out upon the level of the railroad, and drawing nearer to him, saw that he was a dark, sallow man, with a dark beard and rather heavy eyebrows[5]. His post was in as solitary and dismal a place as ever I saw. On either side, a dripping-wet wall of jagged stone, excluding all view but a

---

[1] Sunsets are usually typified as beautiful – sublime at the worst – and seen as having a spiritual, even religious quality. That the sunset is "angry" informs us of the manner of universe that this tale is set in: hostile, indifferent, malicious

[2] The very elements – earth and air, physical and psychical, material and spiritual – are disturbed in this chaotic environment where industry has violated nature

[3] Sudden, steep – it is difficult to reach this sad, isolated man in his spiritual banishment

[4] The signalman is comfortable in his alienation – resistant to accepting company

[5] An earthy, almost underworldly appearance – his exterior matches his surroundings, indicating the nature of his spirit: remote and hidden

strip of sky[1]; the perspective one way only a crooked prolongation of this great dungeon; the shorter perspective in the other direction terminating in a gloomy red light[2], and the gloomier entrance to a black tunnel[3], in whose massive architecture there was a barbarous, depressing, and forbidding air. So little sunlight ever found its way to this spot, that it had an earthy, deadly smell; and so much cold wind rushed through it, that it struck chill to me, as if I had left the natural world.

Before he stirred, I was near enough to him to have touched him. Not even then removing his eyes from mine, he stepped back one step, and lifted his hand.

This was a lonesome post to occupy (I said), and it had riveted my attention when I looked down from up yonder. A visitor was a rarity, I should suppose; not an unwelcome rarity, I hoped? In me, he merely saw a man who had been shut up within narrow limits all his life, and who, being at last set free, had a newly-awakened interest in these great works. To such purpose I spoke to him; but I am far from sure of the terms I used; for, besides that I am not happy in opening any conversation, there was something in the man that daunted me.

He directed a most curious look towards the red light near the tunnel's mouth, and looked all about it, as if something were missing from it, and then looked at me.

That light was part of his charge? Was it not?

He answered in a low voice,—"Don't you know it is[4]?"

The monstrous thought came into my mind, as I perused the fixed eyes and the saturnine[5] face, that this was a spirit, not a man. I have speculated since, whether there may have been infection in his mind[6].

In my turn, I stepped back. But in making the action, I detected in his eyes some latent fear of me. This put the monstrous thought to flight.

"You look at me," I said, forcing a smile, "as if you had a dread of me." "I was doubtful," he returned, "whether I had seen you before." "Where?"

He pointed to the red light he had looked at.

"There?" I said.

Intently watchful of me, he replied (but without sound), "Yes."

"My good fellow, what should I do there? However, be that as it may, I never was there, you may swear."

---

[1] Read: heaven, spiritual health, transcendence of the soul over sin, dread, and misery

[2] A hellish tint suggesting blood and damnation -- the only light (read: illumination, truth, spiritual clarity) in this gravelike place comes from a soullessly practical, industrial tool

[3] Symbolic of the unconscious, the cosmic void

[4] The exchange is bizarre and redolent with subtextual meaning. The narrator questions the signalman's responsibility for the manufactured illumination, and the operator responds defensively, asserting his ownership of and comfort with the subterranean world

[5] Gloomy, morose

[6] This questioning of the signalman's sanity casts him as a somewhat unreliable narrator

"I think I may," he rejoined. "Yes; I am sure I may."

His manner cleared, like my own. He replied to my remarks with readiness, and in well-chosen words. Had he much to do there? Yes; that was to say, he had enough responsibility to bear; but exactness and watchfulness were what was required of him[1], and of actual work—manual labour—he had next to none. To change that signal, to trim those lights, and to turn this iron handle now and then, was all he had to do under that head. Regarding those many long and lonely hours of which I seemed to make so much, he could only say that the routine of his life had shaped itself into that form, and he had grown used to it. He had taught himself a language down here,—if only to know it by sight, and to have formed his own crude ideas of its pronunciation, could be called learning it[2]. He had also worked at fractions and decimals, and tried a little algebra; but he was, and had been as a boy, a poor hand at figures. Was it necessary for him when on duty always to remain in that channel of damp air, and could he never rise into the sunshine from between those high stone walls? Why, that depended upon times and circumstances[3]. Under some conditions there would be less upon the Line than under others, and the same held good as to certain hours of the day and night. In bright weather, he did choose occasions for getting a little above these lower shadows; but, being at all times liable to be called by his electric bell, and at such times listening for it with redoubled anxiety, the relief was less than I would suppose.

He took me into his box, where there was a fire, a desk for an official book in which he had to make certain entries, a telegraphic instrument with its dial, face, and needles, and the little bell of which he had spoken. On my trusting that he would excuse the remark that he had been well educated, and (I hoped I might say without offence) perhaps educated above that station[4], he observed that instances of slight incongruity[5] in such wise would rarely be found wanting among large bodies of men; that he had heard it was so in workhouses, in the police force, even in that last desperate resource, the army; and that he knew it was so, more or less,

---

[1] The signalman is a paragon of Victorian duty – a watchful, alert, industrious exemplar of British expectations for the lower-middle class and public servants. He attends to his duties unquestioningly, performing them with a passion that confines his soul to his work

[2] He has learned a language (likely French or German, possibly Italian), but only by sight; he has no expectations of speaking it to another human soul, only of reading the sterile print

[3] His physical, psychological, and spiritual well-being is restrained by the duties of his job, and he happily forfeits their care in the pursuit of his responsibilities

[4] Critically, the signalman has demonstrated that he is capable of elevating himself beyond his job. Having educated himself beyond the expectations of a minor railway functionary, he could – if he so chose – remove himself from the grave-like cutting

[5] Inappropriateness

in any great railway staff[1]. He had been, when young (if I could believe it, sitting in that hut,—he scarcely could), a student of natural philosophy[2], and had attended lectures; but he had run wild, misused his opportunities, gone down, and never risen again[3]. He had no complaint to offer about that. He had made his bed, and he lay upon it. It was far too late to make another[4]. All that I have here condensed he said in a quiet manner, with his grave, dark regards divided between me and the fire. He threw in the word, "Sir," from time to time, and especially when he referred to his youth,—as though to request me to understand that he claimed to be nothing but what I found him[5]. He was several times interrupted by the little bell, and had to read off messages, and send replies. Once he had to stand without the door, and display a flag as a train passed, and make some verbal communication to the driver. In the discharge of his duties, I observed him to be remarkably exact and vigilant, breaking off his discourse at a syllable, and remaining silent until what he had to do was done[6].

In a word, I should have set this man down as one of the safest of men to be employed in that capacity, but for the circumstance that while he was speaking to me he twice broke off with a fallen colour, turned his face towards the little bell when it did NOT ring, opened the door of the hut (which was kept shut to exclude the unhealthy damp), and looked out towards the red light near the mouth of the tunnel. On both of those occasions, he came back to the fire with the inexplicable air upon him which I had remarked, without being able to define, when we were so far asunder.

Said I, when I rose to leave him, "You almost make me think that I have met with a contented man."

(I am afraid I must acknowledge that I said it to lead him on[7].)

"I believe I used to be so," he rejoined, in the low voice in which he had first

---

[1] The signalman's excuse is that he is not an anomaly, and that his education would do him no good because plenty of equally knowledgable men continue to toil as lower middle class functionaries in the nation's service organizations

[2] The philosophical study of nature and the physical universe – in a word, science, but with an inclination towards theoretical philosophy

[3] A typical Dickensian character, the signalman has been diverted from a more personally and spiritually fulfilling life by the forces of society and the industrial revolution, and has become mired in a depressing and dehumanizing occupation that pits vital nature against cold industry

[4] Psychologists would say that the signalman has an exterior locus of power: he believes that he is at the mercy of a hostile world and that his actions to benefit himself will be useless. In short, he is a pessimist who resists any suggestion that he act to improve his life

[5] Although he is demonstrably more than a minion of the railway, he resists any possibilities

[6] Efficient, dutiful – an obedient underling to the class-conscious demands of society

[7] The signalman avoids honest conversation, so the narrator attempt to lure him into a dialog

spoken; "but I am troubled, sir, I am troubled."

He would have recalled the words if he could. He had said them, however, and I took them up quickly.

"With what? What is your trouble?"

"It is very difficult to impart, sir. It is very, very difficult to speak of. If ever you make me another visit, I will try to tell you."

"But I expressly intend to make you another visit. Say, when shall it be?" "I go off early in the morning, and I shall be on again at ten to-morrow night, sir."

"I will come at eleven."

He thanked me, and went out at the door with me. "I'll show my white light, sir," he said, in his peculiar low voice, "till you have found the way up. When you have found it, don't call out! And when you are at the top, don't call out!"

His manner seemed to make the place strike colder to me, but I said no more than, "Very well."

"And when you come down to-morrow night, don't call out! Let me ask you a parting question. What made you cry, 'Halloa! Below there!' to-night?"

"Heaven knows," said I. "I cried something to that effect—"

"Not to that effect, sir. Those were the very words. I know them well." "Admit those were the very words. I said them, no doubt, because I saw you below."

"For no other reason?"

"What other reason could I possibly have?"

"You had no feeling that they were conveyed to you in any supernatural way?" "No."

He wished me good-night, and held up his light. I walked by the side of the down Line of rails (with a very disagreeable sensation of a train coming behind me[1]) until I found the path. It was easier to mount than to descend, and I got back to my inn without any adventure.

Punctual to my appointment, I placed my foot on the first notch of the zigzag next night, as the distant clocks were striking eleven. He was waiting for me at the bottom, with his white light on. "I have not called out," I said, when we came close together; "may I speak now?"

"By all means, sir."

"Good-night, then, and here's my hand." "Good-night, sir, and here's mine." With that we walked side by side to his box, entered it, closed the door, and sat down by the fire.

"I have made up my mind, sir," he began, bending forward as soon as we were seated, and speaking in a tone but a little above a whisper, "that you shall not have to ask me twice what troubles me. I took you for some one else yesterday

---

[1] A tremendously eerie and ominous experience the suggests the presence of a great, hurtling force of destruction lurking in the signalman's underworld, and prefiguring events to come

evening. That troubles me."

"That mistake?"

"No. That some one else." "Who is
it?"

"I don't know." "Like
me?"

"I don't know. I never saw the face. The left arm is across the face, and the right arm is waved,—violently waved. This way."

I followed his action with my eyes, and it was the action of an arm gesticulating, with the utmost passion and vehemence, "For God's sake, clear the way!"

"One moonlight night," said the man, "I was sitting here, when I heard a voice cry, 'Halloa! Below there!' I started up, looked from that door, and saw this. Some one else standing by the red light near the tunnel, waving as I just now showed you. The voice seemed hoarse with shouting, and it cried, 'Look out! Look out!' And then again, 'Halloa! Below there! Look out!' I caught up my lamp, turned it on red[1], and ran towards the figure, calling,

'What's wrong? What has happened? Where?' It stood just outside the blackness of the tunnel. I advanced so close upon it that I wondered at its keeping the sleeve across its eyes. I ran right up at it, and had my hand stretched out to pull the sleeve away, when it was gone."

"Into the tunnel?" said I.

"No. I ran on into the tunnel, five hundred yards. I stopped, and held my lamp above my head, and saw the figures of the measured distance, and saw the wet stains stealing down the walls and trickling through the arch. I ran out again faster than I had run in (for I had a mortal abhorrence of the place upon me[2]), and I looked all round the red light with my own red light, and I went up the iron ladder to the gallery atop of it, and I came down again, and ran back here. I telegraphed both ways[3], 'An alarm has been given. Is anything wrong?' The answer came back, both ways, 'All well.' "

Resisting the slow touch of a frozen finger tracing out my spine, I showed him how that this figure must be a deception of his sense of sight; and how that figures, originating in disease of the delicate nerves that minister to the functions of the eye[4], were known to have often troubled patients, some of whom had become conscious of the nature of their affliction, and had even proved it by

---

[1] A sign of warning or distress to oncoming trains – *"Beware!"*

[2] Very telling – the signalman, despite his protests of contentment, is made tremendously uncomfortable by this symbolic reminder of the unconscious – replete with regrets, fears, anxieties, and anger

[3] Separated by a matter of several miles, signal boxes lined the railroad. The signalman telegraphs his colleagues on either side, but neither reports trouble

[4] Politely, and sugarcoated with jargon, the narrator advances his theory that the signalman might be going insane

experiments upon themselves. "As to an imaginary cry," said I, "do but listen for a moment to the wind in this unnatural valley while we speak so low, and to the wild harp[1] it makes of the telegraph wires."

That was all very well, he returned, after we had sat listening for a while, and he ought to know something of the wind and the wires,—he who so often passed long winter nights there, alone and watching. But he would beg to remark that he had not finished.

I asked his pardon, and he slowly added these words, touching my arm,—

"Within six hours after the Appearance, the memorable accident on this Line happened, and within ten hours the dead and wounded were brought along through the tunnel over the spot where the figure had stood.[2]"

A disagreeable shudder crept over me, but I did my best against it. It was not to be denied, I rejoined, that this was a remarkable coincidence, calculated deeply to impress his mind. But it was unquestionable that remarkable coincidences did continually occur, and they must be taken into account in dealing with such a subject. Though to be sure I must admit, I added (for I thought I saw that he was going to bring the objection to bear upon me), men of common sense did not allow much for coincidences in making the ordinary calculations of life.

He again begged to remark that he had not finished.

I again begged his pardon for being betrayed into interruptions.

"This," he said, again laying his hand upon my arm, and glancing over his shoulder with hollow eyes, "was just a year ago. Six or seven months passed, and I had recovered from the surprise and shock, when one morning, as the day was breaking, I, standing at the door, looked towards the red light, and saw the spectre

---

[1] An Aeolian harp – famously the subject of Coleridge's "Ode" – is a form of wind chime that creates pleasant notes as the wind crosses its strings ; it is associated with the idea of nature producing designs of spirit (much like nature appears to be producing the signalman's apparition out of thin air)

[2] On 25 August 1861, three locomotives left Brighton in southern England within only minutes of one another. As a result of complicated miscommunications between the signalmen at the opposite ends of a tunnel through which all three were due to travel, the bloodiest train wreck in British history up to that date occurred. Not wanting the second train to plow into the first as both flew into the Clayton Tunnel, the first signalman urged the second train that a train was already in the tunnel by rushing out of his box and flagging the engineer down. But both trains shuttled into the tunnel despite his warnings. The signalman on the other side of the tunnel, seeing the first train pass through safely, signaled all clear, which the first signalman took to mean both engines had made it out. Tragically, the second train had seen the flag in time to stop before hitting the first, and was in the act of backing out of the tunnel. Thinking that both trains were cleared, the first signalman signaled "all-clear" to the third locomotive which plowed through the reversing second train, killing 23 and wounding 176. Many of the deaths were particularly gruesome, being caused by scalding from the steam or incineration from the coals from the obliterated engine that bored into the passenger cabins. This is almost certainly the event that inspired Dickens' first tragedy

again." He stopped, with a fixed look at me.

"Did it cry out?" "No. It was
silent."

"Did it wave its arm?"

"No. It leaned against the shaft of the light, with both hands before the face.
Like this."

Once more I followed his action with my eyes. It was an action of
mourning. I have seen such an attitude in stone figures on tombs.

"Did you go up to it?"

"I came in and sat down, partly to collect my thoughts, partly because it had
turned me faint. When I went to the door again, daylight was above me, and the
ghost was gone."

"But nothing followed? Nothing came of this?"

He touched me on the arm with his forefinger twice or thrice giving a ghastly
nod each time:—

"That very day, as a train came out of the tunnel, I noticed, at a carriage
window on my side, what looked like a confusion of hands and heads, and
something waved. I saw it just in time to signal the driver, Stop! He shut off, and
put his brake on, but the train drifted past here a hundred and fifty yards or more.
I ran after it, and, as I went along, heard terrible screams and cries. A beautiful
young lady had died instantaneously in one of the compartments, and was
brought in here, and laid down on this floor between us."

Involuntarily I pushed my chair back, as I looked from the boards at which
he pointed to himself.

"True, sir. True. Precisely as it happened, so I tell it you."

I could think of nothing to say, to any purpose, and my mouth was very dry.
The wind and the wires took up the story with a long lamenting wail.

He resumed. "Now, sir, mark this, and judge how my mind is troubled. The
spectre came back a week ago. Ever since, it has been there, now and again, by fits
and starts."

"At the light?"

"At the Danger-light[1]."

"What does it seem to do?"

He repeated, if possible with increased passion and vehemence, that
former gesticulation of, "For God's sake, clear the way!"

Then he went on. "I have no peace or rest for it. It calls to me, for many minutes

---

[1] In one sense, that the ghost haunts the danger-light is only natural – it is a harbinger of
danger. In other, it is more nuanced, laying the onus of responsibility at the feet of the
railway, the industrialism that has forged this subterranean hell by violating nature and
dehumanizing menial men like the signalman. The danger-light is the manufactured sun
of the railway – symbolically, its truth, its gospel – and the ghost haunts this "gospel" of
industrialism, blaming it for the tragedies – both physical and spiritual – that occur in
the bowels of the cutting

together, in an agonised manner, 'Below there! Look out! Look out!'
It stands waving to me. It rings my little bell—"

I caught at that. "Did it ring your bell yesterday evening when I was here, and you went to the door?"

"Twice."

"Why, see," said I, "how your imagination misleads you. My eyes were on the bell, and my ears were open to the bell, and if I am a living man, it did NOT ring at those times. No, nor at any other time, except when it was rung in the natural course of physical things by the station communicating with you."

He shook his head. "I have never made a mistake as to that yet, sir. I have never confused the spectre's ring with the man's. The ghost's ring is a strange vibration in the bell that it derives from nothing else, and I have not asserted that the bell stirs to the eye. I don't wonder that you failed to hear it. But I heard it."

"And did the spectre seem to be there, when you looked out?"

"It WAS there."

"Both times?"

He repeated firmly: "Both times."

"Will you come to the door with me, and look for it now?"

He bit his under lip as though he were somewhat unwilling, but arose. I opened the door, and stood on the step, while he stood in the doorway. There was the Danger-light. There was the dismal mouth of the tunnel. There were the high, wet stone walls of the cutting. There were the stars above them[1].

"Do you see it?" I asked him, taking particular note of his face. His eyes were prominent and strained, but not very much more so, perhaps, than my own had been when I had directed them earnestly towards the same spot.

"No," he answered. "It is not there."

"Agreed," said I.

We went in again, shut the door, and resumed our seats. I was thinking how best to improve this advantage, if it might be called one, when he took up the conversation in such a matter-of-course way, so assuming that there could be no serious question of fact between us, that I felt myself placed in the weakest of positions.

"By this time you will fully understand, sir," he said, "that what troubles me so dreadfully is the question, What does the spectre mean?"
I was not sure, I told him, that I did fully understand.

"What is its warning against?" he said, ruminating, with his eyes on the fire, and only by times turning them on me. "What is the danger? Where is the danger? There is danger overhanging somewhere on the Line. Some dreadful calamity will happen. It is not to be doubted this third time, after what has gone

---

[1] Stars, like daylight sky, symbolize spiritual health, transcendence, and heaven – something beyond reach in the miserable cutting

before. But surely this is a cruel haunting of *me*. What can *I* do[1]?"

He pulled out his handkerchief, and wiped the drops from his heated forehead.

"If I telegraph Danger, on either side of me, or on both, I can give no reason for it," he went on, wiping the palms of his hands. "I should get into trouble, and do no good. They would think I was mad. This is the way it would work,—Message: 'Danger! Take care!' Answer: 'What Danger? Where?' Message: 'Don't know. But, for God's sake, take care!' They would displace me. What else could they do?"

His pain of mind was most pitiable to see. It was the mental torture of a conscientious man, oppressed beyond endurance by an unintelligible responsibility involving life.

"When it first stood under the Danger-light," he went on, putting his dark hair back from his head, and drawing his hands outward across and across his temples in an extremity of feverish distress, "why not tell me where that accident was to happen,—if it must happen? Why not tell me how it could be averted,—if it could have been averted? When on its second coming it hid its face, why not tell me, instead, 'She is going to die. Let them keep her at home'? If it came, on those two occasions, only to show me that its warnings were true, and so to prepare me for the third, why not warn me plainly now? And I, Lord help me! A mere poor signal-man on this solitary station[2]! Why not go to somebody with credit to be believed, and power to act?"

When I saw him in this state, I saw that for the poor man's sake, as well as for the public safety[3], what I had to do for the time was to compose his mind. Therefore, setting aside all question of reality or unreality between us, I

---

[1] Overwhelmed by his sense of responsibility, the signalman is failing to understand that he cannot possibly be held responsible for all such things in a scenario such as this, but he takes his job duties seriously to the point of masochism, and languishes under the guilt that he projects onto himself from the standpoint of the railway company. It must surely be his fault, he reasons, because his sole task on earth is to ensure safety on the line. While his concern is certainly in part humanitarian, it is undoubtedly fueled by a sense of obligation and obedience to the company, from whom he derives his self-worth, identity, and soul

[2] The signalman's torments stem from his comfort in isolation: he does not ask to partake in the affairs of men, only to do his duty. But this self-banishment cannot protect him from the inevitability of being touched by human traumas and events. Emotion and social congress is, perhaps more than prevention, the message of the ghost. Remove yourself from here; resurrect yourself and rejoin the flock of mankind. As the poor man himself observes, there was absolutely no chance that he could have influenced the second tragedy – the ghost's appearance seems to serve more as an indictment of the society and culture, and as a call to re-humanize himself before he too is destroyed. The warning is unheeded

[3] If he is insane or maddened by anxiety, the next accident might be due to his negligence

represented to him that whoever thoroughly discharged his duty must do well, and that at least it was his comfort that he understood his duty, though he did not understand these confounding Appearances. In this effort I succeeded far better than in the attempt to reason him out of his conviction. He became calm; the occupations incidental to his post as the night advanced began to make larger demands on his attention: and I left him at two in the morning. I had offered to stay through the night, but he would not hear of it.

That I more than once looked back at the red light as I ascended the pathway, that I did not like the red light[1], and that I should have slept but poorly if my bed had been under it, I see no reason to conceal. Nor did I like the two sequences of the accident and the dead girl. I see no reason to conceal that either[2].

But what ran most in my thoughts was the consideration how ought I to act, having become the recipient of this disclosure[3]? I had proved the man to be intelligent, vigilant, painstaking, and exact; but how long might he remain so, in his state of mind[4]? Though in a subordinate position, still he held a most important trust, and would I (for instance) like to stake my own life on the chances of his continuing to execute it with precision?

Unable to overcome a feeling that there would be something treacherous in my communicating what he had told me to his superiors in the Company, without first being plain with himself and proposing a middle course to him, I ultimately resolved to offer to accompany him (otherwise keeping his secret for the present) to the wisest medical practitioner we could hear of in those parts, and to take his opinion. A change in his time of duty would come round next night, he had apprised me, and he would be off an hour or two after sunrise, and on again soon after sunset. I had appointed to return accordingly.

Next evening was a lovely evening, and I walked out early to enjoy it. The sun was not yet quite down when I traversed the field-path near the top of the deep cutting. I would extend my walk for an hour, I said to myself, half an hour on and half an hour back, and it would then be time to go to my signal-man's box.

Before pursuing my stroll, I stepped to the brink, and mechanically looked down, from the point from which I had first seen him. I cannot describe the thrill that seized upon me, when, close at the mouth of the tunnel, I saw the appearance of a man, with his left sleeve across his eyes, passionately waving his right arm.

The nameless horror that oppressed me passed in a moment, for in a moment I

---

[1] Note, the red light is absolutely not portrayed as a simple, innocuous prop. It is the symbol of the soul of an industrial nation that dehumanizes its citizens and violates the realm of nature (i.e., the cutting), and the narrator is sensitive to its sinister nature

[2] The narrator explains that he is not ashamed that he is unsettled by what might be a genuine haunting, and what – in either case – is certainly a series of tragedies

[3] He begins to inherit the signalman's crippling responsibility

[4] The menial workmen that keep the nation running are not robots or machinery, Dickens asserts: no, they are psychologically complicated, and may become infected by the dehumanizing contagion of their isolated existences

saw that this appearance of a man was a man indeed, and that there was a little group of other men, standing at a short distance, to whom he seemed to be rehearsing the gesture he made. The Danger-light was not yet lighted[1]. Against its shaft, a little low hut, entirely new to me, had been made of some wooden supports and tarpaulin. It looked no bigger than a bed.

With an irresistible sense that something was wrong,—with a flashing self-reproachful fear that fatal mischief had come of my leaving the man there, and causing no one to be sent to overlook or correct what he did,—I descended the notched path with all the speed I could make.

"What is the matter?" I asked the men "Signal-man[2] killed this morning, sir." "Not the man belonging to that box?" "Yes, sir."
"Not the man I know?"

"You will recognise him, sir, if you knew him," said the man who spoke for the others, solemnly uncovering his own head, and raising an end of the tarpaulin, "for his face is quite composed."

"O, how did this happen, how did this happen?" I asked, turning from one to another as the hut closed in again.

"He was cut down by an engine, sir. No man in England knew his work better[3]. But somehow he was not clear of the outer rail. It was just at broad day. He had struck the light, and had the lamp in his hand. As the engine came out of the tunnel, his back was towards her, and she cut him down. That man drove her, and was showing how it happened. Show the gentleman, Tom."

The man, who wore a rough dark dress, stepped back to his former place at the mouth of the tunnel.

"Coming round the curve in the tunnel, sir," he said, "I saw him at the end, like as if I saw him down a perspective-glass[4]. There was no time to check speed, and

---

[1] Almost as if its mission to destroy and squelch had been completed, the light is darkened

[2] Not "*The* signal-man," not "John (or Bob or Jack or Will) the Signal-man..." "Signal-man." His identity is seen as indivisible with his work. He is not viewed as a soul or a mind or a heart, but as a job. As "signal-man"

[3] It is no mistake that Dickens qualifies the signalman by his nation: he is described as one of the best of his kind in the entire nation – an exemplar of duty and responsibility – and yet he is mowed down like dry fodder by the machinery of his dehumanizing occupation. If this is the fate of the best in the country – to be tortured with self-doubt, anxiety, and misery – what then are the psychological and spiritual conditions of the rest of Victorian Britain's menials like?

[4] A mounted magnifying glass used to examine pictures, giving them a 3-D appearance. The tunnel objectifies the signalman – just as the first lines of the story do – framing him in its ravenous gaze. When looking into it, he saw only blackness, stains, and murk – the crude blots of a turbulent unconscious – but from the other end he (the supposed viewer) becomes the viewed. It brings to mind Nietzsche's famous comment "when you gaze long into an abyss, the abyss gazes also into you"

I knew him to be very careful. As he didn't seem to take heed of the whistle[1], I shut it off when we were running down upon him, and called to him as loud as I could call."

"What did you say?"

"I said, 'Below there! Look out! Look out! For God's sake, clear the way!'"
I started.

"Ah! it was a dreadful time, sir. I never left off calling to him. I put this arm before my eyes not to see, and I waved this arm to the last; but it was no use."

Without prolonging the narrative to dwell on any one of its curious circumstances more than on any other, I may, in closing it, point out the coincidence that the warning of the Engine-Driver included, not only the words which the unfortunate Signal-man had repeated to me as haunting him, but also the words which I myself—not he—had attached, and that only in my own mind, to the gesticulation he had imitated[2].

---

[1] Perhaps the most outstanding mystery of "The Signal-Man" is the scenario of the signalman's death. Why was he so effortlessly mowed down? What was he doing standing in the tunnel's mouth? It stands to reason that while the train barreled down the tunnel he was staring into its recesses. This is curious, since the signalman had "a mortal abhorrence" of the place, which symbolically represents the forbidding turbulence and desolation of his troubled unconscious. Staring fixedly into this dark mirror, possibly – though not necessarily – lured there by the apparition, the signalman is caught off guard while in an existential stupor. The signalman's sole solace in his diabolical surroundings is the assurance that his job matters, that his dedication and obedience have been done faithfully in pursuit of a noble calling. But the red light at the tunnel's face – like the green one across from Jay Gatsby's mansion – is a flase light, luring him onto the rocks of a crisis in purpose and identity, and we may wonder if the full import of this reality has dawned on him while gazing into the brooding tunnel. Fixatedly stunned by the reality of his alienation and cosmic insignificance, he is absorbed in existential terror when the train cuts him down

[2] His demise was the tragedy the ghost foretold, and critics have pointed out that while the previous disasters were beyond his control, this final one was indeed within his power to divert

DICKENS lures us into a Dantean purgatory where the abilities and realities of willpower, personal agency, and human transcendence are repeatedly called into question and affirmed – doubted and established. The signalman is simultaneously helpless and empowered, incapable of altering fate and amply armed to release himself from approaching destruction. This humble functionary – a man who willing works below the station of his intellectual ability, resisting upward mobility on the grounds of obligation – presents a chilling indictment of the British cult of status and duty. As he learned from his own life-rattling brush with death, Dickens avows that the only thing which we can be held responsible for in life is our own fate. The signalman tortures himself over his failure at duty, but fails to remove himself (in spite of his mobilizing capabilities) from his station, stubbornly standing at the helm of a floundering ship due to his stunting and self-deprecating fetish for duty. In his final moments, the nervous little man is run down while staring into the tunnel's black mouth – a void which suggests the other end of his purgatory, a hell which ultimately swallows him when he refuses to ascend to the available salvation yawning above him. The railroad-man is either unwilling or incapable of questioning the status of his menial station or the infallibility of his masters, and (as Dickens wants us to understand) a society which urges its best and brightest to settle for what they are allowed, will ultimately sink into a hell which devours individuality and crushes potential. Dickens does not hesitate to doubt the cruel riptides of life – as he learned at Staplehurst, it can suddenly surge and consume, and we cannot expect to save everyone or be responsible for the whims of fate – but he charges his readership: if you can save no one else, at least save yourself – ascend, transcend, rise above what life deals you, or be prepared to be destroyed; when we are given a chance to better our lives – when warnings and opportunities come – we must understand that the abyss is close behind.

About the Editor and Illustrator

Michael Grant Kellermeyer -- OTP's founder and chief editor -- is an English professor, bibliographer, illustrator, editor, critic, and author based in Fort Wayne, Indiana. He earned his Bachelor of Arts in English from Anderson University and his Master of Arts in Literature from Ball State University. He teaches college writing in Indiana where he enjoys playing violin, painting, hiking, and cooking.

Ever since watching Bing Crosby's *The Legend of Sleepy Hollow* as a three year old, Michael has been enraptured by the ghastly, ghoulish, and the unknown. Reading Great Illustrated Classics' abridged versions of classic horrors as a first grader, he quickly became enthralled with the horrific, and began accumulating a collection of unabridged classics; *Edgar Allan Poe's Forgotten Tales* and a copy of *The Legend of Sleepy Hollow* with an introduction by Charles L. Grant are among his most cherished possessions. Frequenting the occult section of the Berne Public Library, he scoured through anthologies and compendiums on ghostly lore.

It was here that he found two books which would be more influential to his tastes than any other: Henry Mazzeo's *Hauntings* (illustrated by the unparalleled Edward Gorey), and Barry Moser's *Great Ghost Stories*. It was while reading through these two collections during the Hallowe'en season of 2012 that Michael was inspired to honor the writers, tales, and mythologies he revered the most.

Oldstyle Tales Press was the result of that impulse. Its first title, *The Best Victorian Ghost Stories*, was published in September 2013, followed shortly by editions of *Frankenstein* and *The Annotated and Illustrated Edgar Allan Poe*.

In his free time, Michael enjoys straight razors, briarwood pipes, Classical music, jazz standards from the '20s to '60s, sea shanties, lemon wedges in his water, the films of Vincent Price and Stanley Kubrick, sandalwood shaving cream, freshly-laundered sheets, gin tonics, and mint tea.

Printed by Amazon Italia Logistica S.r.l.
Torrazza Piemonte (TO), Italy

10499165R00103